Infinity Series

Realm Speaker

Laura Livingston Snyder

ISBN: 978-1-7351913-1-7

Photography: Laura Livingston Snyder
Infinity Series logo photography: Anatoli Photograffi
Publisher: Laura Livingston Snyder
Publisher email: applesnyder6@gmail.com
Cover design and art design: Laura Livingston Snyder
Cover art: Allison Snyder
Artist address: alliedrawsart01@gmail.com
Instagram: AllieDrawsArt

For my mother, Marcia Livingston
who always believed in me

And for those who helped:

My 'born spooky' talented daughter Allison Snyder,
for her fine artwork
and my wonderful friend Alexandra Butterfield,
for her corrections and hesitant critiques

One

*I*T FINALLY HAPPENED.

After all the years of dreaming and worrying, she had gotten through it without breaking a sweat—not that she had expected a problem. She took a huge breath and exhaled as the last of the evening's strangers disappeared in the darkness. And now was clean up time.

Jenna Stevens walked through Orchard Creek's Historical Association taking in each room, her senses on alert for anything out of the ordinary. The great room—a huge area directly off the main door—was to the right and showcased a majestic winding staircase that led to the second floor. Jenna remembered the night of the first Halloween Masquerade Ball. Kids dressed as witches and princesses danced to Monster Mash in the corner. Right now, there were rows of tables and glass cabinets holding treasures of years gone by. Paintings and moderate-sized farming and salt-mining equipment, overcome with rust, hung on the walls. On the floor were items too big for elevating. Small placards were posted close by each item. Jenna's eyes scanned and searched the length of the great room that extended all the way to the outer walls. Her attention was captured by the bright red dots of the apple trees outside, still visible in the floodlights. Nothing was amiss.

She marched left and popped her head inside the enclosed room there. It was the perfect size to host several families for a sit-down dinner, as the museum had done since its inception. Display cases and shelves full of antiques lined the room. One wall was dedicated to black and white photographs and diagrams of how waterwheels worked. Another side highlighted the 1920's in the nearby vicinity. This included several speak-easies and Loew's State Theater—now known as the Landmark Theatre—in Syracuse. Jenna didn't see anything out of the ordinary and circled clockwise to carry on.

She opened the first door against the far wall. Usually this room was a catch-all, but in the autumn, it was cleaned out for the Culinary Arts students to use as a kitchen. Only two sturdy farmhouse tables and a homemade ladder refurbished from pitted trusses—used to exhibit more historic items—took up the floor space. The walls were covered with vintage utensils and a few framed pictures from an ancient women's magazine called *Godey's Lady's Book.*

One large-framed picture in particular caught her eye and Jenna smiled as it drew her near. It was of her and her best friends, Tina Levy and Toby Jacobs, all re-dressed in period costumes from the first Ball, holding an oversized check from Lincoln-Grant Community College. Channel four had covered the story twice that year. No one but Jenna, her friends, and their fathers realized Jenna looked just a bit differently in this photo than on that actual night. The space was exactly as should be, so she clicked the light off and continued.

Muffled voices could be heard from the modest office, quaintly confirmed by a block of aged wood hanging over the door with the words "Orchard Creek Historical" burned into it. She kept walking, her sights back on the great room.

Looking up, Jenna sighed, admiring the height the architecture highlighted with the small walkway that wrapped around the upstairs rooms. It made it possible to see a good portion of the building from that floor. So, as seventeen-year-old Jenna began ascending the stairs, she smiled. It was 9:01 p.m. on a humid Wednesday evening in September. It was the museum's closing time on her first day of work as a real docent—a professional tour guide—in a position that generated a paycheck. Her birthday was back in February, but it took this long to have the Association's blessing and financial ability to pay for employees. Looking back through the blood, sweat, and tears, she was where she wanted to be. Where she felt she belonged. That had been nothing to be afraid of, after all.

Her shoes made scuffing sounds as they reached each stair, the stairs she helped sand and polyurethane. Her fingers caressed a century's worth of nicks and cuts in the wooden banisters. Jenna couldn't help but be mindful of how many other hands touched those railings over the last hundred years: the owner of the old Orchard Creek Mill, Seth Sawyer, his younger brother Joseph Sawyer, and all the loom workers like Elizabeth Avery.

Pulling her long blonde hair to the side, Jenna walked to the room at the far right chewing her lip without realizing it. Time has a way of diffusing traumatic events, even ones that

3

have no logical explanation. Like what happened in this place, specifically in that room, half a decade ago.

Recollections bubbled to the surface as they usually did, of her first experiences. In 1996, the Historical Association had finally gotten the green light to fix up 713 Sentinel and turn it into a museum. Unfortunately, 150 years of history had been waiting for the perfect person to bridge this world and the one beyond. In this case, the bridge was the window on the second floor, known as the Sewing Room back when the place was a mill. That was the gateway. And Jenna Stevens, then a precocious twelve-year-old new to the area, had a gift for walking dreams and connecting with others. She had been the perfect vessel for a restless and desperate soul—Elizabeth—to reunite with her long-lost love, Joseph.

Even today, Jenna wasn't old enough yet to be a member of the Historical Association, but she had stayed involved anyway as a junior volunteer. Her experiences gave her an edge if an oddity arose, but nothing major had. Those strange events had righted a wrong, and Jenna's life was back to normal. Well, normal for her.

On occasion, she would have dreams that seemed to connect with others. Most of the time she didn't know the people in them, and didn't understand the dreams at all. Just lately she had dreamed about a gypsy lady. The woman seemed nice enough, but there was an urge to make her dress like everyone else. Actually, there were arguments about this.

She knew the people in other dreams. She randomly dreamt about the town's librarian Mary Kathryn, who had helped Jenna check out books at the library for years. Jenna didn't know her personally, and yet she knew a lot of details of her life she couldn't have known otherwise. In the dreams, Jenna felt certain she knew Mary Kathryn was becoming frustrated with her husband's complaints of indigestion after dinner each night. It wasn't more than that, but Jenna was certain she gleaned access into her mind. Learning things like this was something that had always been a part of her. It defined her just as much as having big, brown eyes.

It was a good thing her mother had no knowledge of that crazy night because she didn't understand what Jenna was able to do, and chose not to question it. Her dad did. He kept tabs on both her and the museum, but he didn't need to. She understood the importance of the group's decisions from that night. What he didn't know was what occurred shortly after that maiden Halloween.

Jenna had had another direct encounter with the magic that building held. She briefly touched the frame of the Sewing Room window and the word 'soon' whispered through her mind. It was exactly the same experience she had the first time she touched the building the day she moved into town. Even though she had promised to share if anything strange happened, Jenna kept this to herself. She swore she would tell the others if more developed from it. Months went by where she walked on pins and needles, hypervigilant to every creak and cold spot. But nothing more happened. Sometimes Mr. Levy or Mr. Jacobs—her friends' dads who ran the place now—would question whether a door had been left closed or open, but it didn't matter either way. Ultimately, the place stayed quiet and the Historical Association moved forward.

Jenna unconsciously rubbed her head at the memories she held of the Sewing Room of what should have been impossible:

portals, possession, concussions, ghosts. Her eyes scrutinized every inch of the troublesome window overlooking the orchard, thankful it was still closed and sealed as it had been since that first Halloween night.

The rest of the room consisted of several rows of foot-powered sewing machines set into wooden frames very much like old-fashioned desks. They were also in a classroom arrangement. A large bin near the door held a bunch of giant-sized spools with yards and yards of material in retired patterns. For some reason, almost every group she took on tour had to touch them or the large wicker baskets that sat at the end of each sewing row. Jenna readjusted the spools so they would rest against the wall, easing the weight on the ancient bin. She straightened the baskets, subconsciously naming them off in her head: Ruthie's station, Gert's station, Helen's station, and Emma's. Having that knowledge was a remnant of Jenna's unique gift. Bringing herself back to the present, she started towards the landing to the other rooms.

This old place still held fascination for a history lover such as herself. It hadn't deterred her in the least. The building had originally been built as a boarding house in 1846, and then turned into a mill in the 1890's. Along with its past it was a mystery, the supernatural that resided in this building. Of course, Jenna wondered about her part in all of it, especially connecting with the ghosts.

But that had been ages ago. Even so, Jenna shuddered a little and walked to the other rooms upstairs for a quick peek. She straightened a few of the larger antiques in the Display Room so tomorrow's tourists wouldn't trip over them. Somehow, even though she'd been allowed to do this job a hundred times, it felt more important today, now that she was a real employee. A minute later, Mr. Jacobs's voice from the downstairs office reached her.

"Jenna, are you still here?"

"Just making rounds to close down. I'm almost done," Jenna hollered, bounding down the stairs. She rounded the corner and skidded to a stop, almost walking into a young man her age. Five inches taller than she, he was solidly built. He held himself with an air of confidence without pretention.

"Ah, there she is," Mr. Jacobs confirmed. The years hadn't changed him except for some subtle thinning of his blond hair. "Will, this is Jenna Stevens. She's, well, really one of the founders of this museum. She'll be able to show you the ropes. Jenna just started working as full-fledged staff, but has been active here at the museum since she was about twelve. Will is going to be working your opposite days here, Jenna, as soon as he's trained. He just moved into town a few weeks ago. You both have a lot in common. Of all the Orchard Creek kids we interviewed, none were as qualified as Will—familiar with New York's history, experienced in tourism, first-aid trained. And he's a junior, too. Oh, have you already met?"

Jenna blushed. "No, but the first full week of school is always chaotic." She wasn't prepared at all for introductions this late at night, and this was not the way to meet the new guy she had heard about, especially when she wasn't looking her best. She wasn't wearing makeup, and the wavy ends of her hair were a bit snarled, tickling her elbows. Of course, she could count the number of days she wore makeup on a single hand. Tonight would have been another, had she known. The gossip at school was right, though, he was definitely GQ material.

"Will Greenley. It's nice to meet you, Jenna," he said quietly, extending his hand and nodding his head down briefly as if bowing.

Jenna felt a small parade of butterflies pass through her stomach. As goofy as it was on television when people did that, it seemed purely gentlemanly to her. He smiled easily and seemed comfortable in the unfamiliar surroundings. He certainly didn't look like the other kids that applied. There was a professional edge to him despite his hair, a rich chocolate brown, which framed his face and just skimmed his shoulders. It matched his eyes. His dark pants were understated but contrasted nicely with an unlabeled, plain white shirt. It was refreshing to meet someone who didn't conform to the teenage image many of her friends hid behind. No piercings were obvious, no ear buds, just an observant stare. It caught her off guard.

"It's very nice to meet you. Welcome to Orchard Creek. I haven't seen you around school yet. Where did you move from?" Jenna asked, trying to compose herself without looking obvious.

"Libertyvale, not too far away." A hint of a smile played around his lips. His voice was deep, but soft spoken. It didn't quite match his physique. On second thought, it fit him perfectly. "It's a small town, too. I worked in the tourist office there a few summers until August when we moved here."

Jenna's attention wandered to his eyes. Framed by thick lashes and strong brows, they were intriguing but guarded, and held a depth to them that was compelling. For the first time in her life she was without words, captivated by the boy and the way he held her gaze. Out of nowhere a rogue feeling swirled through her that deep down her soul was being called to, or a missing puzzle piece was being set into place. She could see herself melting into those eyes. All of this transpired in a nanosecond that was a bit too long. Mr. Jacobs snapped her out of her musing as he continued walking toward the sign-in podium that had two wooden chairs next to it. He dragged a third that was tucked away over to the others.

"As I was saying, the new positions are more out of need. Our foot traffic is light but we can get busy around holidays and summer. It's been hard to count on until now. I'm proud to share we've recently signed contracts with Denim Miles Tours of New Jersey, and Queen Victoria Touring in Canada to make our museum one of their fixed stops. They've been crisscrossing New York for years and this bid finally includes us. The number of travelers will ultimately determine if the buses actually stop, but the museum will get a percentage regardless."

"How did you operate before that?" The question was directed at Mr. Jacobs but his eyes remained on Jenna as they each took a seat.

Mr. Jacobs smiled and nodded in approval. "That's a great business-minded question, Will! The museum never really generated enough revenue to sustain itself so the Association has had to be imaginative to find other sources. We have an annual Halloween Masquerade Ball; it brings in the bulk of our money. We also work with the town to host community events too, like the Strawberry Festival in the spring. We open the building for the library's Ice Cream Social fundraiser each summer since the library isn't big enough. This way we get publicity and help causes at the same time."

"That's impressive, but much different than my old job."

"It's not that hard, though," Jenna interjected. "I help catalog and display the tons of antiques the Association owns, and it's all computerized now. It was harder when we first started because Mr. Jacobs and Mr. Levy needed to set up the programs. We had to empty what was packed in the tiny room they initially used at the Town Hall, and also a good deal of items from the president's own house. Mr. Robertson's collections of Erie Canal and salt industry memorabilia are better than what official museums hold. We have an edge over the others because he inherited items his father amassed, and he won't part with anything. Never has. And yet, I still don't think we have everything from his place."

Mr. Jacobs shook his head, chuckling at the inside joke.

"Somehow, I think he's managed to stuff half the continent in there," she fake-whispered leaning towards Will. He smelled good. Earthy. "Anyway, other than our events, we're usually busy just giving tours or looking online for new items."

"Sure, only that," Will agreed, returning the grin.

"The bosses are the lucky ones. They get to go on road trips for big items."

Mr. Jacobs put his hand on Jenna's shoulder and pat it a few times. "Don't forget she cut her teeth on this years ago. Anyway, the Historical Association wants to change things up a bit here. The request to divide the rooms to showcase the years of the mill—around 1845, as well as the 1890's of the boarding house—was brought up at our last meeting. Gotta stay fresh and competitive in this day and age, you know. Our next objective is to concentrate on finding bits and pieces that would fit that earlier period and switch over a few rooms for them." The smile on Mr. Jacobs face got bigger. "Oddly enough, that brings us to Will and a happy coincidence. He and his mom just moved into the old house on Miner and Fallow."

"Wow, that's a big place."

"It is, and they found pictures that must have been there for over a century. They're of this place when it was the old boarding house, if you can believe it!" The phone rang in the office and Mr. Jacobs got up. "Excuse me, please. What luck, huh?" he asked, shaking his head as he disappeared.

Trepidation filled Jenna, not that she would let that show on her face. Nothing felt wrong, per se, it was just strange. She wasn't sure she believed in luck or coincidence. "You found pictures of this building in your house?"

"Yes, a few boxes of pictures when we were cleaning it out." Will's face still seemed friendly but for a brief instant something like apprehension flickered in his eyes. "We were in the basement and they were tucked away in a dark corner."

"How'd you know it was this particular place?" Jenna concentrated on keeping her tone light. A trickle of unease had seeped into her blood making her heart race. For a fraction of a second, Will's attention seemed to focus inward on something else before catching Jenna's eyes. The moment passed, and Jenna's rising adrenaline slowly chilled out. Strange.

"There are a few of the front of the building and a few showing the creek. It wasn't hard to piece together."

"Huh. I wonder why—"

"So, now that the papers are signed, you're on the books," Mr. Jacobs interrupted as he returned with his keys in his hand. They all made their way to leave while Mr. Jacobs briefed Jenna on Will's responsibilities, and how Will would be working with her for the next week or so to learn the ins and outs.

"Oh, hold on!" Jenna jogged back to the podium to grab a copy of their brochure for Will. His expression was patient but she could swear he looked a bit restless. Jenna scolded herself. Here he was, new to town, and she was grilling him over photographs. She realized he must be as nervous as she was and tried to reassure him. "Sorry about the inquisition. I'm a bit protective of this old place. I am excited about the pictures, though. It's a part of the history I don't know much about." She nodded towards the paper. "Here's a map of the building and basic history of the place. If you're back tomorrow we'll go through it together. Maybe there'll even be a quiz. I mean, there isn't really a test. That would be weird." Jenna squeezed her lips together so she'd stop this mindless babbling.

"I'm looking forward to it."

Still feeling self-conscious that her mind would wander and her brain to mouth connection would jam, Jenna was hesitant to meet his eyes. When she finally looked up at him, he smiled, his eyes again holding hers warmly without reservation. A wide smile grew on Jenna's face in spite of herself.

Two

THE NEXT EVENING, Jenna showed up promptly at five expecting to be shadowed by Will—or so she thought.

She had devised a list of questions a few years back to narrow down which people might really believe what had happened at the museum. Today was the day she wanted to ask them. She wasn't ready to share with Will details that centered around the paranormal; what sane person talks about ghosts and spirit embodiment anyway? It was important to Jenna that anyone who spent a considerable amount of time in that building be of strong mind. As cute as he was, he might not be the best person to work in a place with so much…heavy history.

So far, no one outside their small circle knew, but she always kept the questions tucked away just in case. She had hoped to find Tina after Physics to bounce her ideas off her at lunch, but Tina wasn't in school the whole day. There was also no time to call between dismissal and when Jenna was scheduled at the museum. And it looked like she wouldn't even get a chance to talk with Will. When Jenna arrived, all the men were at the door, talking. Mr. Jacobs looked a bit stiff.

"Hang on, Jenna," Mr. Levy said before she could put her keys away. "We've got to change things around for tonight. We need to pick up a pot-bellied stove at Lieutenant Kowalski's grandfather's home."

"Nice Nick?" Jenna asked, putting the purse strap over her shoulder. She looked inside to find Will and smiled a greeting. The smile she received in turn was polite enough. Jenna was sure he was excited to see her, too. The butterflies kicked up in her stomach only to be smothered by the night's agenda.

"Yes, Charlie Kowalski passed and the stove was left to us. We need to get it tonight if we want it. Ol' steel arms here was going to help," Mr. Levy inclined his head towards his partner, "but he pulled a neck muscle dragging a bookshelf in his classroom today and can't lift anything."

Mr. Jacobs struck a pathetic body-builder's pose. Jenna giggled. "Oh, I'm sorry to hear that Mr. Jacobs. I'm sorry to hear about Nick's grandpa, too."

Orchard Creek's police force was small, but involved. The Lieutenant usually did a presentation at the end of each school year on "stranger danger" and saying no to drugs. He was a down to earth guy who was very approachable.

"Thanks, Jenna," Mr. Jacobs said. He winced when he moved his head to the left. "It's not too bad, but I don't want to overdo it. Will's agreed to help retrieve the antique and it'll take a good part of the evening breaking it down, shipping it over, and putting it back together. At any other time, I'd have you cover here. Unfortunately, the hours you'll be putting in to train will add up fast, so we'd like you to work only the days Will is on. You can take him on a tour and go over the history tomorrow. Tonight, I'm going to stay. I wish I'd known earlier. I could've called so you didn't have to make a trip out."

Jenna had been sneaking glances at Will, who still seemed very pleased to see her. Knowing she would be working exclusively with him buoyed her mood, even if it wasn't until tomorrow. "Oh, it's not a problem. It'll be nice to have some down time with the family."

Jenna drove home with a grin plastered on her face. To say she was distracted through dinner would be an understatement, but only her mom and dad noticed. Her brother was too busy shoveling food into his mouth.

"Slow down Pete. There's enough for seconds."

"Yeah, I know but I'm hanging with Ryan after dinner. It's my turn for dish duty and that always burns too much daylight." He sounded a lot like their father since his voice had changed.

"Don't you have homework to finish first?"

"No, mom! Not the first week I don't. Can you pass the potatoes?"

"So, Jenna, today was the big day. How does it feel to be a productive part of society and earn a paycheck? Still in the honeymoon phase?" her dad asked, picking up the bowl.

"I just met him," Jenna replied without thinking. She was miles away, imagining what it would be like to go out with Will.

"What?" her mother asked, putting her fork down. She cocked her head to the side the way moms do when juicy news is brought up. It was too late to do damage control; the radar had gone off.

"Yes, my only daughter, do tell," her father added. He was always busting on her for something.

"Nothing."

"Gwen, did that comment seem like nothing to you?"

"Why no, Jack, that comment seemed like a whole lot of Let's Hear More," her mom answered, playing along. Jenna knew her face was red. Even her ears felt hot. They looked at her expectantly and she knew there was nowhere to go but forward.

"We have a new employee at the museum."

"And…"

Jenna knew it wouldn't be that easy but it had been worth a try. "His name is Will."

She watched her parents as they tried to figure out who in town fit this description. None would. Will wasn't a common name in Orchard Creek. In fact, no one had it. There were two Williams (married and retired), a few Bills, and one Billy, but not a Will. The town was also small enough that both knew of just about everyone in the high school. Their faces confirmed as much. Finally, her mom's forehead wrinkled and she pursed her lips in worry. "Is he a lot older?"

"No, mom, he just moved into town. He's in my grade."

"The house on Fourtney, Oak, or the one on Miner?" her dad asked. He was a credit analyst for a company that leased and sold backhoes and bulldozers. Of course, he would know who was building or renovating.

"Miner and Fallow."

Her father nodded in appreciation before a Cheshire grin grew on his face. "And…"

"Ugh, dad, stop. Mr. Jacobs hired him to work opposite me. That's all."

"That's all, Gwen. Nothing more to it than that."

"You guys are impossible."

"And we love you so be good," her mom added.

"Geesh, we just started working together. It's not a big deal." Jenna had gotten up and started to clear the table. Both her parents had a smirk on their faces as they watched her. She didn't know what made them look that way, until she was done with the dishes and realized it had been her brother's turn. Peter had conveniently neglected to correct her, instead, ran out the door before she remembered. Getting into bed that night, Jenna couldn't help the butterflies that stirred within her. A moment later, she was on the phone with Tina.

"Jenna, it's late," Tina said, sniffling.

"Sorry. Are you okay? I didn't see you in school today."

"Sore throat and runny nose. First week of school and already my perfect attendance record is shattered. Besides, my mom babies me too much. What's up?"

"Guess who I met last night?" Jenna teased.

"Who?"

"Will Greenley, the new guy at school," gushed Jenna.

"No way! Where?" Tina asked excitedly.

"He's working at the museum with me. Well, the days opposite me, but still. And, I get to train him."

"Is he cute up close? I can't really tell. The most I've seen him is across the lunch room."

"Oh, yes, he is! His eyes are to die for. He's different, though. Quiet," Jenna mused.

"What's this?"

"What's what?"

"Miss Fickle's interest has finally been piqued by something that's not a book or an old building?" Tina kidded, covering the mouthpiece while she coughed.

"Hey, I've had boyfriends," Jenna reminded her.

"Boyfriend," Tina corrected. "We're juniors now, Jenna. The clock counting down high school life has only two years left to tick, and sadly, you've turned down quite the handful of hotties." Jenna started to protest but Tina plowed on. "And Alan Houghton from sophomore year doesn't even count. You went to one movie with him and held hands in the hallway for, like, two weeks, max. It doesn't count."

Jenna made a raspberry sound. "This is different."

"It must be, although he sounds like my type, not yours."

"That's because I don't really know what my type is yet!" Jenna defended, knowing her face was growing warm again. Tina snickered on the other end.

"Huh. He must be all that and a bag of chips for you to be blushing. Go ahead, try to deny it." There was no way Jenna could, her best friend knew her too well.

"Shut up," Jenna replied playfully. "Anyway, you've got

Rob, the guy who's made eyes at you across orchestra since the beginning of sophomore year." Jenna hesitated. "At least that was true a couple days ago. Did something change?"

"Naw, I'm just giving you a hard time. Ooh, I'm jealous though. He seems mysterious. He didn't join football, and he's not in the drama club. What does he do?" Tina asked.

Jenna thought about that herself. "I don't know. He didn't talk about himself. So, he's not involved in sports or music. Maybe he's too shy right now. It is a new school and all. I think he might like me which is cool."

"Hmm, how convenient to work with your boyfriend," baited Tina.

"Now you're rushing things. Not that I wouldn't mind. Anyway, he smiles at me a lot. That's good, right?" Jenna asked.

"Uh, yeah, that's good. Rob and I have been dating for almost 250 days now. Nothing exciting happens anymore. Keep me posted."

"You know I will. Feel better."

Friday took forever. Jenna was able to catch sight of Will during lunch only briefly. She didn't have the nerve to go see him at his table, so she kept getting up to throw something away so she could steal a glimpse. He dressed the same way for school as he did for work. It wasn't preppy, just nice. And she couldn't get Tina's opinion because Tina never made it in. Jenna heard from Toby who had talked to his mom that Tina had gone to the doctor and had strep. Jenna chickened out telling her plans to Toby so she kept them to herself, counting the minutes.

5 p.m. finally arrived and Jenna blew her bangs out of her

face as she shut the car off and made her way inside. Will was already there, reviewing the pamphlet on the museum, waiting patiently. Even though Mr. Jacobs wasn't with them, Will greeted her in the same polite fashion with no slang or high school mannerisms. He did not have the typical football player attitude Jenna was used to expecting with someone as toned as he was. Instead, he continued to come across as very well read. And again, he was wearing nice clothes: pleated khakis and a button-down shirt. Jenna wasn't sure if all of this was his professional demeanor for work or his true personality.

"Mr. Levy had given me a key so I let myself in. I hope that's okay."

"Yeah, of course, you're one of us, now." Jenna hadn't planned on what she said, it just came out. She thought how nice it sounded. "So, how'd the move go?"

Will looked confused for a moment before he understood. "Oh, it went well."

With effort, Jenna forced her thoughts to focus on work. "It's just us tonight, I guess. We'll try to get through as much of our tour as we can, Friday's are usually busy."

"That's good, actually. I'll be able to see exactly what you do and how you lead into all the details." He bent down to brush off a piece of lint on his pants. His hair hid his face. "Whenever you're ready."

"Okay." Jenna looked out the window for the tour buses. So far it was still only the two of them so she tried to figure out how to approach him with her questions. She still needed to know how he would handle the museum, but now it would help her in other ways. It would serve a secondary function, to find out what Will had in common with her. She couldn't get more of who he was with what little he was offering. She certainly was attracted to him—who wouldn't be—let alone intrigued by his atypical behavior. Most people try to sneak in a forbidden trinket or conversation piece in an interview. If anything, it would serve as a reminder on how unforgettable they were. Will hadn't. And who doesn't let their guard down when the boss isn't there, even a little? She couldn't pick up on anything other than what he put out for public display. She motioned for him to follow. "Time for an interest check. Wanna play along?"

"What do you mean, 'interest check'? Ah yes, the quiz from the other day," Will guessed. He had a beautiful smile.

"No, well, yeah. Just be truthful," Jenna suggested as they went through the main room. She gestured to the area where glass display cases of salt mining equipment were being reorganized. "Besides, if there was a quiz it would be the new vocabulary words you'll be using here: terminology like bittern pans and muddles. This is something different."

She pointed out a few items that she thought were pretty cool, and lingered over the cabinet watching him. Propping herself up on her elbows, she rested her chin in her cupped hands and sighed. "It's more like a game of favorites." The way he studied her caused stomach jitters that derailed her train of thought. She broke his gaze and pointed her finger. "Um, we think this smaller room off to the left of the staircase was originally a dining room for the boarders, and we believe the Historical Association's office on the right might have been part of a kitchen. These larger rooms were turned into the business area when the mill was established. You can tell because the upstairs rooms all have holes on the floors. That was where the machines were anchored down. Okay, so," she took a deep breath and dove in. "First question, Fourth of July or Halloween?" She started walking down the small corridor noting small structural details.

"What? Oh, ok, favorites. Hmm, Halloween."

"Ski lodge and conquests or camp fires and ghost stories?"

"No doubt, camp fires with ghost stories," Will replied with mock seriousness. "If we were meant to slide down snowy hills, I'm sure our creator would have made our feet longer." For an instant, it seemed like the comment slipped out. He said nothing more but looked at her as if to say "sorry about that."

Jenna tilted her head to the side, an expectant expression on her face before it morphed into a grin. Now she felt she was getting somewhere. Shaking her head to dismiss the idea Will planted, she stopped to make sure he was ready to go down the stairs to the basement. He looked back towards the front door, concerned.

"Don't worry, we'll hear if someone walks in, and we won't be long. Come on."

Will was right behind her, his eyes alight with humor, his hands casually in the pockets of his pants. He leaned in towards her to turn the knob and open the door, an old-fashioned gesture. How was it he was still making an impression on her? Her biggest problem now was trying to reign in her stupid smile. A faint hint of a woodsy cologne caught up to Jenna and her stomach fluttered again. Without losing her rhythm she turned the lights on and started down the steep steps. The humid smell of musty basement reached her nose bringing with it a sense of familiarity she liked.

"Obviously, this is the basement. The generator is down here, as you can see, as well as the electrical box in the back corner. All the holiday decorations are kept off to that side, including what we'll be bringing up soon for Halloween. There is an old storm cellar door to the outside, but we don't utilize it." She paused. "Next question is mystery adventures or playing football?"

"Adventures, but I'm always up for a good game."

Maybe the opinion on skis was an anomaly. He was back to simple answers without small talk or reason. No jumping into any stories. Noticeably though, there was also no gloating. His voice was smooth, like caramel, and Jenna decided she could listen to it indefinitely without tiring.

They went back upstairs to the main level and started up the grand staircase. Jenna thought a second and spoke without thinking it through. "Wood or metal?"

Will just looked at her puzzled. "Are we talking elements or structure?"

"Just a question, never mind." She shrugged her shoulders and sighed again. They had taken a right off the stairs. The view from up there showed just how large the building was. Jenna stopped in front of the Sewing Room. She felt comfortable around Will, drawn to him. As much as she was psychically abnormal, this building was a part of her. She felt compelled to share that with anyone close to her, and was surprised to find she was starting to wish very badly that she could get close to him. Her quiz didn't yield enough answers to help in her quandary. She couldn't do it. There was too much hesitation to step outside her comfort zone to talk about beliefs that could scare him away. No better off than when she started, she bit her lip, torn with indecision.

"Did I pass?"

The question pulled her from her reverie and she looked up at him. His eyebrows arched as his lips quirked to hide a smile. Somehow Jenna was sure through the smug look she could see worry in his eyes.

"The first half anyway. But, let's just say this building has a lot more than history to it, and if I say this room needs special handling, I want you to take it seriously."

Will's eyebrows dipped down. The smug look vanished, replaced by a somber alertness. "Okay."

"This is the Sewing Room. There is a particular history to this room especially that is a little, um, odd. Just be extra careful in here. More than anything that window across from us must never be opened."

He took the time to study her face. She could imagine a million thoughts going through his mind. Thoughts like how crazy she just sounded. It surprised her at how quickly she worried what he would think of her.

"Okay. The window stays closed," he pledged with confidence. Jenna almost sagged in relief. She wouldn't need to go *there* just yet. "But, will I ever get the real reason why?"

Man, he was smart, too.

"In time, I'm sure. That would be the other half of the quiz. But if the window stays shut it won't have to be a pop quiz."

Three

THEY HAD TO break twice for a tour bus and a carload of people from Pennsylvania.

Will remained observant and somehow blended in with each party. The bus group was large, and it was easy to tell the museum was the last leg of their tour. Several small children started to chase each other once inside, and wouldn't behave even when their parents reprimanded them. Unfazed, Jenna continued to talk about a handheld food mill from the depression era as she walked behind one of the displays and pulled out a sturdy rocking horse. The kids stopped and stared when Jenna pretended to mount it. A mass of squeals ensued.

"What? I shouldn't get on? Then how about this, I promise you all a turn and a lollipop but there's a condition. Does anyone want to hear it?" She had their attention now. "Everyone can have a ride but afterwards you all will have to help me find George the Bear. This is his favorite toy, you see. He was just here and now he's gone hiding. I bet all that running scared him off. You'll need to walk slowly and talk soft like mice while we go through each room. Maybe, if you're all quiet enough we can find him. If you do, I'll give you each a treat for helping me. Deal?"

Immediately, the chatter stopped and Jenna held her hand out for tiny high-fives. While each child took a ride, Jenna pointed out the craftmanship and how it was a popular toy during the 1930's. The entire display was reviewed while the kids were occupied, and Jenna continued the tour at a comfortable pace. The girls and boys kept their promise and were quiet as they searched for the elusive George. When the tour concluded and everyone was back in the main room, a boy with sandy hair jumped up and down.

"There he is, there he is!"

Jenna gave him permission to run ahead to a counter where the tan head of a teddy bear was peeking out. "You found him! Thank you, friends." She opened the door to the counter and took out a plastic barrel full of colorful pops. Wide eyes and anticipation met her as she rewarded her search party. It was obvious the adults were happy with the tour and impressed with the way she involved the kids.

"I am amazed," Will announced as the lights from the bus faded down the road.

"All in a day's work."

"Who thought of the bear trick?"

"I did. I've done some babysitting and nothing gets kids to mind better than to include them in something they have a stake in. And if that fails, sweets do it." Bright white lights in the window made Jenna look up. "Aw man, there's another car."

"That's okay, I'm learning a lot this way."

Even though the carload from Pennsylvania was smaller and only with adults, it proved difficult in another way.

"So, these are willow baskets make locally in Liverpool. This was a sustainable craft and this industry helped the town thrive," Jenna explained, pointing to a basket large enough to be used as a hamper.

"These were all made by hand?" a woman asked, bending over and lifting her glasses to study the details.

"Yes, ma'am, they were."

"These look too perfect. Like they were made in China off some production line." The woman was clearly in a bad mood. She had been attempting to find fault with every exhibit.

"No, those who weaved baskets day after day became experts, that's all," Jenna said patiently. "We have pictures proving authenticity. Each family had their own special detail or characteristic to identify them. This one was made by the Besaws." She thought a moment. "But there is some truth in referring to China."

The woman lifted her head, clearly feeling superior. Jenna continued. "Willow trees were native to China before they were brought to America." And just like that, Jenna smoothly turned back to the topic at hand. "They like their feet wet, so to speak, that's why they're found lining lakes and rivers. We have a lot of waterways around here. They made good raw material and since they grow so fast, they were plentiful." She ignored the lady's "humph," directing everyone's attention to a few Iroquois Indian artifacts from the Ithaca area.

Finally, the museum was empty and Jenna concluded Will's private tour. She had taken him through the rest of the upstairs and outside to the right, around the water wheel and creek. She finished up in the west in the apple orchard just before seven. Now they sat by the podium to take a break and get a drink before starting in on the ledgers and record keeping. Mr. Jacobs had stopped in and left in a matter of minutes. He had complete confidence in Jenna.

Jenna, however, still had no feel for who Will really was. He had been practically invisible with the visitors, and he only listened and nodded as she led him from room to room, talking about the history and the items. Opportunities for socializing and small talk were met with questions appropriate to the job description, what he had done as a tour guide in Libertyvale, or to clarify information on an antique. The most he divulged was his ability to decipher a map upside down. She couldn't read him at all and it was making her frustrated.

"You're an enigma, you know that?" Jenna said impatiently.

"What do you mean?" Will asked, defensively.

"I can't figure you out."

"Why? What is it you need to know?" He stiffened. "Do you not think I'm qualified for this job?"

"No, you're absolutely qualified," Jenna answered without hesitation.

Now Will look frustrated. He put his bottle of water down and cupped his hand around his temple to pull the hair back from his face. "Then what is it?"

Jenna hesitated. "It's just sometimes this building might seem a little strange and I don't know you well. I worry that you might misinterpret it."

"Like drafts and creaky doors? It's an old building," Will stated. Jenna noticed he skipped over the topic of himself. Again.

"It's more than that."

"You'll have to be more specific if you want me to understand."

Jenna's heart was hammering in her chest. "It's going to sound mental. A lot of old places have a personality. Kinda like it's based on the history it's seen. Ours does. Do you believe in anything like that?"

She watched him closely as either surprise or apprehension, or both, colored his face. He was obviously caught off guard, and immediately Jenna worried, hoping this wouldn't become too awkward. What would Mr. Jacobs do if his first outside hire decided to quit the week she started because she sounded like a nut job?

"You mean karma?" His brows knit down in suspicion and he gave her a sidelong glance. "Have you met my mom?" Before Jenna could answer, he continued. "Yeah, I do believe in that." The comment was assured and certain. Jenna released the breath she didn't realize she was holding.

"Okay, good. Good."

Will waited for more but nothing came. "That's it?"

"Um, yeah, for now." She was tired, as if she had used all her courage. She kept her head down, swirling the flavored water around in the can and listening to the carbonated fizz.

She could feel Will's eyes on her. When she spoke again her voice was quieter. "I need to think where I've left off on our agenda. We'll go through bookkeeping another day."

"Okay."

"Usually by this time, I'm finishing up with the particulars of having a table at the Autumn Harvest Festival," she said after a brief pause. "It's at the end of this month. There's food and craft vendors there, and games. We bring some of our heartier antiques to showcase."

With the uncomfortable conversation behind her, Jenna once again became animated about her passion. And there was something about Will that made it easy for her to relax. "Every other year we alternate between things used for harvesting and canning crops, and our school-themed items. Like Mr. Jacobs said, we really do try to stay involved with the town. October is our busiest month by far. Every Halloween since the bid to restore the building, we've held an annual Halloween party. It's our big fundraising event for the year and has become a town favorite, even though no one has a clue what actually happened at the first one." She was on a roll and it slipped. Her snicker dried up as soon as it left her mouth. She tried to keep going but Will held his hand out to stop.

"Each year it's gotten a little bigger—"

"What happened at the first one?"

"Creaky doors," Jenna blurted, feeling her face heat up. "It's okay though, as long as the Sewing Room window stays shut." She pushed on, refusing to elaborate. "Anyway, I'd be working on the Harvest Festival already but I've had all this new rearranging to do. Mr. Levy and Mr. Jacobs started the Halloween event stuff on their own well over a week ago.

"Besides, the boxes you brought from your home need to be cleaned out to see what is usable. Mr. Jacobs said some of the pictures are damaged beyond saving, and those that are usable can be cleaned off, framed, and put up. There's a specific process to bathing photos. We'll need more supplies first."

"Sorting it is. Show me what to do."

Jenna and Will sorted through only the first box in an awkward silence that was only broken a few times by sneezes and coughs from all the dust. Most of the pictures were small, three and a half by five with scalloped edges. All were in black and white. The photos on the top and bottom had been damaged the most by moisture. Several were covered in mold, which had distorted the images. The ones in the middle had fared better.

Jenna would have loved to concentrate on the pictures but was too distracted by Will. He was definitely lost in thought, oblivious to her scrutiny. She noticed his face held every emotion, and after a few minutes concluded his expressions were mainly directed by his eyebrows. There was a lot he was considering, and something she took as him weighing his thoughts. Confusion and concentration were easy to see. For a guy, he was very observant. She had never seen her dad or brother internalize this much. Will was inconspicuous but she found him studying the rooms around them. It endured him to her. It didn't seem to matter, though. She was lost as to how to reconnect with him and it made her feel lonely. What a shame. She thought they had hit it off so well at first. He was probably trying to puzzle out a way to give his notice this soon, or how he could work alongside someone like her, saying what she had about the building. Will's gentle voice pulled her from her thoughts.

"Jenna?"

"Hmm?"

"I'd really rather you weren't upset, and I promise not to judge. Tell me what happened at the first fundraiser party."

Jenna studied the green smudges on the cloth in her hand. Her stomach twisted in a very uncomfortable way. It pinched and started to sour. There was no way she could face Will and tell him the truth.

"Jenna?"

She raised only her eyes to meet his. There was something so inviting about them.

"Please?"

All the apprehension she was holding left her body. It wasn't like she had calmed down; it was more like the worry had never been there in the first place. He did need to know and now it was unavoidable. She knew the task had anxiety attached to what she had to say, and yet it didn't hold the fear it once did. It was a bizarre sensation. Maybe it was because Will was no longer a stranger.

Jenna took a deep breath and began. It had started raining and there were no more tourists, so she was able to finish the whole story without any interruptions. Will had kept his end of the deal and had been patient and attentive. He had also not shown any particular emotion. The last thing she wanted to do was spook him. She wasn't sure how to proceed.

"Well? What do you think about this building's history? Do you believe anything I just told you?"

"Yes, I do. I don't have a problem with it. I'm not scared, if that's what you're hinting at," he added, an edge to his voice.

Jenna apologized. "I didn't mean to offend you; you just seemed so unfazed. I would think most people would be skeptical or disbelieving. Regardless, I think they'd have something to say."

"Well, I'm not like most people," Will shot back quickly as he raked his hand through his hair. He got up and took a few steps from her before turning back. "I'm sorry. Things like that are not that uncommon in my world. Let's move on, shall we?"

Jenna was perplexed by Will's sudden change in demeanor and his last statement. "Sure. Let's just finish these up."

While they emptied the most damaged package, she discussed the layout of the new arrangements for the museum, but it was still a long night.

Closing time finally came, and Jenna looked around at what she would need to pick up for tomorrow. She mumbled to herself, calculating how long the rest of the job would take. They hadn't even gotten to the other two boxes. They'd still need to separate the pictures, figure out the years, and organize them for the wall in the room upstairs.

Jenna looked up briefly and realized Will was watching her. It really looked more like admiring, but she wouldn't flatter herself. She did a quick double take, looking back at the pictures to regroup her thoughts. The butterflies stirred again. She felt a brief surge of anger that dissipated quickly only when she realized she was angry with him for being short with her. When she thought it through, she wasn't sure how she expected Will to act. He was definitely distant, almost defensive. Regardless of all that, he had been studying her. Maybe it would work out after all. She smiled, unable to concentrate further to be of any help for the job.

"Good for today, yeah?" she asked, purposely looking at everything but Will.

"Sure, it was very informative," Will answered.

Jenna tried to figure out how such a subdued tone could hold her full attention.

With each busy with their own thoughts, they quietly moved the boxes into the office and gathered the pictures that were in good condition into a pile. Finally, everything was tidied and locked up. Will motioned for Jenna to lead at the front door but she needed to switch places once they were outside so she could lock the door behind her. This created close quarters and Jenna giggled as they shuffled in a half circle. The alarm system was activated, and she smiled tentatively at Will as she said she'd see him at work tomorrow. Smiling back, he started for his car and wished her a good night. They were both too preoccupied to realize they were both off the next few days.

THE NEXT DAY was Saturday and by the late afternoon, Jenna had her chores and homework done. "Mom, I'm running to the store to pick up some supplies for the museum. Do you need anything?" Jenna asked, walking into the kitchen as she pulled on a sweater.

Jenna's mother was setting the table for dinner after helping Peter with his freshman algebra. "We could use some bread," she answered. Jenna pecked her on the cheek, grabbed the car keys, and headed out the door.

Putting forks at each setting, Gwen shook her head. Jenna had never gotten over her infatuation with that building. After the first Halloween fundraiser and the costumes, Gwen thought the novelty would have worn off well before high school. It was hard for her to understand the attraction that old building held for her daughter. She had to admit Jenna was a good kid, though. Very grounded, good in school, involved with her family and things that benefitted others. But those dreams she had as a young child, they were a bit unsettling.

Gwen allowed herself a moment to think she was a good mother, despite all the time she spent away from home for work. When she accepted the position as the regional representative with the homecare company three years ago, she knew the kids didn't need her to be home after school to supervise like when they were little. However, she had no idea how much time she would spend on the road. Then after the territories were reorganized, her area was increased to include part of Pennsylvania and Michigan. The weather in the northeast could be unpleasant eight months out of the year, so when she needed to make her rounds out-of-state, she clustered them together so she'd only be gone a few days at a time for each state. It had always bothered her when she felt she was an invisible parent, only there sporadically. She was glad Jack worked in town and was a hands-on father who stayed connected. He was especially close to Jenna and for that, she was thankful.

Four

*J*ENNA DROVE TO the Wal-Mart on the other side of
town. She had just added a loaf of bread to the cart
full of frames, nameplate kits, and other items, and
didn't see the woman in front of her. Jenna skidded the cart to
a stop to avoid a full-fledged head-on, but still, she knocked a
few items out of the woman's hands onto the floor. Only when
she stood up after retrieving the woman's items did she get a
good look at the lady.

She was a large woman, about middle age, wearing a
renaissance-looking floor length dress. It was a deep cranberry
in color with tiny black beads decorating the low-cut, well
endowed, fitted bodice. She wore a dark red, floor-length cloak
over it that had small, silver, mock coins as fringe around the
open-slitted three-quarter length sleeves. There was a dragonfly
pin the size of a silver dollar above her right breast. Behind
silver framed glasses, her amber eyes matched her textured hair

which was short to the nape of her neck and accented by red streaks. As she rearranged her items in her arms, Jenna noticed she had several rings on each finger. All were silver with a large prominent stone or design of a star within a circle. A peculiar perfume, reminding Jenna of the outdoors, caught her nose. The woman laughed and a book slipped from her hands, the coin fringe of her outfit chinking away.

"I am so sorry. I wasn't paying attention. Please, let me get that for you," Jenna said, embarrassed. They both reached for the book on the floor, their hands meeting. As their fingers touched, the woman gasped, and Jenna's mind went blank for the briefest instant. The woman withdrew her hand only to purposefully grab Jenna's hand a moment later.

"You have channeled," the woman said, focusing her amber eyes on Jenna's face.

Jenna was dumbstruck. "Wh…what? I'm sorry. Channeled? I've what?" She stood up awkwardly, removing her hand from the woman's grasp. She clutched her cart and looked at the flamboyantly dressed woman. There was something vaguely familiar about her.

The woman's expression softened. "I sense that you have served a purpose other than your own. You have a gift, a very strong one, but you know that. You are very strong."

Immediately, Jenna thought of Elizabeth, but was baffled as to how this stranger could know about the part she played in that incident.

The woman laughed at the confused expression on Jenna's face. "My name is Sulis, and we haven't met before. I sense things in others. It comes and goes, but you…it is very strong in you. You know what I'm talking about, right?"

Jenna slowly nodded her head. A million thoughts rushed at her. How did she know? Who was she? Jenna had never seen her before, and this woman had too distinctive an appearance to have not been noticed—and remembered.

"I don't want to make you nervous, but I would like to talk with you sometime. I think it would be interesting for us both. Here, take my card."

The woman tried to shift her load and handed a few things to Jenna so she could rummage in her tiny, satin, pull string purse. It bulged with the movement of her hand, distorting the hand sewn willow tree on the front until she produced a small card. She collected the last two items from Jenna and turned away. Jenna just stood there, numb, staring at the back of the woman as she went down the aisle to the register and began to check out. Only then did she look at the card in her hand. It was a light lavender color with sculptured edges. An outline of a willow tree had been punched in the top. It gave her name as Sulis with the title of Soothsayer under it. There was a phone number printed for tarot card readings and palmistry. When Jenna looked up again the woman was breezing through the door, her long cape billowing out behind her. Jenna went about the rest of her shopping with those thoughts wandering around in her head.

Sulis walked out of the store and stopped to the side to reorganize the canvas bags in her hands that held her purchases. Taking in a large breath of air, she looked up at the stars just becoming visible in the evening sky. She loved the smell of autumn.

The mission she went on tonight had indeed been fruitful. It wasn't the usual night for her to shop, but something told her she needed to. She never questioned that inner voice. Just as she was beginning to become impatient whether the motivation was just because her notebook was on sale, she was run into by the young woman, quite literally out of nowhere. She hadn't heard her coming. It didn't dawn on her that this was why she had felt the need to come out until their hands had touched as they reached for the same fallen item.

Touching the girl's hand sent a thousand images through her head. It connected to her on a common wavelength that she recognized as channeling. There weren't that many people out there whom she had encountered that had done that, at least who hadn't been more aware of their talent. The girl, truly, looked dumbfounded, and anxious. It reminded Sulis of the first time she came across someone else who could do what she was able to do. It was like looking in a mirror reflection of oneself. In all those years since then, she had also not encountered anyone who came across as forcefully. The girl didn't just have a fleeting moment of intuition as some had, she was truly gifted.

Some of the images that came to her were unsettling, repeating. The girl was an innocent and very vulnerable to those who willfully held onto their mortality after dying. It was these entities who were most responsible for ghost stories. In a matter of speaking, they fought crossing over to the other side, and part of them remained in this realm. And, like an infinity circle—a never-ending loop that repeated. However far the girl wandered, she would be brought back in by others to do their bidding. She was very intrigued by her, though. Something else connected Sulis to her, something she still couldn't identify. But she knew, eventually, all would become clear.

THE FOLLOWING WEEK started quickly with schoolwork and family obligations. Jenna occasionally thought about her meeting with the odd woman at the store, Sulis. Why hadn't Jenna called her? Part of her was fascinated, inquisitive, and downright nosy, but something held her back, and she wasn't sure if it was nerves or fear. Maybe it was somehow all a ruse. But Jenna had to put it all away so she could concentrate on her school work.

4:30 P.M. ON Wednesday, September twenty-first came around quickly after a full day of classes. Jenna was a bit late for work and tore through the door. She hadn't had a chance to change out of her jeans from school into something more appropriate. Will had already arrived and was organizing the pictures. Jenna felt out of sorts for a moment, wondering how awkward it might be now that she let the proverbial cat out of the bag. She began to relax when Will looked up and smiled at her just as he had the very first day. *It's going to be a good night*, she thought. She put the bags of frames and cleaning solution down next to the pictures after leaving the receipt on the podium.

"Look at this one. Can you imagine wearing this with our summer heat?" Will asked, showing her another picture.

They had been working for over an hour, and it had been quite enjoyable. He hadn't mentioned the building's past, and for once she was happy not to have to dwell on it. Will was also a little more talkative which she found encouraging. He described his teachers and classmates while she tried to guess who they were. Since she had been going to school with the same group of people since fifth grade, she was able to give background info on them and their family. With each story, Will was astounded. He admitted he moved too many times to know anyone well. She reminded him that was how she felt only a few years back. She even told him of an overly simplistic map she drew when she first moved to Orchard Creek, laughing at how awful it was, even if it did help her find her way around.

"Those clothes must have been itchy," she replied, leaning over Will's shoulder to look at his picture. His hair smelled so good. She was really beginning to like woodsy. She had two photographs in her hands, trying to decide where they should go.

They were trying to put the prints in an aesthetically pleasing arrangement as well as figure out the chronological order. They dotted the floor in a huge pattern. Some had dates and names inked on the back, but some didn't. None were familiar to Jenna.

The picture Will held showed a woman standing next to a small Boarding House sign in front of the building. Her hair was swept up in a knot showing off her high-collared blouse. The leg o'mutton sleeves were larger than her head and tapered down to tight cuffs at her wrists. The woolen skirt looked heavy and extremely warm. Jenna looked behind the woman to the rest of the picture. It must have been summer because the trees in the background were full. The structure of the building had changed little, but the area around it looked bare. Except for the trees by the creek, there was nothing else to be seen, just open fields. There were no apple trees at all as they had been planted decades later. The date on the back indicated it was August 7, 1846. It was the oldest one.

Something still felt a little 'off' to Jenna about the photographs. There was nothing alarming about them, actually. They were just plain, old photos. But who would take so many of this building when there was other more pleasing architecture to capture? Granted, they found a few of the town scattered throughout, one or two of the bridges, three of the cemetery across from the building, and one of Will's new home, but most were of 713 Sentinel. Why? And more importantly, why weren't they boxed up and stored here? Was there a reason they were hidden at a house miles away?

"No wonder no one smiled in those pictures, huh?" Will added, breaking Jenna out of her thoughts. The tone was light but there was concern etched in his face. "Don't you wonder if they went skinny-dipping in that creek?" Will went on. The comment sounded forced to her ears. Jenna just looked at him, not sure how to answer. Was he messing with her or flirting? His cologne was nice. It smelled like a combination of citrus and sandalwood.

"Oh, I never, I mean, I wouldn't have thought about it," Jenna stammered.

Will's face reddened as he bent towards the picture in his hand, straightening out the corner even though it wasn't bent. "So, is there something wrong with the pictures?"

"Huh? Why do you ask?"

Will shrugged and shook his head. "Just a feeling. You look worried when we work on them."

Jenna studied his face. It was clear of teasing or joking. She wasn't aware of making it obvious. "I just don't get why they were kept at your house."

"Are you sure that's all?"

She sighed. There was no reason to hold back now. "It doesn't sit right with me." Will frowned, thinking. She didn't want him doing too much of that. Just then, her stomach growled. "I know I could go for one of the Pound apples outside, though. They're just about ripe. How about you go get a couple, I'll bring these pictures upstairs, and we'll take a quick break?"

"Sure. I wouldn't mind breathing in some fresh air anyway. I like that old musty smell, but mold is only good to a point. Wouldn't it be great if you could bottle the smell of a crisp night? It's gets me feeling, I don't know, kinda anxious." There was a pause. "That sounds stupid, doesn't it?" He looked embarrassed.

"No, actually, I feel the same way, kind of excited, like I have to go outside to do something, but I don't know what," Jenna said smiling. She picked up a few of the framed pictures and a handful of ones that were still loose.

"Exactly!" Will replied, grinning at her as he made his way to the door.

Jenna started up the staircase to the room on the left. That's where they would be hanging a collage of pictures that weren't in good enough condition to merit a display downstairs. She heard Will open and close the front door as she looked down at the photographs in front of her. Barely visible, having faded from years of storage was a shot of the inside of the building. Jenna was unsure which room was pictured, as all her landmarks had changed. It was one of the rooms, she was sure of that, because it had the same woodwork and trim. It was a large room with an interior staircase and a window. Where had the stairs come from? She tried to picture each of the rooms against the photograph to see which one fit. The stairs just didn't make sense. The building was tall, but other than the basement and main staircase, there were no other stairs inside. It was assumed the false attic was a lot of dead space that had never been utilized.

When nothing seemed to come to her, she gave up and looked at the picture underneath. It was stained, but looked like it had been taken from the road. It showed a side view of the boarding house and the storm cellar door which led out into what would eventually become the apple orchard. She took a moment to think about how differently it must have looked with tiny apple trees and how long it had taken for them to grow so big.

All at once, she vaguely heard Will yell just as there was a loud shattering of glass. Jenna jumped, startled, and a very bad feeling washed over her. Her heart was pounding in her chest as she looked down. The loose pictures she was holding had fallen to the floor. The framed pictures began to vibrate on their own in her hands.

Jenna froze, her jaw dropped, as the pictures in her hand kept vibrating. What was happening? Again, she heard Will yell from outside. She began to move towards the stairs on weak legs to look for him, holding tighter to the pictures. As if her legs were weighted, she made her way across the hall into the Sewing Room just as his voice became louder and clearer. She stopped dead in her tracks. She could hear Will crystal clear now, his voice coming from a hole in the window in the Sewing Room. There was glass on the floor, and at her feet, was a large, smashed apple.

"Oh Jenna! I'm sorry, I'm sorry! It was an accident! It's the wrong window. Please, tell me the apple went in any window but the Sewing Room!"

Jenna walked stiff-legged towards the window, feeling that cold, achy feeling, deep in her bones. The closer she got to the window, the more the pictures in her hand vibrated. She looked from her hands to the window, not knowing which to think about first. Her brain was stuck in neutral, and she just stood there unaware of time passing.

"Ouch, hot!" she cried out, dropping the pictures. The frames bounced off the floor, cracking. The glass, however, broke into a million tiny pieces. She held her hands up to her mouth to soothe them and felt arms come around her from the back. She squealed, trying to throw her arms wide and break free while cupping her palms outward to protect the fresh burns. She immediately had flashbacks of Seth Sawyer coming at her with his hands outstretched, and began wrenching away from what could be trying to restrain her.

"Jenna, it's me, Will! Stop! It's okay! Stop!" Will was saying. He was trying to turn her around so she could see who he was. He needed to lunge and duck her flailing arms. It took a moment for Jenna to realize it was Will.

"Oh, Will, what just happened?" Jenna sobbed and sagged against him, allowing herself to be wrapped in his arms.

"I… it's my fault. I was trying to get this huge apple off the tree by knocking it down with another. I wasn't thinking. I was throwing towards the building, and it missed and went through the window. Oh, this is bad," Will admitted, clearly upset as he looked from the window to her.

"I don't understand. I was just holding the pictures, and they began to shudder on their own. Then they got really hot." Jenna held out her hands, which were still shaking badly to reveal red spots on her fingers. Only the fingers that had been touching the frames were marked. Will tenderly took her hands, then looked down, distracted, as his boots crunched in the glass.

"I've never seen glass from picture frames break into so many pieces. Usually it's four or five, you know? This looks like it was blown up, except they resemble pebbles more than jagged shards," Will observed.

They both stood there for a minute, looking at the mess of glass, trying to absorb everything that had just happened. A strong breeze swept over them, and they looked towards the window. The hole was only apple-sized, but the breeze that came through was much greater. Jenna's hair blew off her shoulders. That sinking feeling came back, and she looked up worriedly at Will.

"That window. Oh, man. It had to stay shut. I don't know what to do now; I don't know what will happen," Jenna said quietly, feeling sick and numb.

"Tell me the details again," Will urged.

"Every time that window is opened, it somehow links us to the other side, the afterworld. I know it sounds stupid and sci fi, but it's not. It's a threshold that has allowed those from the past to cross over because I saw it firsthand. So did Toby, Tina, and our dads. From what we've learned and experienced, if the building is left alone, it doesn't seem to bother anyone. But this place is a museum now. When we started renovating, the window would open on its own and that's the room where I saw Seth. He thought I was Elizabeth and tried to kill me. That night on Halloween, when Joseph came back, many others did too. It was in this room and the window was open again. Somehow after Elizabeth and Joseph were reunited, the ghosts took Seth away. When they left, the window was shut behind them. We haven't opened it and nothing bad has happened since."

"And now the window is open. It's open, and it's my fault," Will said. His disgust was directed towards himself.

"I'm not sure if repairing the window will fix it," Jenna admitted.

They left the pictures where they had fallen, moved the broken glass off to the side for now, and tried to patch the window as best they could with an old board from the basement. But the damage had been done the instant the apple went through, and they both felt it.

A quarter of an hour later, they were back up in the Sewing Room, this time with Mr. Jacobs. He sighed, puzzled, and was quiet. Several different expressions crossed his face, but none seemed to make him happy. Jenna had called him at home after they had collected themselves, and asked that he come over. They weren't sure what else to do.

"Jenna, do you really think it'll be that bad?" Mr. Jacobs asked, scratching his head as he inspected the makeshift repair. Jenna shrugged as if to say she didn't know. "Maybe it has to be the whole window, you know, the sash has to be opened," he suggested hopefully.

"No, it's open," Will replied. He seemed very assured of that.

"He's right. I could feel it. How would you explain this and the pictures?" Jenna asked, holding her hands palm up for him to see the faint burns.

"Yes, but you had that thing with Elizabeth Avery going on. That business is finished. Maybe it's not too late to close it," Mr. Jacobs offered.

"Only time will tell, I think. You don't know how sorry I am," Will apologized again as they all filed out of the upstairs room. Mr. Jacobs put his hand on Will's shoulder as if accepting the regret. Will's tensed stance relaxed a little. They walked down to the main floor to call it a night with Mr. Jacobs looking over at Jenna.

"Let's lock up."

"I've got to hang here for a just a little while, if you don't mind. My mom had to take my car for appointments," Will stated. Just then the main door opened, and Sulis, the woman Jenna had run into at the store, walked in.

At first Jenna didn't make the connection. The woman suddenly stopped walking and frowned. She made eye contact with Jenna and her eyes widened in recognition. Walking farther into the room she looked around her.

"It's this place. That makes sense. However, I didn't feel

this when I was here a few weeks ago. There is a very negative energy in here: anger, despair, stifled voices. Something has been upset. The balance is off," She said, walking in farther and looking up the stairs.

Five

"MR. JACOBS, IT'S very nice to see you again. Pardon my thoughts. I'm sure I must seem to be a pessimist. I make a good portion of my living off of what I see and feel. I can get a really good sense for people and places, and something is different here from when I came in to give you the photographs."

Mr. Jacobs looked confused and a bit anxious. He didn't know what to make of any of this. Up until this evening, his life had been business as usual without any reason to think about the goings on of five years ago. Now, with Halloween fast approaching once again, here stood someone with no connection to the museum, who was reaffirming it held a life of its own.

Sulis was walking in a large circle in the great room, looking up and around in the corners. The three stood there, watching her intently. She was again wearing a long cloak, this time a black velvet one with a hood, pinned low under her chin by a large broach. Underneath was a long wine-colored dress with a lace overlay. Her auburn hair was scrunched into wavy curls with deep purple-red low lights, and five sets of earrings curved around her ears. She was without her glasses. Her makeup was done heavily with black eyeliner and smoke gray and plum shadow that extended past her eyes, and she had on the same peculiar perfume. On her hands were black half-finger lace gloves. She began to talk to no one in particular.

"I'm wondering if anyone can tell me what happened here tonight. I did several readings, and each time I went to take my cards out of my satchel, the death card would fall to the floor, the picture upside down. That is not a good sign."

"I broke open a gateway," Will confessed quietly. His face was tightly controlled but bits of anger and frustration broke through. Sulis frowned at him as he continued. "It could just mean change. You know as well as I, it may not necessarily signify death." Sulis was now glaring.

Jenna's confusion dissolved as she realized this was Will's mother. The confusion returned when she didn't understand what they were talking about. Mr. Jacobs stared at the two of them as if watching an interesting play on surrealism.

"Hold on. What is a death card?" Jenna asked Sulis.

Sulis approached the group and studied Jenna for a moment. Her gaze wandered slightly and became fixed on something just behind Jenna as if she were deep in thought.

"You've channeled here." She broke out of her musing, her eyes meeting Jenna's once again. "Tarot cards. It's a way of interpreting someone's life and their potential future. Each card represents something particular and when picked and laid down in a group, it pieces together a story, so to speak.

"The death card is a card in the deck. It has many meanings, depending on what card is drawn before it and after it, as well as what direction the card is facing. Drawn reversed means something different that being placed face up. Obviously, its literal meaning is death, but when placed upright it could stand for transformation. Something ending so something new can begin. But when it is upside down, as my cards were this evening, it represents painful change or exhaustive absolute ending. Usually I don't drop my cards at all, but I seemed to be off a little tonight. It caught me as odd that I consistently dropped the death card. It's making more sense to me now that I am here."

With that, she looked over at Will. "We have a conversation waiting for us, do we not?" she asked him.

Will nodded once and looked down at the floor briefly before walking toward the door. Sulis swept out in front of him, muttering to herself.

"I'll see you tomorrow at five for work, Mr. Jacobs. Jenna, good night." He walked out behind his mother. It was quiet for at least a whole minute.

"All right, then. I think it would be in our best interest, at this point, to close off the Sewing Room completely. No visitors. No one, Jenna," Mr. Jacobs said, holding her attention with his eyes.

"I'm sorry, Mr. Jacobs," Jenna whispered.

"I know, kiddo. What does all this mean? The window breaks, glass shatters into a thousand pieces, somehow your hands get burned, and now this. I certainly don't know Sulis other than meeting her the day she brought the box of pictures over a few weeks ago. How could someone so new to town feel something wrong here?" Mr. Jacobs thought out loud.

"I accidentally knocked her down in the store last week. She knew just by touching my hand that I was able to, well, whatever it is I'm able to do in this place."

"I think we may be in for another ride," he admitted, his face scrunched in concern. He looked very much like Toby in that moment. "We're so close to Halloween as it is. Maybe they'll be able to help us out. I just hope whatever it is they stand for is on our side. At least we know what we're working with here." He looked upstairs apprehensively as he turned off the main lights to lock up. "The window will be replaced first thing in the morning."

It was foggy outside and frigid for so late in September. It was a cold ride home and Jenna was worried. It didn't feel the same as last time. This time she had a feeling of foreboding.

EVEN WITH HER long gown and shorter strides she beat him to the car. Will closed the door and waited. The car started and made its way across the bumpy gravel parking lot.

"We're not here two weeks and already you're dabbling with gateways?" He braced himself figuratively and literally. Angry stones bounced off the undercarriage. He opened his mouth to speak but didn't get the opportunity. "And on your own? Is this something new now? Do you know how dangerous that is with a fully prepared coven let alone a fledgling seventeen-year-old going rogue?"

He wanted to roll his eyes but didn't dare. Not when she was this upset. "I wasn't going rogue Mom, you know that." His voice was low and calm. "And you're not giving me a chance to explain."

"I felt what I felt Will. My senses don't lie."

"I've never doubted that. It just looks worse than it really is." Even in the dim light of the cabin he could see the scowl on her profile as the car hit the pavement of the main road. He let out a moan. "Okay, it is bad, but I didn't do it on purpose. I didn't actively seek this out. I'm not ready for something like that, and you know I wouldn't do anything alone."

Sulis took a cleansing breath and eased her foot from the pedal. The car slowed to a more legal speed. "Do I? I wouldn't be able to stop you if you tried, you know." Her voice had leveled off and Will was hoping she would become more reasonable. The feelings coming at him, stinging him really, were of fear and vulnerability. As an empath he rarely felt them from her. She was the most level-headed person he knew. "We can't turn these things on and off. I thought you were aiming for discretion here."

"I was. I mean I am. I got nothing out of the ordinary from Mr. Jacobs or Jenna the first couple of days. She had some nervousness and insecurities, but I thought it was from having to train a new guy she didn't know. She mentioned a room upstairs that we needed to treat carefully, but never in a million years would I have guessed it housed a gateway and the building was active."

"Its tone was muted the few times I went in but nothing like this. Now it's like an achy cavity in a tooth." She paused. "You weren't showing off, were you?"

His face reflected the hurt he felt. She knew him better than that. It had only been the two of them since his father died years ago and their relationship was closer than most parent and child. He opened his senses to pick up what she was really feeling.

As an empath he was prone to being affected by the moods and energies of those around him. His intuition about others was rarely wrong. But sensitivity to those around him could be detrimental. At an early age his mother discovered this, nurtured it, and educated him on blocking. It had taken awhile to understand each particular emotion but the older he got, the better at it he became. Always being 'on' to other's feelings was an extremely exhaustive state.

Not only could Will absorb feelings, he was also susceptible to projecting those emotions as his own. Being around those who were negative or depressed could become downright unbearable so he learned how to tune in and out when he needed to. It was second nature now but he rarely needed to use it with her. He was picking up worry, protectiveness, and a feeling of loss. Feeling of loss? He put his wall back up. Now was not the time.

"I would never abuse those gifts," he answered. She reached over, her bracelets chinking against each other, and moved a lock of his hair away from his face.

"I know. I'm sorry. I didn't think the move would be hard for me."

"We've moved before." Several addresses flashed through his mind. So did the times he realized he was different from his classmates. His holidays revolved more around the Wheel of the Year equinoxes instead of anthropomorphism and Christian beliefs. Having a mother who clearly didn't subscribe to jeans and sweater sets didn't help. Being an empath he knew this. She continued, pulling him to the here and now.

"Yes, true. I didn't have to worry about you driving and holding down a job and finishing your last years of high school back then. Your independence is wonderful and exciting and inevitable. Having you away from me—growing up—is a harder adjustment than I thought it would be."

"You've done a good job. You've raised me right," he murmured, watching the dark trees pass his view. There were few street lights in this town.

"I'd like to think so, to think I encouraged the right values. Although I don't think any parent feels they've done the job justice. If anything, I hoped you understood and respected the spirit realm."

"Of course I do. Discreetly." With anyone else he would think hard and clearly about glassy seas and tranquil fields. Along with being able to feel the emotional tide of others he was good at projecting the atmospheric mood he wished to be embraced. He wouldn't dare with his mother. She would pick up on it right away. Her sensitivity was amazing even while irate.

She pursed her lips together before speaking. "We are not discussing my wardrobe again, Will. Right now, we're talking about what happened back there."

"It'll take a while to explain."

"Then I'll put on some tea. We have all the time in the world."

WILL OPENED THE door to his room and let out a huge breath. The ride home from work was too uncomfortable. Actually, the later part of the evening was uncomfortable. Being yelled at like he had been by his mother was rare, but never good, and it did nothing to relieve the guilt he already felt.

He lay down on the bed, putting the back of his socked feet up on the wall and the heels of his hands against his eyes. What a mess.

He was really hoping that moving to a new town was an opportunity to start over in more ways than one. His thoughts went back to the car ride and how he had always been an outcast, the strange kid with the weird-looking mother. Memories of his old elementary school flashed through his mind. He was the kid who called Halloween Samhain, and celebrated it as the New Year. In third grade, he was the only one who brought in Christmas cupcakes decorated with ivy vines and red candies resembling holly berries instead of Santas and reindeer. He didn't understand the confused looks from others.

THE MOVE DURING middle school was when he learned he was different from everyone else in their beliefs. He had brought home a pile of papers from his new teacher Miss Nash, and his mom was going through them while he washed his hands and fixed a snack.

"An 85 on your spelling test is great, Will. 'Musician' is a tough word. Math homework is due tomorrow so don't forget to put it in your folder when you're done. Oh, Strong Museum. I'll need to sign the permission slip for the field trip there. That's a fun place."

He sat down at the tiny table next to the counter, chewing his crackers with peanut butter and pointed to another paper. Their apartment was small and compact, it was only two steps. "You'll need to sign this one, too."

His mom picked up the green half sheet of paper, reading it through. "No, not this one," she said casually.

"Yeah because I can't go to these classes until you sign it," Will explained, picking up his glass of milk. "Lots of kids go."

"This is for Religious Education, honey. We don't practice what they would be teaching. Maybe, when you get older and would like to learn about other religions that would be okay. Not right now."

Little Will frowned, confused. "Other kinds?" His mom snagged a cracker and winked at him.

"Sure, why not? The world is a big place. We're Pagan, specifically Wiccan. This paper is for Methodists. There are Protestants, Catholics, Lutherans, Agnostics, atheists, those who practice Buddhism, Judaism, the list goes on. Some share similarities and others seem the opposite."

"You mean my new friends that go to Religious Ed don't have ceremony? What do they do?"

"No, not ceremony. They have a church service, but the idea is roughly the same. Take a napkin, sweetie, you have a milk moustache. We are duo theistic."

"Huh?" Will said, wiping his upper lip.

"What's duo mean?" She got up and started pulling items out of the fridge to make dinner.

"I love your mac and cheese."

"Focus, Will."

"Sorry." He slid out of his chair and reached up on tip-toes to grab the cheese grater from the cupboard. "Well, the dynamic duo is Batman and Robin, so two?"

"Yes. We worship both a Goddess and a God, the Moon Goddess…" She handed him the bricks of sharp and Muenster.

"And the Horned God."

"Very good. Some religions don't practice idolatry so they don't have a god or worship anyone particular." She started in on the white sauce.

"How do you know all this?" He turned away from her to sneak a mouthful of grated cheese.

"I saw that. Because I made a point to learn about what's out there. We are earth-based and value the elements of air, fire, water, earth, and spirit."

"I know. Do you think they'll send a paper around for Religious Ed for Wiccans?" He noticed his mother winced a bit.

"No, I'm very sure they won't."

Will opened his eyes and stared at the unfinished walls of his room. He remembered being excited to have learned something new that afternoon and tried to explain it to his two new friends, Scott and Mikey. Within a few days Scott told him his parents had decided not to have a birthday party at the bowling alley and to not bother going. By the next school week, all Will heard from his classmates was how great the party was. It seemed he was the only one who wasn't there. Within the next month both boys had changed lunch tables and were also sitting with different kids on the bus. This pattern repeated year to year, not only isolating him, but stigmatizing him and his family.

Six

*W*ILL REMEMBERED THE years in Libertyvale weren't much better for him. Word gets around fast when the town's psychic reader is your mother. It was easy fodder for stories of devil worshipping and evil witchcraft. Even though none of the rumors were true, they still hurt. Who knew the few years he was in that town they would see an upsurge of religious families steadfast in their own faith that held no room for nonconformists. He and his mother always took the high road, but didn't change the way they lived. For once, Will had wished he could have a do-over. He knew now what not to do and wanted to reinvent himself at his own pace. Orchard Creek was his last chance.

But then he had smashed the stupid apple through the worst possible window and there was something very bad attached to that. He tried to be blasé about that particular building's past, but it was hard to ignore after the apple went through. Of course, it had to be a portal to the after-life. He felt it. Usually he had a rough time 'feeling' a place. Not this one, no matter how much he hoped he was wrong. He knew better. This was a full-body electrical charge that also made him feel cold. It was so intense he had felt it while still outside. In the last hour he was in the museum he realized it had more activity than the strongest place he had ever experienced paranormal action. And that was saying something considering his upbringing.

As the only child of a single parent who was psychically talented, he found himself in places no one else his age would be in. He tagged along with his mom and her sisters—their coven—first out of need, and then for practice, to places with a reputation for hauntings or negative energy. The coven was well known in metaphysical circles around Libertyvale for being hired, so to speak, to clean areas the proper way. That included recognizing paranormal activity, how residual energy felt, and how to safely call forth entities to allow them to pass the living world to where they needed to go.

They had discovered Will's talents early in his life. He had trouble remembering that far back but one memory always stuck in his head. He had been about four. It was cold because he had his favorite Snoopy hat on. He was with his mom and her sisters: Diane, Lee, Mina, and Whitty, and they were at Fort Ontario in Oswego. A historic landmark today, it had been a military post for over a hundred years starting in the mid 1700's. The buildings there had seen harsh life conditions as well as death, components well known for creating restless spirits.

The women had been trying to connect with a Lieutenant Colonel Bishop, who was well known in the Guardhouse.

They had all held hands while his Aunt Mina had tried to call him forward. Will, trying very hard to fit in, had squeezed his eyes shut and listened while his aunt tried to reach the man. A frequent game he played to stay out of trouble was to repeat in his head every word the ladies said. This time when he repeated the words she used he also heard a man's voice, but didn't understand what he was hearing.

"He wants to play tag," Will said, his mood brightening with excitement as he looked up to his mother's face. Will loved to play games and was seldom able to since he was the only child in the family. She drew a breath, ready to scold him for talking out of turn when she stopped herself.

"What Will?"

"He said 'good tag,' Mommy."

"Honey, no one's said anything."

"Uh huh. The man did. I heard him." The women looked at each other, confused or amused, Will couldn't figure out which.

"This can't be possible," Whitty said. All the women were older than his mother, but Whitty was the one closest to her in age. She was thin and very pretty with light blond hair and bluish-gray eyes.

"No, it's not probable, but it is possible," his Aunt Diane replied, thinking. She was the oldest of the group, and the shortest, with baby-fine dark brown hair. "Remember last fall when we were at the old restaurant in Sterling? I'm almost sure the spirit showed up when Will started to sing the ABC song."

"What about the time Will repeated our greeting at the house on Westcott? We got activity as soon as he started to talk," Mina added. She looked a lot like Aunt Diane, being only a year younger than her.

Will watched his mother as different expressions crossed her face. "He was only three then! You think he can bridge the realms?"

Even if he didn't understand what they were talking about, he knew he wasn't in trouble. He still held her hand which was conveniently near his ear and snuck a finger under his hat to reach an itch. The deep voice spoke again and this time Will knew the tone of the words meant he wanted something even though the words were strange.

"He wants to talk, mommy."

"You're very talented, Sissy. Why should Will be any different?" Aunt Diane posed. "I took six years of German in school. Guten Tag is German for 'good day,' and I'm pretty sure Will isn't bilingual."

"Oh, Goddess, he's so young."

"Yes, but we can teach him and he'll be able to control it." Will looked across the circle at his Aunt Mina. She looked happy, so Will spoke to the man he heard.

"Hello?" He remembered how his voice sounded so little in the echo of the cavernous chamber.

"Hallo!" It was a whisper of sound, but clear and distinct, and one everyone heard.

"That wasn't exactly our English, was it?" Whitty asked.

"No. "Ah-low" is how it's pronounced in German," Aunt Diane replied. "I think we have ourselves a very talented young man."

Staring at the newly painted ceiling, Will grinned at the memory. Maybe being an empath like his mother gave him an edge for communicating with spirits. Maybe that was why he could bring them forward better than any of the ladies in their coven.

Actually, he was better at it than the other covens they sometimes worked among. In the northwest New York area, at least, there was no discrimination between groups in this field. Each felt comfortable calling individuals with a particular affinity to help with certain jobs.

So that spark of talent was encouraged, molded, and refined. At seventeen, his ability was incredible. It came easily to him, and didn't drain his own energy like it initially had. He was probably in a league with only a few others if he was ever interested in bragging.

But throughout all the years of doing house cleansings, ceremonies, and exploring places with a past, he had never experienced glass shattering like in Orchard Creek's museum. Or objects burning people. So much for trying to impress her with the largest apple he could find. His plans to begin again had been smashed apart tonight just like the apple that broke the window.

It couldn't get worse than that, right? Then his mother walked in. And she was wearing a work outfit. He had asked her nicely if she could limit the public places she wore those kinds of clothes. It was a delicate conversation. One he probably didn't do too gracefully because she became defensive. She reminded him she was being true to herself and was disappointed if he was embarrassed by her. The few times he had broached this it had gone the same way. He couldn't make it clear it had less to do with pride as it was about keeping it low key.

"Maybe I can salvage it," he thought out loud. "Jenna wasn't completely freaked out. If anything, she seemed hesitant, concerned." That kept his attention. "I might have to say something a little sooner than I wanted, but still." He sighed as he ran his hands through his tangled hair. He hadn't even made it past September. There was just too much room for failure. What had started out so well was now fractured. It could never be repaired as if it had never happened. Realizing the damage done at the museum would be harder to fix than just replacing the window, he worried again.

Opening a portal through ceremony with those trained to do it was purposeful, and invited in only the positive forces beyond. Breaking a portal without intension asked for trouble. It would be vulnerable and unguarded. Like having a huge hole in a screen door on a buggy summer night, it was an open invitation for anything bad to get in. Especially with the stories Jenna had told him. He wondered how she would react to how he and his mother would need to be involved to fix it. If they could. A bit of panic settled in his chest. If it were true that this spirit, Seth, had actually tried to kill Jenna, they might be in over their heads. There were limits, despite how talented he and his family was. For one, his mother never dropped her tarot cards. Ever. Especially the death card.

He undressed for bed. There was so much that needed to be fixed up. It bothered him their house was still a shell. He wasn't used to living in sheetrock and disorder. When they had bought the large old house back in the beginning of summer, they had commuted on their days off from work to gut it and renovate. Even after moving in August they had only completed what they had named the Red Room downstairs, most of the kitchen, and both upstairs and downstairs bathrooms. His room still needed painting, and the floors needed to be buffed down and polished. It was dreary and depressed him.

Taking a deep breath, he closed his eyes and exhaled slowly. He centered himself, focusing his concentration on his body and thoughts being one. He would pull some positive energy, up from his toes if he needed to, and find good here. He visualized a running brook in a deep wood, its journey led by nature's gentle motion. It was quiet with faint bird song in the distance and the rustling of leaves whispering to each other when the breeze picked up. He imagined his troubles as easy to overcome as the water over the smooth stones, its energy filling and renewing him. Imagining a white light molding to the outline of his body, he acknowledged it before allowing it to seep into his very being. He pictured what he wanted to happen in his life. The tension in his muscles eased. His breathing smoothed out.

Jenna. His thoughts had once again turned to her. Her smile seemed to stay in his mind's eye. It took his breath away every time and left his mind blank. More than once she sidetracked him and his carefully laid plan. She was nice—different—and pretty in a natural way. She had caught his attention at school a few times in the hallway and from across the cafeteria, and he was a more than a little surprised when he realized she worked at the museum. She had friends, but didn't belong to the popular crowd. And she wasn't at all like the cookie-cutter girls with the same hair style and clothes. He had a thing for girls with long hair anyway, and hers smelled like a bouquet of hyacinths. It lingered in her wake, and he found himself walking by her just to enjoy it. Her brown eyes were always warm and trusting, and her full lips were mesmerizing. When she smiled her whole face filled with genuine happiness.

They even shared several things in common. He noticed right away she was left- handed like he was. That usually indicated someone creative and talented in the arts. Still smiling, he opened his eyes. She not only worked in a type of place he enjoyed working, she had been there for years. As if that wasn't incentive enough to pursue, she had experience with the paranormal. She said it herself she felt it. It was more than that, he reminded himself, she believed and didn't seem completely terrified it was starting again. What were the odds he could find someone that might actually understand and accept him? Could it be that easy?

His overall mood was much brighter as he got ready for bed.

SLEEP ELUDED JENNA for quite some time. She half expected to have dreams of the museum but didn't. At first, her dreams were broken, vague, and disorganized. For a while, Will was there along with his mother. They had been sitting around a table decorated with sunflowers, sipping tea out of mugs. They talked a lot about their approach and what tools they'd need. Will said he didn't think it would be like any job they'd come across, and he was worried about safety. Their planning involved a lot of things Jenna didn't understand.

Then the dream faded to a thinner Sulis and younger Will. He was maybe five. They were at an outdoor concert with several ladies that Jenna was almost sure were related to Sulis due to their similar appearance. They were helping little Will work on something but Jenna couldn't figure it out.

"Will, what are you feeling right now?"

"Um, hungry," he said confidently. His voice was higher and lighter and it made the dreaming Jenna smile.

The one who looked like the oldest of the bunch threw her head back and snorted a little, wiggling her stubby, painted toes. They were all sitting on beach blankets, enjoying the warm summer evening. "He's ours, that's for sure," the woman replied. Sulis gave her a faux glare as she tucked her long auburn hair behind her ear and turned back to Will.

"Concentrate, honey. Reach out, hmm, try not to think of anything. Focus on your breathing, just like we taught you." Will didn't hesitate to close his eyes. His little lips puckered as he blew his breath out. Barely touching him, Sulis began to rub her hand up and down his arm. Jenna soon made the connection. As Sulis swept her hand up, Will breathed in. When she brushed down, Will exhaled. There was a tiny line of tension in his eyebrows even then. Within a few seconds, his face smoothed out and his mouth slackened. "Good. Now, with each breath out I want you to try to listen to what people are doing around you. Not to their words but the energy around the words."

"Describe the energy again, Sissy. He forgot last time." This came from the woman closest to Sulis. She had lighter hair with the start of some gray in it. Sulis nodded but held her hand out as if to say 'hold on."

"Remember, anger feels pointy, and sadness is like water, but heavy."

"Why aren't you reminding him what happiness feels like?"

"Lee, please," Sulis answered quietly.

"Because Rebekah wants him to concentrate on something he has to search for," the oldest whispered, rolling her eyes. "There's too much happiness here for him to isolate."

"Oh. That's pretty clever. Good idea."

"I found two," Will announced a moment later, his eyes still closed. No one spoke. The women looked at each another, some with trepidation, others with awe. "Over by the speakers near the water."

Everyone turned to the right, trying to see what Will had found. The woman named Lee pointed. There, quite a way from them was a couple by one of the speaker systems. It was too loud for their words to be heard. The guy had just rolled over and was still lying on his back. His girlfriend or wife was gesturing with her finger to him and the stage. Her face was red. If he had fallen asleep during the concert she had good reason to be embarrassed and upset.

"Winner winner, chicken dinner, Will. That was much faster than last time."

"Awesome!" he said, clearly proud of himself as he riffled through their cooler for a juice box. "I hope we have grape, that's my favorite, right mom?" Sulis ruffled his hair and he ducked out from her hand to straighten it. Jenna smiled again as she rolled over. The dream morphed again to something Jenna couldn't recall later.

The next day at school, Jenna searched for Toby during lunch. She would have to talk with Tina later. Even though Tina shared the same lunch hour, she was seldom there, preferring to spend her time in the band room with her boyfriend instead. Jenna found Toby back in line for seconds and briefed him quickly on what happened the night before.

"Yeah, dad was talking about it last night while my mom was teaching her ceramics class. The new guy broke the window, huh? That's like, what, seven years back luck?" he managed to say between bites. His voice had dropped an octave, and he was over a foot and a half taller since the last time they had problems in the old mill. No longer wiry, he was muscular and fit. His blond hair, a bit darker now, was cut short and neat.

"No, Tobe, that's breaking a mirror, although I don't know how this would be much different. Something feels wrong, and Halloween is next month. I never know what to expect there." Jenna sounded so worried, Toby stopped eating and looked at her.

"We'll be there if you need us. You know we will. Try not to worry." He leaned over and smacked a kiss on her cheek without giving it a second thought. Jenna leaned into him, smiled, and nodded her head in agreement. Across the room, taking his tray up to the trash was Will, watching everything with a frown on his face.

Seven

THE NEXT NIGHT, Jenna arrived for work and found more cars there than usual. She knew Will would be there, but didn't expect to see anyone else. Tina was with there with her father, Mr. Levy, standing by the staircase. Mr. Jacobs was introducing them and Toby to Will and Sulis. Sulis was wearing more normal clothes than Jenna had ever seen her in before. She had on stretchy black pants tucked into ankle boots and an oversized white tunic with three long necklaces. Still, all her fingers were decorated with rings. Slung over her arm was her black cape. Her amber hair was without accents and her face clean of makeup. She was very attractive.

"Great, Jenna's here. Let's pow-wow," Mr. Levy stated.

"Hey Toby, Tina, good to see you," Jenna said. She smiled at Will who smiled back at her. "Hi Will. What's going on? I didn't know there was going to be a forum."

"Jenna, last minute thing, you know. Meeting of the minds, if you will." Mr. Jacobs seemed uncomfortable.

"Mr. Jacobs filled us in on what happened last night and thought maybe we could brainstorm ideas on what to do. We tried to get your dad but he was tied up a management meeting," Tina explained. She was still petite, standing only five feet four, but had filled out nicely. Her bright blue eyes dominated her features, despite the wire-rimmed glasses she now wore. Her black hair, cut just below her shoulders, was tied back neatly in a clip. She still wore conservative clothes: brown corduroys with a cream- colored mock turtleneck and ballet flats. Across her chest was an ever-present messenger bag. Replacing the Hello Kitty purse she had when she was younger, was a simple brown one with a magnetic snap.

They talked for a while filling Sulis in on what they knew of the building's past and listening while Jenna described what she saw and felt when the apple crashed through the Sewing Room window. She held out her hands to show what was left of the burns, they had healed with only a faint pink remaining. Even though Will had been introduced to everyone, he kept his gaze on Jenna the whole time.

"I just have a bad feeling. I really think that window is the doorway to something beyond and now it's back open. We don't know how to shut it," Jenna said.

"Well, we do shut it. Often," Mr. Jacobs admitted. "Yesterdayay morning it was wide open. The window pane was replaced by eleven and when I checked after work it was open again. A lot of the smaller antiques in that room were tipped over this morning. When I checked just a few minutes ago one section of the bolts of material were all collapsed onto each other like dominos. The window was open—no surprise there—but the things that were disturbed couldn't have been from the wind."

"And you all believe it's a portal, a literal doorway between our world and the after world?" Sulis asked to clarify.

"Sounds nuts, but yeah," Toby admitted.

"That window was where a young man lost his life over a hundred years ago. It's documented as fact," Jenna stated. "There's been mention of the same window in diaries, and even when the renovation was attempted around 1929 that room was to blame for many accidents. I looked into it further and found an article from the Orchard Creek Chronical. It mentioned the accidents only briefly because they could be reasonably explained. What shut down the whole operation was the fatality. The construction company had at least three different guys who said they saw the foreman being dragged to that window by a man in his early twenties wearing black clothes and black top hat. They all swore they tried to stop this mystery man. But they couldn't touch him, it was like he was invisible. Together, the men pulled their boss back when it became apparent he was going to be dragged out the window, but this man was stronger."

The room was silent with everyone's attention on Jenna while they listened.

"The article said they struggled and tugged, three on one. They managed to keep their foreman in the building, but the window let loose and he was under it. It wasn't that heavy, but it crushed his ribs and lungs. He died instantly. The mystery man pulling him disappeared through the second story window laughing, but was never seen by the workers outside.

"It might have gone down as a murder or something, but those three workers had never complained about management, were good employees, and none had a legal record. All three were well regarded in the community."

"Actually," Tina interjected, "the man who died was the uncle of Mrs. Travers. She was the nurse at the middle school."

"And I'm pretty sure the man wearing black was Seth Sawyer, except there is no way Seth, who would have then been around fifty-four years old, could pass for someone in his early twenties. This event sounds incredibly close to my own experience, except something somewhere stopped me from actually getting through the window. Instead, I wound up in the hospital for a couple days."

"Seth materialized at our first Halloween fundraiser and didn't seem much older than us." Toby flexed his arms absent-mindedly with the memories. "Tina and I were in the middle of it. We tried to rush him and we couldn't touch him either. Later, when Jenna found this info, it kinda freaked us out. What we experienced was too close to what had happened before."

"And you three were only twelve or so." Mr. Jacobs expression showed exactly how he felt about the dangers they had faced.

"Ultimately, the other ghosts in the room got rid of Seth. That power or whatever built to a head. When they all disappeared, the window was closed and sealed. That seemed to do it," Toby added. Sulis nodded, considering everything.

"Jenna, have you had any new dreams or anything?" Tina asked hopefully.

"No, it's different this time," Jenna replied.

"If I may, I'd like to stay here a while, walk around, and see what I can pick up," Sulis offered.

"I mean no disrespect ma'am, but you weren't here five years ago and have never dealt with what we have encountered," Mr. Levy interjected defensively.

"I have had many encounters in my time, but you're correct, not here. I understand your protective stance with this building. Right now, I might be helpful to you," Sulis offered gently.

Mr. Levy, who had never truly wanted to believe in the paranormal, was still skeptical. "I don't believe so in this case."

Sulis sighed as if this confrontation came up often. She closed her eyes and concentrated. "I know you doubt what this building holds, but I also know you would protect it to uphold the memory of the childhood your grandparents carved for you. That is, despite the potential to be hurt by it. You struggle with what you've seen and what you believe. They war with each other."

Mr. Levy's mouth dropped open so quickly, everyone could hear the audible pop. "How did you…? Who did you talk to?" He already knew there was no one who knew that information. His grandparents had been gone for over a decade.

"I can also sense how the success of your fundraisers dictate how long this establishment remains open."

It was Jenna's and Mr. Jacobs's turn to look uncomfortable.

Jenna looked up cautiously at Will, but again, he had on a poker face she couldn't read.

"Now, I've had experience in many different kinds of interactions, and I believe I can help here if you would like me to try," Sulis offered quietly.

"I'm all right with you doing a walk through. Do we have any other suggestions?" Mr. Jacobs asked. Everyone, still surprised, shook their heads. "We don't have anything to lose at this point. Jenna, please let your dad know when you get home. We need to have everyone who was here five years ago up to speed. Hopefully, we won't need an intervention this time. If we want to maintain our credibility and the town's perception of our sanity, I know we really can't let anyone on the outside be involved in this, uh, situation. Except maybe Sulis." Mr. Jacobs looked over at Sulis and smiled slightly.

"Who ya gonna call?" Toby mumbled in a sing-song voice, stuffing his large hands into his jeans pockets.

"We handled it before, so we can do it again if needed. If we do, though, this is the team to do it. Is everyone on board?" Mr. Jacobs asked. Everyone nodded in agreement.

Tina and Toby stayed behind with Jenna, Will at her side.

"So, you haven't been looking through old magazines and newspapers to find another girl like you, right?" Toby asked, mock-punching Jenna in the arm. She scrunched up her face before it relaxed into a comfortableness that tolerated her friend's sense of humor.

"No, Tobe."

"Remember how we thought all those ghosts were people from town?" asked Tina.

"Oh yeah," exclaimed Toby, becoming animated. "That's right! Their clothes were so much better than ours."

Jenna laughed. "If I recall correctly, your mustache was too big for your face. By the end of the night, the adhesive stopped working and one side kept flapping every time you'd say something. It was kinda cute."

"For a brother," Tina snickered. Jenna chuckled, joining in on their old joke of how brothers stink.

"Tina smelled like my mom's make-up area."

"You're such a guy. That was all the hairspray."

"And Jenna, your eye color got a little strange," Toby stated. He frowned and leaned into Jenna's face. "Well, at least you're still you right now."

By this time, Will had drifted off by himself to the pictures they had cleaned for the display. Sulis went outside to walk the grounds, and Mr. Levy and Mr. Jacobs took around a bus tour group of eight that just arrived. A few minutes later, Jenna hugged her friends, lingering a bit longer with Toby, who was whispering in her ear. Jenna reddened, giggled, and waved goodbye as they left. It was suddenly quiet and the air seemed heavy in the room. Will had been shifting pictures about on a table, trying to look occupied.

"So, that's your mom," Jenna started. She was consciously trying to be as neutral as possible to let Will lead.

"Yeah. Her real name is Rebekah. Rebekah Willowby Greenley. She goes by Sulis for her part time job, but prefers Sulis anyway."

"That's pretty," Jenna remarked, now joining Will in

rearranging the pictures haphazardly. "I bumped into her a few days back. I think she can help us here."

"Oh," Will commented, not really hearing Jenna. "What?" he asked, finally realizing what she was saying.

"I literally bumped into her in the store the other day. She knew about the thing I had with Elizabeth and all. She seems to be a cool mom."

Will seemed relieved and smiled a little. Then he looked over at the door, frowned momentarily, and then resumed his poker face. "That's great. I'm glad you're okay with her. Not everyone is as accepting," Will admitted, still guarded.

The evening was a complete wash when it came to talking to Will. There was too much going on in the building, and now there was an odd distance between them that Jenna couldn't understand. Both were preoccupied with every little noise in the building, but Jenna was sure it had nothing to do with that. She kept replaying her conversations with him in her head, unable to figure out what had changed.

Sulis walked back inside, a bit winded from the lengthy walk just as the tourists were finishing up. She pulled the hood of her cloak off her hair and exhaled. "There are layers everywhere. Overlapping layers outside in the orchard, down by the creek, near the storm cellar. It is the coldness of death. I would like you to accompany me as I do a walk-through in here, Miss Jenna."

Jenna's head shot up to look at Sulis. A cold shiver ran down her spine. "Why did you say that? Why did you call me *Miss* Jenna?" she asked.

"It's like picking up an accent when you hear it enough. And I've heard it a lot here."

Memories of Mrs. Forrester instantly flooded Jenna's mind. She hadn't really thought about her in a long while. Jenna's face softened as she remembered her and Tina's afternoon visits for stories and lemonade, and how Mrs. Forrester had called her Miss Jenna from the very first day. Coming back to the present moment, Jenna nodded, and walked toward Sulis, feeling a bit exposed. A lot of things Sulis said mirrored her own thoughts. Will came over, and the three of them decided to do a walk-through from the basement up.

Jenna flipped on the light as they walked down the steep, small steps to the dirt floor basement. The light cast shadows, and Jenna was at once uncomfortable. They walked slowly, Sulis pausing occasionally, cocking her head to the side and saying 'hmm'. She seemed to be listening or concentrating very hard.

"Ooh, this place needs a good smudging," Sulis finally stated.

Jenna was curious. "What's that?"

"It's a way of purifying a space and getting rid of bad spirits," Will answered. If Jenna hadn't been used to the quiet tone, she would have missed it. Then again, everything he did caught her interest.

"Sage is used for smudging because it has healing properties. We use a bundle of dried sage wrapped together with twine. We light it and blow out the flame. The smoke is then taken from window to door to clean and bless a house. We make our intentions known by asking any unwanted spirits to leave and to clear the space of negative energy," Sulis added.

"Oh. We could sure use that here," Jenna agreed, nodding her head. She was intrigued and surprised. Will seemed to know so much about what his mother did. Jenna had never heard of smudging before, but it sounded interesting. She had heard of house blessings, but the only image that came to mind was of her pastor visiting a house with a Bible and maybe some Holy water. Her family wasn't particularly religious.

They reached the far corner where the storm cellar door was, and Sulis stopped walking. It was one of the old-fashioned types, with stairs starting from the basement floor and going up and outside to the ground level. Inside the basement there were five steps before the large forty-five-degree angle door separating the interior from the exterior. Jenna and Will turned around.

"I can't go farther. There is something here that is preventing me from going on: a young girl, two men, someone with keys. I can smell gunpowder. Can you smell the gunpowder?" Sulis asked.

"No, I can't," Jenna stammered. The hair on her neck stood on end with what Sulis observed and how Will was taking in every inch of the room. Jenna wanted to leave that area, but was having trouble getting her feet to move. "Let's go this way, okay?"

Sulis nodded and seemed more at ease after that, walking around the rest of the basement. Her face relaxed, and she didn't hold herself quite so stiffly. Neither seemed bothered by the cobwebs and grime from the stone walls. For the rest of the walk downstairs everyone was silent. Jenna thought at first Sulis had been talking about Elizabeth, Joseph, and Seth, but the keys Sulis mentioned didn't fit. And she was almost certain they didn't have anything to do with a gun.

"There have been a lot of arguments here, very strong emotions. They feel just as strong from above as well."

The three walked up the main staircase. Jenna asked if she wanted to go in the Sewing Room first, the Display Room, or the other smaller rooms that were upstairs. Without answering, Sulis began walking toward the new Display Room. Jenna and Will followed. Just inside the door, Sulis stopped. She cocked her head to one side again.

"I almost expected something worse here," she said, her eyes resting on the pictures scattered about on the floor. She went in farther, moving her long dress to one side so as not to disturb the pictures. Slowly she waved her hands over the grouping, then picked up each one, flipped it over, and turned it around. "Will's told me you have concerns about the photographs."

"There's nothing wrong with them. It's just something doesn't feel quite right about what they're of or where they were found. The museum was about to redesign this room to focus on the boarding house. Then you drop off these photos." Jenna took a deep breath and continued. "I don't believe in coincidences."

Jenna thought she'd see a patronizing look, or maybe even indifference from Sulis. Instead, it was more like she was impressed and pleased about it. "Nor do I."

When Sulis had held each of them, she stood up, looked out onto the landing and walked to the left, putting her hand behind her as if to signal for Jenna and Will to stay behind. Jenna ignored the motion and followed Sulis out of the room as did Will, keeping up at Jenna's side.

A cold chill passed over Jenna as she neared the door at the end of the landing just as Sulis pulled her cape close and stopped in front of the door to the Sewing Room. She motioned for Jenna to open the door and waited while Jenna fished the keys out of her pocket. The door swung open and they could see that the repaired window was – once again – open, the wind whipping into the room as soon as they walked over the threshold.

"It is bad here," Sulis winced. "This is the room. I hurt in my chest, and I have an overwhelming urge to cry. Don't go near the window, Jenna," she cautioned. "It's not safe there. You have been mistaken for someone else, and they don't realize time has moved on. Ooh, there's too much; I need to sit."

She sat on the floor between the glass pile and the pictures Jenna had dropped when they vibrated and got hot. She scooped up the tiny pieces of glass and poured them gently from hand to hand, lost in thought.

"Oh, be careful, you'll cut yourself," Jenna warned.

"But somehow I'm not. Yes, there are shiny things here too." She tipped her hand and the glass tumbled out. When she reached out to pick up the picture that had been in the frame, Jenna gasped loudly, afraid Sulis would be burned. But Sulis pulled the picture close to her face as if to study the details. Still holding the first picture, she reached for the second and compared them.

"There's nothing wrong with trusting your instincts, Jenna.

I feel the vibration in them too. This 'not quite right feeling' you have, was that when you first started handling them?"

Jenna hung her head. It was still weird to talk to others about this kind of stuff. "No, I felt it on Will's first day when he mentioned finding the pictures."

"I'm not surprised. Those who are sensitive pick things up quicker. There is definitely a radiating energy in these photographs, however. Did you see the date? It's across the top of the picture and has next week's date in it, or on it, it's hard to tell. Did you see the date?" Sulis asked.

Eight

*J*ENNA BLANCHED AND shook her head. She was unable to say anything with her mind racing the way it was. Sulis picked up the picture taken from the dirt road.

"I get very negative feelings when I look at the storm cellar from this picture. Something dark, it's fuzzy to me. I can't seem to zero into it, but as vague as it is, I also keep thinking of bright lights when I hold this picture. Something blinding, maybe? Shiny. Hmm, I'm not exactly sure." Sulis put the picture of the interior room with the unknown staircase down and looked around the room.

"There is a lot of sadness, anger, and horror here. Your imprint is here too, Jenna, and a maternal figure. I'm picking up a person who was older and very protective of both this place and the young people who came inside, but there are too many layers. I can't see what belongs to which. An odd name:

Allie, Amy—no—Amelie. Amelie. Yes, someone by that name is very strong here. There is a relationship to her in a few of these pictures."

Sulis sifted through and brought out the picture of the smaller room off the main staircase. "Things have been moved, though. Something has changed up here." She studied the wall opposite the window.

"I don't know what could have changed, it's just the basement, the main floor, and this level."

"That can't be right," Sulis disputed. "This building is taller than our house and we have two levels above the floor."

Jenna shrugged. "None of the pictures have ever shown a larger building. It can't extend farther because of the creek. This one looks like it'd have an upper floor or attic but it doesn't. Mr. Levy once said something about it having a façade."

"That is odd," Sulis commented, dismissing the questionable dimensions.

"What is it that I'm able to do?" Jenna asked hesitantly. "What exactly is 'channeling'?"

"It's a way of being a voice for something that no longer has one of their own. When a living human becomes a vessel to relay the thoughts or carry out the wishes of something without a tangible body of their own to do so," Sulis explained patiently.

Jenna thought that through for a moment. Then she thought about how Sulis actually believed everyone that gathered, and was puzzled by how much she just knew on her own. "How do you do what you do?" Jenna continued to ask.

"I consider it a gift. Do you know how some people can

pick up an instrument and play it without ever having lessons? It just comes to them?"

"Oh, like Paul McCartney?" Jenna asked, her face brightening.

Sulis smiled. "Ah, a Beatles fan. Yes. It's a lot like that. Images come to mind, feelings wash over me, and words or thoughts pop into my head that I'm not consciously thinking. It takes some time to control. I need to let my mind be at ease in a state of peace and let those things come to me. And, just like you, I need to be able to relay those thoughts out loud."

"Oh. So, you 'hear' a lot when you're in here?" asked Jenna slowly, looking around the room. She was aware Will was watching her intently again, but it was an observation she didn't feel compelled to address. There was so much to think about. Finally, answers to all the things she didn't understand.

"Yes, I do. I feel it is just as strong in here as it is in you on the day we met. The frequency, for a better word, is somehow the same."

"Huh. Wow." Jenna really didn't know how to sum it up better than that. Someone like her, at least in a way. It gave her comfort to know there were others and she tried to put it off to the side to chew on later as there were more important things to think about. "Well, I'm not sure if something was changed here. There are no blueprints or anything else to go by other than the few records we've found and the pictures you brought over." Jenna continued with the previous topic. "Do you want to look at the other pictures again, now that we've cleaned them up?"

The trio met the men in the great room and went over to

the display. Sulis picked up the framed pictures Jenna and Will had been arranging. She examined each one and placed them back down in definite piles like oversized cards from a huge deck. She told the men about what she saw in the photographs upstairs. Both were wide-eyed and uneasy.

"This is an anomaly. I usually can't read pictures, but the feelings and images I'm getting are so strong in here. I can read these as easily as my tarot cards. I am putting these in chronological order."

Jenna shook her head, mesmerized. Will was quiet, still taking in Jenna's expressions. At this, Mr. Jacobs seemed excited and nervous. Mr. Levy just watched, not sure what to make of the situation.

Sulis picked up the picture of the woman standing by the sign in front of the building.

"This boarding house was inherited or given to the owners. I don't believe it was something the couple wanted. There is a disconnected feeling when I see the picture of the owner's wife near the sign. Unhappiness. She is alone. Perhaps her husband wasn't here much or worked elsewhere, and this was her burden. I feel a lot of loneliness and sorrow when I hold this." Sulis put the picture down with an air of finality.

"There is one thing very clear to me, though. It wasn't common for dates to be written this way back then, but each of these pictures holds next week's numerical date of 10-01 in them. There's no way to be sure if it's October of 1801, 1901, 2001 or if it just references October first in general. Regardless, it's a palindrome—the same whether it's backwards or forwards. Obviously, no one but myself can see them. I think it's pertinent to be here on that day to see what the significance is. We may want to bring in more invasive methods too, to figure this out. Are you up for being put to work, Will?" Sulis asked, putting her fists on her hips.

"Yeah," Will replied quietly. "I think it's time."

"What do you mean?" Jenna mustered, feeling uneasy.

"Ouija boards," Will answered, looking down. To Jenna, he looked like he was bracing himself for something painful.

"Oh." Jenna didn't really know what that meant, and was still confused. Mr. Jacobs made a noise of affirmation and opened his date book, searching.

"My mom is great at reading things but you can't necessarily get all questions answered that way. I'm a whiz on the Ouija board," Will explained plainly, his eyes not meeting hers. "I'm a good conductor to what's beyond and able to pick up the vibes of others. Especially those who have crossed over."

Jenna's attention had been on Sulis but did a double take at Will. She felt like a train had just run her over, and she didn't even know one was coming. "You can?"

"He has since he was three," Sulis added offhandedly, wandering towards the wall and straightening a frame.

Jenna felt a bit in over her head. All she could picture was a stupid image of Will in a blue and white stripped train hat, swinging a handheld lantern. "What's an Ouija board?"

"An Ouija looks a lot like a board game, like chess. It has a board and pieces. What makes it different from a game is the way it's used. You don't play on it. Questions are asked of it while hands are on the pointer, or pawn, so to speak. Some believe it can open a window to the world beyond where spiritual forces direct our hands to letters on the board to spell out words to form answers. Some simple answers are already written on the board. Communicating and receiving messages from the spirit world can connect us to those who have died, give insight to what's around us, or what's ahead of us.

"It doesn't necessarily work for everyone who uses it. Some are better at receiving these messages than others." Sulis inclined her head toward her son. "Will has always had a knack for bringing forth the other side to communicate." She turned towards the men. "Clearly though, we were meant to explore. A message has been left for us, but it's a gamble, you know. We'd be taking a lot of chances here that leaves us vulnerable."

"Taking chances?" Mr. Jacobs repeated the warning, perplexed.

"If there really is something lingering, it may not want us to interfere. Especially with the history you informed me of when the renovation started. This doesn't sound like a harmless, mischievous poltergeist."

"In what way would we be leaving ourselves vulnerable?" Jenna asked hesitantly.

"Opening ourselves to the unknown is frightening. You never know what you're encouraging or what may cross over."

"Well, at least that's not new to us," Mr. Levy replied tersely.

"Maybe that date has some relevance in us closing that window for good, Mark. What do you think, Jenna?" Mr. Jacobs asked.

Jenna had grown used to trusting her instincts, especially when it came to this building. She was scared out of her mind, but was realizing that even though she had only known Will for a short time, she felt comfortable with him. Safe. She didn't know exactly why, but she trusted him just as much. What Sulis and Will talked about was intriguing despite how foreign it was to her. In her own way, she was unconventional as well. She nodded and smiled a little at Will, who finally released the tension he had been holding. Jenna closed her eyes and nodded. "I trust you. I'm in."

Nine

"NEXT WEEK'S DATE of October first is on a Saturday. Too bad it wasn't on Sunday, we're closed then," Mr. Jacobs said, flipping through his calendar.

"No matter," Sulis answered, unaffected. "It would be better, though, that the building is at rest from other's influence. Saturday evening after closing would be ideal."

"What do we need? What should we bring?" Mr. Levy asked, tiredly. "I'm willing to go along with this, but I'm not sure if I buy into this whole voodoo thing." Big words and lots of jewelry aside, he wondered if it was possible to have the ability to 'see' things. What happened in 1996 didn't matter. It didn't matter that he knew he had witnessed dead people in the old mill. He didn't have any explanations for that or how those beings disappeared in front of his own eyes. Still, he didn't have to entertain the thought that this kind of stuff was common enough that it existed everywhere.

"Everyone who had the experience of five years ago must be here. Each has some capacity for allowing the transference from before to affect them. With something of this magnitude, we should start with a séance to try to communicate and hopefully receive spiritual messages. Sometimes we must take it a step further and use the Ouija. We can try to figure out what the message means. If we're able to connect with others, we can attempt to see what they want now. Perhaps they are lost or confused and need help finding peace." At this, Will just shook his head in disagreement. "You believe otherwise, Will?"

"It doesn't feel like a request for help. It feels…angry."

Sulis turned away from her son. Whether it was because she wanted to divert attention from what he said, or if she wanted the focus elsewhere, no one knew. "We will need candles for natural light. Candlelight is more conducive to bring the other side forward. I will bring everything else."

"It's getting late, and you two need to get home or you'll be dragging at school tomorrow," Mr. Levy observed. Everyone stood up and collected their belongings in silence, each one trying to absorb what this evening had brought.

"Oh, hey, Will," Jenna called, pink coloring her cheeks. "Tomorrow is Homecoming. I'm sure you still don't know a lot of people, so if you're going and would like some company we can, um, walk around together."

Will's eyebrows perked up before his face settled into the neutral expression he wore most of the evening. "That'd be great, but I thought you'd go with Toby. And Tina."

"Tina's in the marching band so she's busy. Although Toby stopped playing football, he still won't be there. He's now into wrestling and the coach doesn't care if the whole town is celebrating. They have a practice."

"Ok." Now it was his turn to blush. "But I can't pick you up, mom has my car."

"It's okay, I can drive. I know where your place is. How about five?"

JENNA'S SHORT DRIVE home had her reconsidering. What was she thinking? Had she really asked Will out? Yes, she had. No, not really. It wasn't like a real date. And, she remembered too late there was a dance. Usually, she only went to watch Tina play in the parade and to root Toby on. Sometimes she hung out with them after that, but she never stayed for the dance, even when she was dating Alan.

SATURDAY TURNED INTO one of those autumn days that defied Mother Nature's journey toward winter. Bright blue skies were broken up by pure white clouds perfect for lying in the grass, guessing shapes. Changing leaves on the trees became brilliant gems that emitted crisp cinnamon into the air. Jenna missed a lot of it, sitting on her bed, her attention shifting from the pared outfits hanging on her closet door to the shirts and slacks dangling from open dresser drawers.

Should she wear jeans? A dress would imply she wanted to go to the dance with Will. Not that she wouldn't be opposed to saying yes if he asked. Jeans and a nice top would be casual enough without trying too hard, right? This boyfriend thing was confusing. She shut her eyes and shook her head. She needed to stop changing her hope into reality. The afternoon flew by as she second-guessed every choice.

Jenna pulled into Will's driveway, feeling pretty good in a green, scoop-necked blouse and dark blue jeans that seemed dressy. The decision to wait versus walking up to the house was taken away when Will came out before she could shut the car off. He smiled as he shortened the distance between them.

"What a beautiful day. You look lovely, Jenna." Her car filled with citrus and sandalwood as she put it in reverse.

"Thank you. Orchard Creek's been known to have a few. You look very nice yourself." The pleasantries dried up faster than she thought they would. With no work to distract her, she would have to think of something to talk about. There was no way she could make it to the high school without some form of conversation.

"This will be my first Homecoming, so I'm at a disadvantage. I hope you don't mind too terribly much if I ask to cut the evening a bit short. Early curfew until we're settled in a little more, I'm afraid."

"That's brilliant," Jenna exclaimed, as she realized she wouldn't have to stress about the dance. Unfortunately, she realized too late she said it out loud.

"What?"

"Nothing," she stammered, mentally kicking herself.

When she glanced over to Will she noticed his hand was over his mouth but his cheeks were turned up.

"So, tell me about your plans for after school," Will asked. It sounded like a rehearsed line and Jenna grinned to herself. They were exactly alike and somehow, that helped her relax.

"Community College for my liberals just like everyone else here. I mean, for those of us who don't have disposable money and run right off to a four-year university."

"No, it sounds like a smart move."

"It's a start that'll give a little more time to figure things out."

"What do you want to do?"

Jenna tipped her head as if weighing her options. "I really don't know. There's so much pressure to find ourselves. I love history and a career in that sounds good. I'm not sure if I could get a practical, well-paying job out of it, though. What about you?"

"My mom says we all should get jobs doing what we're good at."

"That's good advice. And…" Jenna tried to draw him out.

"So, according to her I should excel at Communications. Apparently, I'm good at talking." As soon as he finished, his mouth hardened. She could almost see him chastising himself.

"Oh? I wouldn't know." Jenna smirked, trying to lighten the moment. "Anyway, we don't have to chat about anything heavy. The stuff at the museum is what it is. That's one thing I've learned about the place. We can't change anything about it tonight."

"I agree." With the weight lifted, both found it easier to have fun. The mild evening brought out a good crowd. The band played songs from *Moulin Rouge* and the latest *Jurassic Park* movie. Will joined in applauding loudly when Tina marched past, clad in the school colors of brown and turquoise. By 8:30 p.m., Toby and Tina found them in the food tent, eating eggplant sandwiches.

"It's about time we found you," Toby said, jogging over. Tina brought up the rear. "Oh, hi Will. Having a good time?"

Will studied Toby, and for a minute he appeared perplexed. His face cleared and he smiled. "I am, thank you."

"Excellent," Toby replied.

"How was practice?" Jenna asked, chewing the last bite.

Toby puffed his chest out, overexaggerating. "Six seconds. That's my fastest time pinning so far."

"Good job!"

He winked at Jenna. "Thanks. I would think that's enough for royalty but they already crowned the king and queen."

"You're not a senior yet, Toby, but keep dreaming. Let me guess. Madison Flagg and Jared Reitman."

"Jared was a no-brainer," Tina piped up, scooting between Toby and Jenna. Her eyes were full of mischief. "Not Maddy."

Jenna contemplated. The more she looked at Tina the more deflated she became. "No way."

"Yes way," Tina answered her. "Chloe Fischer." She turned to Will. "Chloe isn't scholarly, she had to take Home Ec twice. She also not popular because she's a good role model, she's popular because her family is influential."

"And because we believe she bought her way to the crown," Toby finished.

Will thought a moment. "Isn't Madison the one on the morning announcements? The class president who has been collecting donations for the Senior Center?"

"Among other super community involvement activities," answered Tina. "Her volunteer work is envious. The only thing Chloe collects is ex-boyfriends."

"At least she's good at it," Toby interjected.

"That sounds very political."

"More like embarrassing. Our school has so much to offer and this is what will go in the yearbook," Jenna finished.

"You want to go to the dance?" Toby asked Jenna. She shook her head.

"No Toby. Will has to get home."

"Oh, don't let me stop you. I don't mind, really." Will held his hands up and took a step backwards. All the time it took Jenna to get him to relax had vanished.

"Be nice, Tobe. Besides, it's been a long day. I didn't get to sleep until late." With that, everyone sobered.

"Dad went over around eight this morning. He said the window was wide open."

"That doesn't shock me," Jenna said lightly.

Toby choked on a laugh as a thought came to him. "It seems the window and Chloe Fischer have a lot in common."

Toby and Tina laughed and Jenna smirked before wrinkling up her nose. "Ooh, hush. That's not very nice."

"Well, neither is she for hijacking our school image and lowering the bar for us next year," Tina added.

"You're sure you don't want to stay longer?" Will asked, changing subjects while he tossed his napkin and plate in a nearby trash.

"No really, it's okay. See you guys later!" The group dispersed and Jenna and Will headed towards the parking lot. She looked up at the sun setting in the middle of a sky painted in purples and oranges and took a deep breath. "We really lucked out with the weather this year."

"Hey, Jenna?" Will asked. She turned toward him, smiling. Its warmth stunned him.

"Yeah?"

For a moment he forgot what he was going to say. "I really am sorry about the museum."

"I know. It's okay."

"But it's not. It upsets you more than you let on. Like tonight. Hearing the window was open again made you mad."

Jenna's smile dimmed and she cocked her head to the side. "I didn't get mad. That would have ruined the evening."

The opportunity was there but he just couldn't do it. "My mistake. I thought I saw it on your face." He switched gears. "So, can you explain how an osprey became our school mascot?" He watched Jenna replay their conversation of a few minutes before, trying to determine if she let that emotion slip. His words pulled her back and she smiled again, giggling over Orchard Creek's odd representative, diving into the local history.

SUNDAY WAS SPENT with family. It was the first opportunity for Jenna to get her dad aside to update him. She was going to join him on his daily walk, but the rain changed those plans. Her mom had just gone out to pick up subs for dinner, and Jenna was setting the table. Pete was in the garage trying to fix one of the wheels on his skateboard. Her dad was busy checking every cupboard for something crunchy. Her mom tried so hard to keep goodies hidden away.

"You mean that stuff is going to start all over again?" His hand was poised over a bag of nacho chips.

"Well, actually Will and his mother are going to help us. Oh, and we all need to be there on October first," Jenna remembered, setting the last paper plate and napkin.

"How will they do that?"

"I'm not sure, but his mom can do what I'm sorta able to do. She called it 'channeling'." This time her dad's mouth remained opened, orange seasoning framing his upper lip. "Mr. Levy didn't think she'd be helpful. Somehow, she proved it. She said things no one knew about, including me being called Miss Jenna." She sat down in her favorite swivel chair, gathering her hair and releasing it behind her.

He put the bag down and wiped his mouth. After looking at his hand he went to the sink to wash. "You can't make that up out of thin air. Some people can do amazing things. Your Gramp Stevens was one of them. Maybe not to that extent. It skipped over me, of course, so I think you got a double dose." He closed the package while glancing out the window. "She wants all of us there?" When Jenna nodded he continued, walking over to the desk next to the kitchen. "After seeing what I've seen, I'd be happier getting this taken care of in the beginning of October as opposed to the end." He leaned down to look at the calendar. "When?"

"The first. I think it's the same day Pete has a sleepover at Ryan's for his sixteenth birthday."

"You're right. Well, that's also your mom's long week out of town. She won't be home so I guess that's a good thing. I'm surprised Tina's okay with all this."

Jenna looked at her fingers laced on the counter. "I don't know if she is. I'm sure this'll fire up her anxiety. I'd hate to see her needing her medicine again. We don't talk like we used to. Actually, she spends more time with Rob than with me these days. I hate being a third wheel."

"Relationships grow and change, kiddo."

"Yeah, so I've noticed."

MONDAY EVENING WAS Jenna's turn for dinner duty. Her parents didn't get home until almost 5:30 p.m. so she and her brother took turns making the meals. She was making a dish with rice noodles and grilled vegetables when the phone rang.

"Yo, Jenna, it's Toby."

Jenna's stomach twisted. "What's wrong? You hate using the phone."

"It's important. It's the museum."

"Now what?"

"All the doors were wide open when dad went in today: cellar door, cabinet doors in the office, Sewing Room, all of them. At first, he thought someone was hiding out because he heard dragging sounds upstairs. Nope. The security system was working fine. He didn't find anyone, either. Thought you'd want to know before work tomorrow. I have a dentist appointment at noon so I wasn't sure if I'd see you."

"Thanks. Yeah, Will and I will need to be on guard."

JENNA WAS NERVOUS pulling into the parking lot the next day. She opened the museum herself on Tuesdays. She sat for a minute watching the windshield wipers, hoping the rain would let up so she wouldn't get drenched. Crunching stones to her left made her look over. Will was right behind her so she got out. He jogged to the entryway, joining her at the door while she searched for the right key. He greeted her pleasantly, but Jenna could see the apprehension in his eyes.

"Well, let's see what tonight brings." The door opened and the musty smell welcomed her as always, wrapping her in familiar comfort. "We should do a walk-through to see what we're working with. Strange things are happening again. Toby called last night to give a heads up." With this, Will seemed to close down again.

Everything on the first level looked okay. Upstairs, the door to the Sewing Room was open. It was expected so it wasn't a big deal. They heard strange footsteps on the staircase when they were in the basement. Thinking they missed tourists coming in, they hurried back upstairs only to find no one there. It made them both nervous.

"And this is a new display that's currently in progress," Jenna began, leading the group of three college-aged couples into the Display Room about an hour later. "This building has had many functions. After it was a mill it had the life of a boarding house. It—"

"Whatsa boarding house?" one of the guys asked, stroking his barely-there moustache. Jenna could tell he was older than her, but not by much. She sighed internally. This group obviously had been enjoying the wineries beforehand.

"How can you not know what a boarding house is?" his girlfriend asked. She unhooked her arm from his, wavered in her wedge shoes, and put both fists on her hip. "It's where dogs go when their owners go on vacation. Duh!"

Jenna looked to the back of the room at Will who was trying hard to keep his composure at her inebriated ignorance. "No, boarding houses in the mid 1840's were more like a bed and breakfast for travelers. They were mostly for single folks who needed lodging while they moved in search of jobs, took on seasonal work, or were passing through town." Jenna was pretty sure this troupe had only lived in the city.

"See Kara, not for dogs," one of the other girls teased, shaking the drops that remained on her rain poncho out at her friend.

"Well, why didn't they just get a motel or something?" Kara asked, blotting the water from her cheek with the long sleeves of her sweater that peeked out of her jacket.

"There weren't any public chains back then. There were a lot of large houses that at one point were home to big families. When the children grew up and moved out, the house had empty space. The rooms could be rented by week or month, or even by day. Anyway, back then Orchard Creek had—"

"I don't know why anyone would want my room at home after I moved everything out."

"Rent paid for a furnished room: a bed with the linens, desk or dresser, and access to share the house bathroom if there was one. Perhaps the landlady owned books, a piano, or fiddle for entertainment. Some arrangements were half boards meaning they offered the bed and only breakfast and dinner. Full boards provided all three meals. There were no laws they had to follow, they could do what they wanted. Some landladies only allowed the doors open in the evenings so the renters had to be out of the house during the day. As I was saying…"

"Oh," Kara's boyfriend exclaimed. "It was like a college dorm! With an olden day meal plan!"

The girls giggled and started to joke about chicken nuggets. The tallest man, who must have been the designated driver, thought it over. "Naw, sounds more like my grandpa's assisted living place."

"Yes, yes!" Jenna jumped on the comment, pointing at him. "Just like that. And, Orchard Creek had a lot of travelers who—"

"Derek, wasn't your grandpa—"

"And Orchard Creek was not far from the Penn-Can Highway," Will's voice cut over the other as he walked through the tourists to join an exasperated Jenna. He knew all about the problems of losing control of a group. "That was a north-south route from Canada through the eastern states down south, which eventually became our Interstate 81 in 1957. What else can you tell us about, Jenna?"

Jenna looked relieved. "Thank you, docent Will. If you'll all follow me, we'll continue our tour, jumping a decade to the 1850's to a modest exhibit on Harriett Tubman. We're fortunate enough to have one of the biographies she sold to bring in money. We even have some items she used at the Home for Indigent and Aged Negros."

With that save, the night wore on as usual, but an occasional door was found open when they had clearly shut it during a previous tour.

Ten

WILL HAD A lot on his mind later that night. He initially thought he'd have a tough time once in his house, but his mom was on the phone with one of her sisters and was distracted.

He announced he was home and after she waved in acknowledgement, he made his way up the staircase to his room. He hated to see Jenna troubled. That was the real issue. He had been tossing an idea around in his head for a few days now. The idea came from what his mom said a week or so ago. Actually, she had accused him of opening gateways on his own. He really had no yearning to attempt alone what he and his family did. What he was trying to reconcile was intervening just a little before they all got together. After all, he was really good at communicating with spirits. It was all in the approach. He thought it would be easy enough to control the situation if he limited it to a short burst of questions. Five minutes. No harm done. His reasoning was good: it could reduce Jenna's worry, and if it were to calm whatever entity before their intervention, it might make him and his mother look less foreign to those who didn't understand their practice. It wasn't like he was showing off, it was a job that had to be done.

"Jenna, come here," Will whispered with a sly smile. It was Wednesday evening.

He and Jenna were manning the museum on their own while Mr. Jacobs was in the basement, fixing the lights that kept blowing. Jenna walked over to him in the corner of the great room by the displays.

"I thought maybe if we used the Ouija board once before everyone was here on Saturday we could get the spirits to relax a little," Will said, getting out an old board from a thin, beat up box and set it on a display case.

He put the mover piece off to the side. He saw Jenna study it and told her it was called a planchette. It was made of a light wood, and just about the size of her hand. It looked like an upside down elongated heart in the extreme with a round hole near the pointed end that was painted to resemble a sun. Phases of the moon surrounded the sun and two simple stars sat below in the middle of the piece. At the tip end of it was a pretty blue gem. Underneath were three ball bearings near the sides. She had never seen anything like it before.

"Are you sure? Will, this is way more creepy than the last

time. Something here is really getting upset. I think we should wait for Tina. Or Toby at least."

Will clenched his jaw and his nostrils flared. "No! We're doing this now. I'm able to reach spirits better than anyone and can ask the right questions, so we know what we're facing. We need to know what's causing all this before Saturday, right?" Everything he had planned in his head was going wrong, but he didn't know how to fix it.

"What's with you? Why do you get so moody sometimes? What did I do?" Jenna asked, confused. She knew Will was upset again, but now he was scaring her instead of her just being angry with him. She knew the potential this building held.

Will shook off the question and went over to the display they were working on, grabbing the picture off the wall that showed the room with the mystery second staircase. He brought it over to the Ouija board and set it down next to him, needing it as a guide. Jenna was going to ask him again but became distracted when she started to wonder how something that looked like a toy could communicate with the spirit world. She thought it looked like a game board, but had no 'start' or 'finish' or squares for moves. There were only two colors. The board itself was a tan color, with a watermark design as if aged, and all the lettering was black in an old gothic font. Even the pictures were black. In the top left corner was a full sun with a smiling face inside it. The sun was in front of a cluster of clouds next to the word 'yes'. A crescent moon with a face in front of overcast clouds was in the right corner by the word 'no'. In between them was the word 'Ouija'. In the middle of the board, taking up much of the space, was the alphabet in two arcs from A to M in the first and N to Z underneath. Below there were numbers in a line from 1 to 0. At the bottom of the board was the word Good Bye. In the two lower corners were clouds with solid black stars that matched the ones on the planchette.

Will placed his fingertips on the indicator and closed his eyes to focus. His hands glided smoothly across the board. It reminded Jenna of air hockey. She was too curious to go get Mr. Jacobs which she knew would have been the right thing to do. Instead, she stood there frozen, watching.

"Is my name Will Albireo Greenley?" he asked. With his eyes still closed, his hands and the planchette—together as one—instantly moved, the hole lining up perfectly to display the word 'yes' on the board. Jenna's eyes grew wide.

"Do I have more than one cat?" His hands skimmed effortlessly to the word 'no'. He opened his eyes.

"Are there spirits here of those who have died in this place?" Nothing happened.

"To whom am I speaking?" The planchette floated slowly but deliberately, showing a single letter before moving to the next. When it finished, if had spelled out A-M-E-L-I-E.

"Did you work here?" Will's hands swung to the corner that said 'no'. Will was just about to ask another question when the planchette started moving again. It skimmed back and forth across the board with Will's body awkwardly following. K-I-L-L-E-D, it spelled out. A cold shiver trickled down Jenna's spine. Will swallowed hard, his concentration faltering.

"Um, who killed you?" he asked, restrained now.

M-A-N. There was a brief pause. G-U-N.

"Is that who is haunting this place?" he asked. His hands swung about, but to nothing. He blew out a mouthful of air and closed his eyes again to narrow his thoughts. "Are you lingering in this place?" No movement. He considered a moment.

"What can we do to settle the spirits?" He opened his eyes to see letters that spelled out the word L-E-A-V-E. Will was visibly sweating now, and it was becoming noticeable that he was trembling.

"How many spirits are at unrest?"

M-A-N-Y. W-I-L-L S-T-O-P Y-O-U.

"Do they already know what we're doing?" He was whispering now. His hands moved so fast he almost lost his balance in the chair. The hole revealed the word 'Yes'.

"Enough, Will! Put it away. I'm really scared," Jenna pleaded, one knuckle in her mouth. She nervously twisted her hair around her finger with her other hand.

Will's jaw clenched, and he became more determined. "What will happen if we come back on October first?"

F-A-L-L-I-N.

"What's going on?" Mr. Jacobs asked, walking into the great room. He could only see their backs. They jumped, and Jenna gasped. Somehow, she knew she needed to cover up what they had been doing. She walked quickly toward him holding her hands to her chest.

"Oh, you scared me. Is everything okay downstairs?" she asked, out of breath.

"Yes. How about up here?" Mr. Jacobs asked. He was trying to figure out what Will was scrambling with. Will was placing a WWI trench coat on the display counter, studying the stitching.

"Mr. Jacobs. We're good here," Will said, his face flushed. Mr. Jacobs wasn't sure what they were doing, but they sure were acting strangely. They looked guilty, too.

"It's a quarter to nine so I'm going to log off the computer. How about we close early? It looks like the bus had no takers tonight."

Jenna looked around desperately, trying to find a reason to stay there for just fifteen more minutes. She needed to talk to Will about what the board disclosed. "Well, Toby will come by from practice any minute now, right?"

Mr. Jacobs's forehead wrinkled. "Jenna, you know he's off on Wednesdays."

"Oh yeah, that's right. I forgot." Jenna laughed weakly.

"Make sure you both go together to do checks, okay? Anything funny, yell," Mr. Jacobs told them, turning towards the office, trying to figure out why she was acting so strangely.

"Don't worry, I will."

Mr. Jacobs walked away, but Will still looked irritated. Jenna didn't know what to say, so she just motioned for Will to go with her upstairs to start checking the rooms. He caught up to her and passed, going up the stairs first, always the gentleman. She put her hand gently on his shoulder, but he shrugged it off briskly.

"Don't play me, Jenna." He stopped on the stair, his voice a bit deeper, his face turned from hers. She withdrew her hand at once, her face reflecting the hurt the words caused. She was completely bewildered. She was scared and needed to be reassured, but was now given the cold shoulder, literally. Her thoughts circled to find what had set him off. Nothing she remembered saying had insulted or misled him.

They continued without speaking further and found nothing out of place in the small rooms upstairs. She was trying to figure out how to start a conversation when they reached The Display Room, the larger room in the middle. It made them stop cold. The pictures on the wall were still hanging, but each had been turned over and misaligned. The look on their faces mirrored each other. They weren't going in the Sewing Room alone.

"Mr. Jacobs, you better come up here and see this!"

"I'm sure the window is open Jenna, I'm just concerned with what else we—," he began, running up quickly. He stopped talking when he saw the Display Room. He joined them across the hall without saying anything further. They opened the Sewing Room door expecting the worst. The window was open, of course, but the only thing out of place was a clear stone the size of a small marble in the middle of the floor.

"Oh, no!" Will's face went white. "I forgot to do something downstairs. I'm just going to run ahead." Too distracted to wait for an answer, he took off leaving Jenna and Mr. Jacobs standing there. Mr. Jacobs looked at Jenna as if for an explanation. Jenna shrugged her shoulders, just as confused. He squinted at the object on the floor that reflected the light. Intrigued, he walked across the room and picked it up.

"Another piece of glass?" Jenna asked.

"You know," he paused, puzzled, "if I didn't know any better I'd say it was a raw Herkimer diamond, from the mines not far from here. My wife and I went digging there one year during an anniversary get-away. This is a pretty big one, too. It doesn't have the weight of glass, and it's faceted like a diamond. It's ice cold, but feels real. Ones this size are rare and worth quite a bit." He held it in his hand as if gauging its weight.

When they got back to the great room, Will was out of sorts, pacing. Mr. Jacobs went to get his coat and keys.

"What were you doing?" Jenna whispered.

"I totally forgot to take the indicator off the board. That was stupid of me to leave it there, especially in this place." Frustration was clearly etched on his face.

"Why? What would happen if you left it there?" Jenna asked. Panic was rising in her throat.

"You just don't leave it there." Will tried to end the conversation, but Jenna looked so upset he couldn't bring himself to keep her in the dark like that. "It leaves the spirit world open to ours. Either we close it or sometimes the spirits will end it themselves by making the planchette move to Good Bye. Neither happened."

"Super." She thought for a second. "Hey, is what happened upstairs because of that?" She motioned her head upward.

Will shrugged. "I don't think so," he answered slowly. He managed to avoid a conversation as the building was locked up. He got into his car after smiling and waving to Jenna and Mr. Jacobs. As soon as they pulled away the smile disappeared and his stomach soured. He shook his head. It was one of the few times he wished he wasn't a pacifist because he wanted to pound himself silly.

He really screwed things up. First the apple a week ago,

and now this. He had never been this careless before. All he wanted to do was connect with the entity and understand what it wanted. Instead, he did exactly what his mother warned him against, and what he swore he would never do. He opened a portal—on his own—and then left it unattended in an unstable environment. Not only did he blow off Jenna's concerns, he snapped at her. Why?

He traced his thought processes back. Because she made him crazy. He thought it over. No, that wasn't fair. The idea of Jenna being unavailable for him to pursue had been making him lose all common sense. He had also not been this interested in anyone before. It would be one thing if she totally didn't like him, but…that was the thing. Sometimes she made him feel like he was the only guy in the world, and then others he got the impression she wanted to add him to her collection.

He didn't intend to be so sharp with her, especially when things were getting scary. It was almost like he was a stranger looking out through his own eyes. He couldn't stop himself. Seeing the desperation on Jenna's face, his guard slipped for a fraction of a second. Her emotions were daggers to his heart, and her reaction to his words killed him. That wasn't who he was at all. The situation was snowballing with his every decision. He could no longer trust himself.

The only thing going his way was being the first one home. His mom had gone over to his Aunt Mina's for sauerbraten, and wasn't expected home for another hour or so. His three other aunts: Diane, Whitty, and Lee were there also. In addition to dinner, they were discussing the museum. None of his aunts were as gifted as his mom, but they had talent and were quite inquisitive. For the first time ever, he was glad to have had the excuse of working late to avoid the lot of them. So, against his better judgement, he decided to just leave everything alone in the hope that it might resolve itself. And despite the situation, he fell asleep quickly and avoided a confrontation.

It got worse. As if sensing the upcoming intercession, the dominant forces were becoming apparent and more tangible in the days leading up to Saturday. Each day upon opening brought a new mess to clean up.

"THIS IS REBEKAH Greenley."

"Sulis? It's Tom Jacobs. Is this a bad time?"

"No, not at all. I'm in between meetings, actually. What can I do for you?"

"You asked to be kept in the loop regarding the museum. The last few days have been weird, even for this building's standards."

"In what way?"

"Well, we've always had cold spots here and there throughout a year. You know, things that might have logical reasons. Sometimes I wonder if they happen or if we think they do because we almost expect it. That's convoluted, huh?"

"No, I understand completely."

"Well, it's gone beyond that. I've had to replace lights that haven't done so much as flicker in years. This morning it was the office. All the file cabinets and desktop papers were emptied in a pile on the floor. It was the most bizarre thing I've ever seen.

At first, Mark thought we'd been vandalized. He was the last one out Wednesday night and the first one there this morning, but there was no evidence of a break in. All the door locks and windows were secure. The security system is working fine. But the Sewing Room door is constantly ajar despite being locked, too. The window gapes so often I can't keep the building warm, no matter how many times we shut it and lock the door."

"And you're sure it's because a portal's been opened."

"Yeah, I do. We've even been keeping an eye on the place the last few nights. We practically live next door. I've adjusted the motion detector's lights to be a little more sensitive, so I could see if it was tripped. Mr. Stevens actually did a drive-by before retiring for bed. We observed nothing out of the ordinary. It's all from the inside."

"I've discussed the situation with my sisters and they agree with our plan. If people were harmed, obviously, we wouldn't have a choice. As it's not, I'm going to suggest we stay the course until the first. It has significance, I'm sure of it."

"Ok. We'll tough it out. I'll call if I need to."

"Thank you. That would be appreciated."

No one was prepared for what was found on Friday. When Mr. Jacobs unlocked the Sewing Room door that day, he found each antique machine had been ripped from the bolts securing them to the floor and overturned on their sides as if they were felled animals. The sight of the arrangement was disturbing, and the physical strength needed to accomplish that made everyone uneasy.

Work that night consisted of helping both Mr. Jacobs and Mr. Levy set the machines to rights. It seemed to take forever, even with Toby's help. Will was pleasant, but distant. Jenna tried to make the evening more enjoyable by joking with everyone, but Will hardly spoke to Jenna socially, and it had her worried.

Saturday morning, October first, had the four of them wading through two inches of water in the basement.

"No rain in days, and we're flooded," Mr. Jacobs said, leaning into a mop with one arm and wiping his face on the shoulder of the other. There is no natural spring under us. We have no leak or any other explanation for where the water came from."

"Because it's never happened before," Mr. Levy said sardonically. "Not a realistic explanation, anyway. I wish I could stay. I hate to leave this to you but…"

"I know, I know, you can't miss that mandatory three-hour finance seminar for work. It would have been nice to have enjoyed the day. Steph and her girlfriends have a booth at the craft fair. I had the whole weekend to eat take-out, watch football games, tinker around in the garage, and take a nap."

"All that in one weekend?" Mr. Levy asked, squeezing the water from his mop head into a large tar bucket.

"No, that was just until tonight."

"Sorry, buddy. You know our mantra: paying job comes first."

"The sump is still going strong. We'll have this place cleaned up in no time, Mr. Jacobs," Jenna offered.

"No worries," Will added. Mr. Jacobs nodded as he swung the mop back to the ground.

The whole morning was spent scooping the water into

buckets and bringing them upstairs to toss outside. The sump-pump burned out after an hour, and Jenna and Will were left to continue the manual work while Mr. Jacobs went to the local hardware store to get a replacement. Will was at least talking to Jenna but acted as if nothing had happened the other night.

"Will, come on, we need to talk about this."

"About what?" he answered. Jenna couldn't see his face, his back was to her.

"Don't you think we need to talk about using the Ouija this week? The stuff that's happening here is getting pretty heavy-duty. Whatever you did has ticked something off big time. I think we need to tell Mr. Jacobs and your mom."

Will turned toward her and motioned for her to keep her voice down. His jaw tightened. "No." The tone was firm, but his face betrayed him. It upset him to say it.

Jenna saw the crack in his façade. She pitched her voice lower. "Listen, I don't want to get into trouble any more than you do. I'm worried about tonight as it is. I've never seen damage of this magnitude before. We've never had anything rip metal out of the floorboards. I think this is something everyone should know about before we start in. Don't you think it'll make some sort of difference?"

Will looked at her face briefly. The fear hit him hard, and it wasn't just all hers anymore. It came from the men, too. He was still messing things up. The tightness in his stomach didn't help; he only experienced that when he felt cornered. Like now. Telling the others would make it worse. There was nothing he wanted more than to stay on good terms with Jenna, but he also wanted to stay away from being frustrated so he could focus later.

"I don't think we should say anything Jenna, please?"

Jenna searched his eyes and caved. "Yeah, okay." She wasn't comfortable with it, but she agreed.

Eleven

OCTOBER FIRST DRAGGED on as they waited for evening. Jenna didn't know what to expect other than what they'd be doing must be a big deal. And, it was an opportunity to spend time with Will so she figured nice clothes wouldn't hurt. That included her favorite shirt. It was royal blue with pleated, cap shoulders and a fitted bodice with buttons down the front. At the bottom, it flared out a little into a yoke. It was everything she loved about period clothes wrapped into something modern, and it made her feel comfortable and girly. She paired it off with her most flattering blue jeans. Jenna knew it looked good and hoped Will would notice. She didn't like this distant Will from the last couple of days. Brushing out her shiny long hair, Jenna admired the different colors of brown and red mixed with the natural blond as she twirled the ends into their wavy curls. She fiddled with her bangs, couldn't get them just right, and blew them up and out of her eyes with a shrug.

Tina and Toby showed up at six to hang out which put Will in another mood. Jenna was surprised to see what he was wearing. Paired with black pants was a long white shirt pleated at the shoulders and cuff. Frowning, she didn't understand why he was so sullen just when he was allowing more of his true self to show through. The style of the top reminded Jenna of the puffy shirts worn in that Jack Sparrow movie. She admired how it contrasted nicely with his long, dark hair. Even though he seemed to be more comfortable in his own skin—slowly incorporating his own style with the required dress for work—he still wasn't very social. It was almost as if he couldn't wait to go down to the basement with Mr. Jacobs and Mr. Levy.

Jenna wandered towards the front door to better see the narrow hallway to the basement stairs. It was empty. "I really can't tell anymore," she declared, walking back to her friends. "He's on my mind all the time. Sometimes I think he might be interested, but I'm baffled. He smiles at me so I think he is, but he gets angry over stuff I'll admit I don't understand. We both had a good time at Homecoming. There were a few good nights here with the tours, but it hasn't gone anywhere. And it's not like we live in a huge town. It wouldn't be hard to find out where I live. Our number is in the book for Pete's sake. He hasn't called me."

Toby leaned in closer. "Do you think it's because he's a bit different?" he asked in a hushed tone.

"No," Jenna shot back defensively.

"He's got a medieval thing about him that I think is pretty mysterious," Tina admired.

"Yeah, I do too," Jenna sighed.

Toby rolled his eyes. "You girls are too easily distracted by long hair and pirate shirts."

"Are you jealous? You know I love you, Toby. Like a brother," Jenna teased, wrinkling up her nose in mock disgust.

"Yeah," Tina joined in, "like a brother." The girls laughed at a play on words they shared since they were twelve.

"Right back at ya, sisters. That joke is old, you know. Anyway, I don't think I'm the jealous type. In my opinion, I'd say it's mutual. Every time I've been here he can't take his eyes off you."

Jenna smiled, pleased.

"You can't mistake that look. I see it with Mom and Dad." Toby narrowed one eye and gagged a little. "It's got to be hard for him though. I think my parents are weird and they're not into stuff like that. Maybe that's why," Toby offered.

"Try winking at him. See what happens," Tina suggested.

The main door opened and everyone's attention shifted. Mr. Stevens walked in with a handful of different colored candles. Shortly after that, Sulis walked in with a large plastic tote. At her direction, Mr. Jacobs and Mr. Stevens started moving a large table into the smaller room off the main staircase. Items were slowly removed from the tote and placed on the table. By seven-thirty they had closed up early, and with the accumulated loss of daylight hours, it was dark, eerily reminding Jenna of the Halloween Masquerade Ball all those years ago.

By 8 p.m. all were gathered in the great room. The air was

thick with uncertainty. Mr. Levy and Mr. Stevens were bringing chairs to the table as Sulis laid a thin, black veil over the top. It had a spider web-like design on it.

"Why did we have to bring this table over when we had a perfectly good one here in the other room?" Mr. Levy asked, wiping his face with his sleeve.

Sulis pulled open the drawstring of her small violet velvet purse. Blue, green, pale pink, clear, and brown gems tumbled into her lace-gloved hand. She began setting them in the middle of the table. "We need to have a round table. Circles are symbolic in many religions. No beginning and no end. We must remain true to the rituals for this ceremony."

"Everything is so delicate looking. I like the stones, they're pretty," Tina admired. She leaned towards the table to get a closer look, but kept her distance from touching anything.

"They're there for more than decoration. Stones and gems are particularly helpful," Will explained. "They are great for their protective properties and the forces they hold. They become synergistic, or more powerful, when used correctly."

"It's all about energy, right?" Jenna asked tentatively. She had wanted to understand what they were going to do and didn't want to say anything wrong, so she had done some research on her own. The public library had a bunch of books on Reiki, aromatherapy, and Pagan rituals. All talked about different metaphysical properties found in nature. Gems and stones were known to hold and channel energies derived from the earth. This connection accounted for their healing powers. Not all had to be pretty and polished like emeralds or rubies, either. She was surprised to learn that raw river and lake stones could be used in this way as well. Jenna couldn't believe how fast four hours flew that Saturday afternoon. The information was incredibly fascinating to her, and she took it in with a hearty appetite.

Will was impressed. His face lit up and he seemed to regard Jenna in a new light. "Yes, it is."

Jenna relaxed and returned the smile. Moving closer to Sulis she offered her hand and Sulis gave her a very old looking silver chalice. She directed Jenna to the middle of table and Jenna set it down gently. Just about that time, Mr. Jacobs came into the room with a small container of soup. Sulis nodded and the soup was poured into the ancient cup.

That caught Toby's attention who had been hanging out by the staircase. Mr. Jacobs anticipated what was coming before Toby even moved. "Don't even think about it, son."

"Hey, we're having food, too?"

"No, not really. Right now, we need to have something to attract the spirits," Will corrected him.

"It smells good," Toby said, walking over to the table.

"See, it worked with you," Sulis deadpanned, raising one eyebrow. Everyone laughed, and the apprehension in the room lessened. "Afterward, we will have a little something to eat to ground ourselves."

"Ground ourselves?" Tina asked. She looked at her father, an edge in her voice.

"Don't worry, Tina. When we do spell work, we pull up and ask to borrow the energy from the earth and from the elements. Those are the main tools we use. We need to give the energy back, or at least the excess energy, after we're done. We never keep it for ourselves. Sometimes we deplete or drain ourselves after a ritual or a spiritual gathering like this, and need to recharge. It's a way to realign your own body and mind," Will explained. His mother nodded.

"Realigning is very important, regardless," Sulis added, straightening her gown. "Those with too much energy can experience mania, and those who are depressed usually don't have enough of their own energy. It's just a fancy word for equalizing. And we don't necessarily need to eat food to ground. Some people make sure they're touching the earth, and some just visualize the energy leaving their body and seeping back into the ground. No matter what we do, the key is our intention. It's extremely important."

"Oh, that makes sense. Thank you."

Six brass-looking candelabras came out next. Mr. Levy stayed close to Tina who stepped up to Sulis shyly and took them, setting them up upright on the table where Will indicated. She was given several long tapered candles: yellow, green, blue and red, as well as two white ones. Tina squeezed them into the candle holders. Three were to go on one side of the table and three in the middle.

"I don't mean to sound ignorant, but everyone uses candles in the movies. Why do we need them?" Mr. Stevens asked.

"Candles are a natural light source. The calm glow and warmth help set the ambiance we want to offer. Symbolism is essential as well. Fire represents one of the elements, just as the colors of the candles symbolize the elements," Sulis answered.

"Anything else?" Toby asked, resting his large hand on Jenna's shoulder briefly as he peered over at the table.

"Numbers hold significance too," Jenna added, absent-mindedly patting Toby's hand with hers. She looked over at Will. His lips were set in a tight line, and his gaze drifted to the floor.

"Very good, Jenna!" Sulis complimented as she flit about. "The number three or anything divisible by three is good."

"The Father, Son, and Holy Spirit?" asked Mr. Levy.

"Not exactly, but remember, all religions have commonalities." Sulis continued. "The number three is a mythical symbol pretty much everywhere, depending upon its roots. Celtic culture differs from Greek and Norse mythology. Some refer to the stages of woman: maiden, mother, and crone. Others believe it refers to our world, the afterlife, and the land of death. The moon cycle has three phases. Even the past, present, and future is a triad."

"This is confusing," Toby admitted.

"I'm sorry. If you focus your intentions with a clear mind you can't go wrong."

Mr. Jacobs helped put the Ouija board on the table, closest to the side of the table that was by the staircase. He set the planchette on the table and handed the well-worn box to Jenna to put away. She noted it was made in Salem, Massachusetts. Holding something tangible was a slap of reality. What she was about to do was real. At once she questioned her trust in what they were about to do.

"You're sure you know what you're doing? You've done this before?" Mr. Levy inquired, voicing Jenna's concern.

Sulis nodded adding a few more items to the table. "Hmm. Yes, quite a bit, actually. It's always better to have an experienced medium familiar with conducting séances. We'll be okay." She put her glasses on and straightened them studiously on her nose. The last thing she did was to take out what looked like a very small knife. It was encased in leather into which flowery swirls and designs were burned. She withdrew the knife and set it on the table where she would be sitting. It was a straight edge about six inches in length. The blade was clean and shiny, three inches long, and didn't appear to be very sharp. Instead, it had a decoration of a circle carved with a star inside it by the base near the handle. The handle was bound with twine.

"Wait a minute." Mr. Levy held his hands out in a gesture to stop. "What are we doing with that? I am not doing anything sick." His expression was one of apprehension and disgust.

"I understand your concern, Mr. Levy, and I don't want you to worry. Nothing is being killed or sacrificed. We don't do that. This is a ceremonial knife called an athame."

"Ah-what?" Mr. Jacobs asked, intrigued.

"We pronounce it ah-THAH-me, but some people say AH-THUH-may. It is never meant to be used to cut anything other than air. It's a symbolic instrument used to channel energy during a ceremony. It can be used to open a circle, a way to open ourselves to deeper energies that lie around and beyond us. We will be using it to hopefully banish negative energies and entities."

Mr. Levy relaxed a little. "I'm sorry. This is a lot for me to take in."

"That is totally understandable," Sulis said with a gentle smile. "Will, do you want to put yours down as well?"

Will looked into the tote and then patted his pockets, his

face wrinkled with concern. "I can't believe I forgot it at home. I left it on the kitchen table."

"You spent too much time on your hair, again. Too late now, we'll have to do without it. Teenagers," she muttered to herself.

With a few of the old photographs of the boarding house scattered about, she nodded her head and smiled slightly, content with the table. Looking around, she waited for everyone's attention. "And now we start."

Both Will and Sulis showed people to their seats as the seating arrangement was important too, but asked them to stay standing. The table was large enough for everyone to be comfortable and still hold hands. Will was closest to the door with his mother to the side of him, her back mostly to the staircase. Sulis raised her arms. Her bracelets clicking together got everyone's attention. She was dressed in a long gown and velvet burgundy cloak. It unintentionally matched the streaks in her hair. She had a bit more make-up on than what would be appropriate for an evening out, and had several necklaces with large medallions or stones on them and rings on each half-gloved finger. The perfume Jenna remembered from the store—she had learned it was called Patchouli—permeated the room. Jenna was to the right of Sulis and Tina and Toby across from them with her father, Mr. Jacobs, and Mr. Levy scattered throughout. Jenna looked meaningfully at Will as if to ask again to mention using the Ouija earlier. Will shook his head slightly, kept his mouth shut, and said nothing.

"I need everyone to clear their minds. Close your eyes and take a deep breath in and blow it out. No negativity or we'll feel it and it'll follow us. This is not something to be taken lightly."

Sulis explained that directions were also important as they corresponded to the different elements, and any kind of circle or ceremony usually started facing the east. At her lead, they opened their eyes and turned so all were facing the office, which was east, and joined hands. Will's right hand rested on his mother's shoulder.

Sulis raised the athame up toward the sky as she spoke. "I call upon the element of air. Let us drink in your rich fragrance." As air's cardinal direction was east, she lit the yellow candle. She turned and everyone followed. "South is fire, that which warms our body and soul." The red candle was lit. Sulis continued to the west. "Join us water, nourish us, cleanse us, and cool us." When the blue candle flamed, the group turned once again, towards the north. "Earth that grounds us and supports us on our journey in this world, we call on you to come to us." The green candle brightened the room even farther. As Sulis continued, Jenna thought about how it was the oddest religious service she had ever witnessed, and yet its foreignness was intriguing.

"Please sit. We must all remain connected to continue the circle either by holding hands or touching." Maintaining their link to one another, everyone sat. "We ask the spirits here to move about us. Please make your presence known. Show us now by giving us a sign; make a noise, offer a scent, move the air so we know you are here."

The room was still. Mr. Levy looked at Mr. Stevens. Both their expressions clearly showed they had reservations of achieving their goal. After a few moments, Sulis shook her head. She encouraged the spirits to come forth a few more times without success.

"Ouija," Will suggested.

"Yes, we're going nowhere here. Will, please do us the honors."

Will took the indicator, placed it on the board and tried to clear his head to concentrate. Watching a repeat from a few days ago made Jenna remember something that had intrigued her.

"Will, what does Albireo stand for?" Jenna asked.

Sulis looked up quickly and glared at her son. "What? When did you use the Ouija, Will?" she asked firmly.

"How did you—" Jenna began, stunned that Sulis put the pieces together so quickly.

Will reddened and looked uncomfortable. There was no way around this. "A few days ago. Great. Thanks, Jenna," he muttered bitterly.

"What'd I do?"

"Why don't you ask your boyfriend what his middle name stands for?" he asked. Even though he was still holding Mr. Levy's hand, he managed to thumb a finger at Toby. Will knew he was in mixed company, and he could feel he was losing it, but couldn't rein it in. There were too many days being consumed with anger for putting Jenna and himself in this situation, as well as being obsessed with the possibility that Jenna was dating Toby.

"Will!" Sulis called, the same time Jenna started to get angry.

"He's not my boyfriend, Will!" Then it struck her completely. "You think he's my boyfriend, don't you? That's why you've been so mad."

"Will!" Sulis tried again. The drama eclipsed her demand. Despite having done nothing, Toby was now the one blushing and shaking his head 'no,' but Will was focused on Jenna. His eyes never left her, even with his mother in the way.

"I've seen the way he touches your arm and whispers in your ear!" He tried to pitch his reply quietly to Jenna. His voice was low and intense, but everyone heard it anyway.

"That's because he's Toby. And, he was telling me he thinks you like me, you doofus! Because I like you," Jenna trailed off, exasperated. Will sat there sulking, then, slowly, the shadow of a grin bloomed on his face.

An uncomfortable silence fell over the table with everyone thinking the same thing. That should not have had an audience.

Sulis cleared her throat. Finally, the awareness of the table shifted back to her. Her eyes were blazing at her son. Somehow, she kept her temper in check. "To answer your question, Jenna, Albireo is the name of a double star. Of all those in the constellations, Albireo was in alignment with earth on the day he was born, January twenty-first. I knew he had used the Ouija because one always has to start with a factual question that can be answered by 'yes' or 'no,' and Will always confirms by asking his name."

"Oh," Jenna said quietly, studying the web design of the tablecloth. She dared to draw her eyes up, becoming aware that her dad and everyone else had front row seats to that little tête à tête. The expression on her father's face was unreadable. Tina was trying to chew down a smirk, Toby was beet red to his hairline, and her bosses looked like they'd eaten something bad but weren't sure of it. She had the awkward feeling of being a little girl again.

"Tell me. What happened, Will? You can be assured we will have a very lengthy discussion about all this in greater detail, but right now we need to focus on the issues at hand. We need to have all the information to use to our advantage, not the other way around. So, what did you learn? Because you most certainly connected with something."

Mr. Jacobs cut in before Will could answer, his face transforming from an easy going demeanor to one of irritation. "Wait a minute. How many days ago? Did you use it before all this damage started?"

Will and Jenna both looked down again, avoiding eye contact. They were busted. Will decided to come clean.

"Yes, on Wednesday. But I, well, I got distracted. Just for a few minutes," he began.

"And?" Sulis asked, practically facing him.

"I left the planchette on the board."

"Hold on. What does that mean? I don't understand," Mr. Levy interrupted.

"This board is a way of bridging the gap between our world and the one beyond, like a door," Sulis clarified. "It sounds like Will left the indicator without control, which is like not closing or locking the door. Apparently, it has stirred some very nasty spirits who may have crossed over." Will and Jenna reluctantly told the group what had happened.

"If we get out of this unscathed, you've got some grounding business to attend to. Right now, though, we need to be united with our thoughts, focused on this and nothing else. We must be a single mind. Thoughts that are not together may destroy the psychic energy we need. Let's take a few deep breaths and concentrate. Do not break the circle." Sulis warned. She sighed. Though very self-assured and nonplussed about the goings on, it made everyone uneasy to hear her hint at the uncertainty that something could go very wrong with this intervention.

They all regrouped. Sulis and Will reached for the planchette together, and Will nodded to Jenna to join.

"Me? Really?" Jenna whispered. She had butterflies in her stomach again, this time for completely different reasons.

"You're strong, remember?" Sulis asked. However upset she had been moments ago, she had put it off to the side.

Hesitantly, Jenna reached her hand forward, and as if sensing her uneasiness, Will put his hand over hers. With her hand sandwiched between the two, she felt an odd static kind of feeling much like a caffeine rush, except it started in her entire hand and quickly travelled through her bloodstream. It wasn't entirely unpleasant. Her eyes met Will's briefly before all her thoughts left and her concentration relocated.

Jenna watched her hand gliding across the board without any attempt on her part to move it. She felt the warmth of Sulis's hand under hers and Will's hand on top, but could not feel the slight pressure one might feel when they wanted their hand to move in a particular direction. It moved on its own. Jenna felt everyone's eyes but couldn't take hers off the board in front of her. The room was eerily quiet with anticipation.

Will took a deep breath in and blew it out slowly. His eyes were shut, his face smooth, completely absorbed. "Is my name Will Albireo Greenley?"

The planchette easily moved with the hole lining up to the word 'yes'. He opened his eyes. His brown eyes met Jenna's brown eyes and he continued. "Is my cat's name Zeus?" Their hands swung to 'no'.

"All right. Let's begin. Everyone please focus. We want to call upon the spirits that will help guide us to find peace," Sulis began calmly.

The air now was completely saturated with the Patchouli she was wearing. The candlelight gave off just enough light to cover everyone at the table and little else, creating the existence of a bubble of space that included the group and nothing beyond.

"We call upon the spirits who are here. Is there someone here who will talk with us?" Will asked. Their hands moved frantically back and forth as if conflicted. "We're asking to speak again with Amelie. Can you come forward?"

Sulis furrowed her brow, trying to keep up with the letters that were being spelled out. Nothing made sense. "Will, there are too many here. Try to be more specific. Try… try the woman in the picture who owns the boarding house." She nodded her head towards the picture closest to them on the table.

"If you are here, please let us know," Will continued. Their joined hands regained some order and moved to spell out S-Y-L-V-I-A.

"Greetings Sylvia. Were you the owner of this building?" Will asked. The indictor stopped on 'yes,' but moved again to spell out D-O-N-T-T-O-U-C-H.

Will looked up worriedly at his mother. Sulis shook her head, confused. Tina, Toby, and the men looked back and forth to the two leading this group, wide-eyed and uneasy. Something wasn't working out the way it was supposed to.

All at once Jenna's nose began to burn. The Patchouli was suddenly gone, replaced by something sharp and acrid. She slid her hand from between the other two out of habit as she began to sneeze. Before Sulis could stop her, the circle was broken, and for an instant Sulis's hand left the planchette to reach for her, distracted.

Jenna sneezed violently, her hand falling onto the picture of the room with the staircase. All at once she felt ice cold, and the room spun around her, getting darker and darker. Her head was swimming, and she was dizzy, falling, and being squeezed. Jenna grasped for Will's hand, and clutching a few fingers, screamed. It seemed to linger and echo in her own ears. Gravity failed her. She fell hard out of her chair and landed on the floor at the same time a door slammed. She felt so heavy at first, she couldn't even blink. It reminded her of the G forces of a carnival ride.

Slowly she lightened to normal and was able to sit up. Her vision was foggy, and she sat there trying to catch her bearings when her stomach dropped. She didn't recognize anything in the room. For a moment, she was uncertain if she had blacked out. The round table was gone as well as her friends and father. She was disoriented, unable to understand what happened. Her vision was still hazy, and Jenna rubbed her eyes as if to clear them. They stung. The air was still thick and she finally placed it. It smelled of sulfur. Realization hit her hard, and she took in a huge intake of air. The room was silent otherwise. It wasn't fog in the room. Even though she never pulled a trigger she knew what it was. It was the smoke from a gun.

Twelve

*J*ENNA SCRAMBLED BACKWARDS trying to get away from the smoke to see better. She didn't understand where it had come from in the first place She knew she was still in the museum as the trim work was familiar, but why she wasn't in the main room confused her. This was a small room, with a rustic looking bed, small wooden dresser, and a tall wooden panel—a bi-fold privacy screen. The room had two doors across from each other and one on the right wall. As the smoke cleared, she saw Will leaning against the wall by the bed. His eyes alarmed her. They were full of shock and anxiety.

"What happened?" Jenna asked, rubbing her nose. It stung again. Will stared wide-eyed at something across the room, and didn't answer. Jenna slowly turned towards the door and realized there was a girl about their age lying on the floor, her hands and legs out to her sides as if trying to make a snow angel. She wore faded black lace-up ankle boots, and a long gray dress with a linen apron over it. Her light blonde hair splayed in an arc above her head. Her eyes looked above her at nothing, surprise etched on her face. A pool of blood was spreading across the hardwood floor from the deep, red hole in her chest.

"Oh my God! That looks like me! Is that me? Where did everyone go?" Jenna hissed, grabbing her own chest. She tried to get up but lost her balance and sat back down abruptly.

"No, that's not you," Will said. His face was flat now, staring at the girl. "Fall in. That's what that girl in the board told us. Today's date opened a portal. Jenna, I'm pretty sure we fell into the picture," he said, finally looking at her.

"How is that possible?" Then she remembered. "I touched the picture," she whispered. Her thoughts finally caught up with the current situation. "There's a dead girl on the floor, Will! Did I do that?" Her voice rose frantically. Will scrambled to her, unable to get up himself. He shushed her and motioned for her to move backwards towards the wooden screen with him to be hidden. Through the fog, they could hear commotion and men's voices growing louder just outside the door.

"We need to run, Jonas! This wasn't supposed to happen. We're wanted men, and now this. I say we leave now and try to come back for it later."

"It was an accident! If you wasn't intimidatin' her and toying with the gun in the first place Henry, I wouldn't have grabbed it outta your hand and none of this woulda happened. No one'll believe it went off by accident. The girl spooked me, is all."

"Well, she's deader 'n a doornail, and we can't leave it all behind. Someone'll find it. Missus Cabet is coming! Let's get it and get out of here!"

Will and Jenna could hear footsteps creaking on the stairs away from them and then an older woman's voice. The creaking on the stairs grew more pronounced as the female voice grew louder.

"What is going on in here? You all know the rules: no guns! Amelie, you up here? I told you to collect the rent and start supper 'pert near a quarter of an hour ago!"

Will and Jenna made it behind the wardrobe screen as the room door opened. They could just see through the tiny space between the panels. The woman who stepped into the room was the woman from the picture. She was short, but solid, with green eyes and tawny brown hair braided and piled on her head. Her long, dark skirts swished with her movements. She wiped her hands on her tan apron before grabbing it in terror. It was obvious, immediately, that it was Amelie lying in the pool of blood.

"Amelie? My baby? No!!" Mrs. Cabet screamed and threw herself down to the floor pulling her daughter to her. Amelie's limp body hung in the embrace, her arms swinging lifelessly at her side. The girl's head lolled on her shoulder awkwardly facing the screen, her eyes still open. Hugging her and smoothing her hair, Mrs. Cabet sobbed and moaned. Her tears and cries escalated to hysteria. It was heartbreaking for Jenna and Will to watch as Mrs. Cabet broke down over her child, and they clung to each other tightly. It hit too close to home. Jenna burrowed into Will's embrace to get the image out of her head.

Mrs. Cabet began to get louder, an edge to her words. She

was angry and ranting. "Cain't! No longer! He cannot leave me every day with all these boarders and such as I didn't ask for any of this! He took in those two even after I told him I had bad visions of them. He has never listened! Never again! My only baby…I will make today their judgment day!"

Mrs. Cabet stopped rocking Amelie in her lap. She laid her down gently and got up, her face devoid of any expression at all. Straightening her soiled apron over her long skirt, she tried to hitch the tapered arms of her sleeves, oblivious to the blood all over them. Her jaw was squared, her face fierce as she left the room. Her voice was traveling farther away, but she was yelling now. Jenna and Will could hear objects being knocked over downstairs. Jenna sniffled and relaxed her iron grip on Will.

"Bad visions? We need to follow her. She might be able to get us out of here. Stay with me and be quiet," Will whispered as he pulled her toward the door. Making sure they were alone, they left the room and stood in the hallway, perplexed. It took a moment for them to realize there were six rooms upstairs. The room they had just exited looked as if it was above the Sewing Room, like an attic room. It was connected by a lone staircase—the mystery staircase. Quietly they snuck through the Sewing Room which now appeared to be someone's living space, and down to the main floor. No one else seemed to be there, but they caught a glimpse of a skirt as it disappeared by what they knew to be the office. For the moment, the building was surprisingly quiet.

Jenna slowed down but Will went ahead. Her senses were overloaded. It was like revisiting a home you had lived in years before, after a new owner took over. She stood there for a second, trying to take in every detail, even though she knew she needed to stay with Will. It warred with every fiber of her being. Everything was exactly the same, but so different at the same time. All she had wondered about the past: the way the wood smelled, the furnishings, the lights, the newness of it all, it was right in front of her. And it took her breath away.

The building was really a home. Oil lamps sat on tables. There was dining room furniture in what was, only moments before, a museum room with display cases. Where the round table had been, a long rectangular table sat. Instead of chairs it had sturdy, well-worn benches. A candle chandelier hung over it, ready to throw warm light on all who ate there. In the main room, wooden-backed chairs and rocking chairs were situated around the fireplace in the far corner. Needlepoint sat on a table. Kindling and chopped wood rested in a large bin next to a black wrought iron poker and a bellow. In the fireplace were andirons which held the logs horizontally for the fire beneath it. Jenna had seen some decorative ones before but never black cats. The design was beautifully crafted with holes where the eyes were so the fire could light them from behind.

She continued on. A simple bookcase took up the short wall. The long wall was bare except for a shelf with several whittled figurines. Without thinking about it, her feet moved her forward. Her jaw dropped. She found herself looking out one of the large windows and was entranced by the difference in scenery—no parking lot, no paved road, no houses or telephone poles. There was only grass and a dirt path worn into the ground that met a well-packed dirt road. Across the road was a tiny cemetery. The area was so bare she could almost see the whole town from where she stood. A horse and buggy were traveling slowly across what Jenna knew as Rodger's Pike Road because it ran perpendicular to Sentinel.

Other than a persistent noise close by her, it was so incredibly quiet! It vaguely crossed her mind she was standing in the exact spot she had been in not even an hour ago. She knew without a doubt the woman they saw upstairs was Sylvia. She was in the picture, taken back in 1846. Somehow, they were now was a hundred and fifty years back in time. Still, she couldn't wrap her brain around the idea.

Will grabbed her arm and jerked her towards the basement, past a kitchen on the right and into the small corridor where they could hear a heated conversation below them.

"The stairs and basement are too small for both of us to sneak into," he began quietly. "I'll go. I appear to be dressed more appropriately for this era, anyway," he volunteered. He took one hand and brushed his long hair back from his face. He stared at Jenna intently for a moment before squeezing her hand tightly and broke away. He very slowly opened the door and disappeared into the darkness, leaving Jenna to stand just outside the doorway to the basement, alone.

Will stayed in the shadows on the stairs until he had a plan and was sure he wouldn't be seen. Then he tiptoed off the last step onto the sod floor of the basement and circled around quickly to hide behind the staircase. The area hadn't changed much. The dirt floor and the bearing wall that was held up by a massive wooden plank were the originals. There was only one lantern lit. The faint glow barely illuminated the far wall where a sturdy table sat with an upended chair next to some woodworking tools. Two more broken chairs needing repair were next to the table.

"You killed my… what are you digging for Henry?" Mrs. Cabet asked.

Sylvia Cabet did not know Jonas at all and didn't want to. He was just another boarder with his own past and his own agenda that paid his rent late as often as he tried to weasel out of it. Then there was the rash of stolen property in the area. Sylvia knew it was Jonas. It upset her that her husband didn't approach him about it, or suggest they kick him out. Somehow, they seemed to be doing quite well financially and they certainly didn't need that kind of boarder. She hated that James toiled all day in the fields, and she was stuck putting up with all the men. She worried about them being around her young, innocent daughter. Amelie was just seventeen. With a pleasing waistline, green eyes, and long blonde hair, she was bright and friendly and innocent. The men were rude and vulgar. They scared Sylvia, and they knew it, teasing and goading her with no respect or repercussions at all. It was if James turned a deaf ear on who was living under their roof.

Anyone could have figured out what a low-life Jonas was just by his behavior. But Sylvia had a gift. She had a way of seeing things and sensing things. Sometimes it came to her in a dream or a burst of feelings. Most times it came to her when her mind was clear as she was practicing her white magic.

James did not like her visions. Once he learned what she and her family practiced, he kept his distance from them. He disliked his wife telling him there were men close to them they needed to watch out for. The visions she had of Jonas scared her most of all. Her heart beat faster every time he was near her. He was not to be trusted. She knew he was a sly, dangerous man. He was trouble, and now she hated him as well as herself. Oh, why didn't she try harder to convince James? Her daughter was lying dead in a pool of blood in her room, and Jonas and his crony were trying to unearth something in her basement.

Peering through the stair boards, Will could see two bearded men near the storm cellar door, digging by candlelight. It was dim in the basement but Will could see their work clothes: dirty brown trousers held up by suspenders over drab shirts that looked like they may have been white at one time. Their sleeves were rolled up, and they each had on worn-out boots. The men grunted as they worked, their backs to the stairs.

They turned around to Sylvia's voice. The candle's glow bounced off the sweat on their faces. Their shovels and picks gave away their desperation. From above was the sound of a horse approaching, then a man's voice and muffled footsteps quickly going upstairs. It finally dawned on Will that Mrs. Cabet was waving a long, weathered riffle back and forth between the two. The men now looked petrified and backed up, their shovels falling to the dirt floor. The taller man, whose shirt was actually a faint pinstripe, nervously wiped sweat from his red face. His friend put his hands out in front of himself, nearly touching his large belly. The patches on the knees of his trousers eluded to his social status.

"Missus Cabet, please. This one was an accident. The gun went off. We was just horsing around. Put the gun down, Missus, please," the shorter one, named Henry pleaded. His dirty, calloused hands were turned upward in surrender.

Will could hear doors slamming and a man's voice yelling almost directly above him. He knew there was no way he could get back upstairs now and he worried about Jenna. He backed up even further into the tiny crevice as the basement door opened again.

Footsteps coming down to the basement distracted Mrs. Cabet. Sidetracked, she turned around, but it was too late. Henry snatched up the shovel and swung it at the woman, striking her left shoulder and head with the back end of it. She collapsed to the floor, unconscious. He reached for the gun and nearly had it in his hand when Will heard the click of a gun behind him being cocked. Will had been found out, and his heart stopped in his throat. He sighed ever so slightly when the footsteps kept coming down the stairs.

A small man with round spectacles and thinning blond hair stepped into the basement. He was modestly dressed for farm work in olive colored overalls, but right now he was pointing a large pistol at Henry. The walnut-colored handle of the gun curved around and past his fist. The butt of it ended in a wide flower design. The barrel was at least nine inches long supported half way with a continuation of the woodwork with another flourish at its end. Will, who enjoyed learning about old weapons, knew by those distinctive features it was a Belgian pistol. Mr. Cabet staggered, just noticing his wife's body.

"What'd you do Henry? I trusted you. We had a deal, remember, Jonas? I'd keep your cover here while we mined, and we'd split the profit three ways. Two more murders can't be hid. And now you're burying my family," Mr. Cabet choked.

"No, James, Mr. Cabet, sir. Honest. We wasn't burying your family," Henry whined.

Will knew this wasn't going to end well. With his one good chance gone, he started to inch towards the staircase to sneak out as fast as he could. Suddenly there was movement, a struggle, gunshots, and breaking glass. It was completely dark now, the room filling with smoke.

Will started coughing, his eyes tearing. There was grunting, yelling, heavy breathing, footsteps on the stairs, and Jenna's scream. Will had just come around to the front of the stairs when he heard a thud in front of him and tripped as he tried to leave. A faint whiff of hyacinths made him stop. That was the smell of Jenna's shampoo. He bent down, his hands sweeping out in front of him.

"Knock it off, leave me alone!" he heard Jenna yell.

"Jenna, it's me, Will. We need to get out of here," he whispered in the darkness. Jenna crawled into his arms.

"I had to hide when that guy came through. I didn't know what was going on down here. I couldn't hear a thing. Then guns went off, and it was so loud! I thought you were shot, too, and I would be left here all by myself," Jenna sobbed. "I'm scared, Will. I want to go home!"

Will stood up, both his hands on Jenna's arms to get her up as well. They started to fumble forward when they ran into something solid. They both froze when they heard the cocking of a gun by their heads.

"I can't see, but my Colt Paterson will find you. I only spent two rounds so's I have three left. More than I need. And I can shoot just fine in the dark," a man's voice drawled directly in front of them.

Thirteen

HERE WAS A scuffling of feet, and Jenna and Will were pushed forward and up the stairs into the daylight by a firm hand.

"Who are you?" the man called Jonas asked apprehensively, looking Jenna and Will up and down.

"Um, I'm Will. I… just walked into town. This is my, uh, sister."

"Aye-uh. Runaways, I reckon. Well, now I got me some lee-ver-age."

He went to the hoosier just inside the kitchen. The freestanding large wooden cupboard was like a baker's table with a tabletop, and cabinets above and below used for storage of flour and spices, as well as preparing food. Searching quickly through the small drawers, he grabbed a candle and some match sticks all the while pointing the revolver at them. His gun had a simple, small wooden handle with a pronounced cylinder. The business end started wide but graduated down to a long, thin barrel. Will squeezed Jenna's hand, tipping his head towards Jonas's. Her eyes followed his direction and she squeezed his hand back. Jonas was bleeding quite badly from his temple. Oblivious to this interaction, Jonas scooped an empty lantern onto his forearm and shoved it at Jenna.

"We're goin' back downstairs," Jonas ordered. He pushed the candle into Jenna's other hand and struck the match against the wall. He lit the candle and barked at Jenna to place it in the lamp. They all walked through the hallway and back down the stairs. The light threw dizzying shadows in Jenna's unsteady grasp. She almost fell twice, her legs were shaking so badly. Will put his hand on her shoulder. When they got to the bottom, their eyes acclimated to the faint illumination. It was then that they realized the man called Henry had been shot as well. He lay sprawled on the floor, face first, not far from where he had reached for Mrs. Cabet's gun. Turrets of blood darkened the dirt floor underneath him. Mrs. Cabet herself had not moved from where she fell. There was blood by her head but her face was turned so the injury was not visible. Glass from the lantern had shattered, surrounding the small holes the men had been digging, the candle broken in half. Mr. Cabet was nowhere to be seen.

"Pick up the shovels and axe, and start over there," Jonas drawled, pointing to the sod side by the storm cellar stairs. He staggered a step and sat down on the bottom stair. Will and Jenna cautiously walked by Mrs. Cabet and stepped over Henry's body. Jenna slowly started shoveling the earth Will loosened with the axe. Will kept glancing toward the gun in

Jonas's hand. After a few minutes his axe hit something hard. Confused, he looked at Jenna and stopped. She stared back at him as Jonas got up.

"What is this?" Will asked him. He didn't get an answer.

"Ha, Henry, I knew it was over that 'a way," Jonas said, waving the gun at the mound of dirt. He brushed Jenna off to the side and motioned for Will to keep going. Will put the axe down and took the tool from Jenna. When he could no longer pull up a shovelful, Jonas grunted at him. Will bent down and started clearing the dirt away with his hands, unearthing a package.

The basement was now full of the iron smell of blood and the deep earth. It took some effort for Will to pry off the caked soil to reveal a large bundle wrapped in brown burlap. Will brought it to the surface and wiped his forehead on his pleated sleeves, which were now both brown.

Jonas laughed and let his guard down, dropping the gun onto the floor as he lunged for the parcel. As he did, Will moved forward to reach for the gun. Jonas didn't seem to notice. Will had just about reached the gun when Jonas opened the ties and Jenna gasped loudly, making Will turn his head back to her in fear. The window of opportunity Will had to grab the gun was gone. That split second was long enough for Jonas to reach back and reclaim the gun, his face sinister from the blood oozing down his temple. Once again, the barrel faced Will and he put his hands up in defeat.

"Oh wow, look!" Jenna exclaimed, fascinated.

The biggest, shiniest stone Jenna and Will had ever seen sparkled up from the rough cloth wrappings at them. It was about the size of a softball, and its many facets sparkled in the beam of the candlelight. Jonas kept his eyes on Will as he moved his left hand to spread the burlap out in front of them. A dozen smaller stones, the size of ice cubes tumbled out to the floor, glinting in the candlelight.

"Pick 'em up!"

"Are those diamonds? Real diamonds?" Jenna breathed, as she scrambled to pick them up.

"I've never seen any that big before," Will admitted, shaking his head, as he helped.

"A-uh. Found a brand-new vein just a while back. This'll have to do for now. Wrap it back up straight away, y'hear? Time to leave town. Now alls I have to do is get my gear. Move!" Jonas ordered.

"Are we leaving town, too?" Jenna asked timidly. She couldn't help but look at the wound on his head, and wonder how in the struggle he got hurt. It was bleeding quite badly.

A wicked grin grew on Jonas's face before it instantly cleared to innocence. "Uh, no ma'am. Just me. You two can stay here, a-course." He motioned with his head for them to keep moving. With that gesture, small beads of blood dripped onto the floor.

Jenna picked up the lantern, her free hand finding Will's. Jonas took the burlap bag. Once again, they climbed the steep stairs with encouragement from the weapon at their backs. Up they went to the main floor. Jonas told Jenna to blow out the candle and set the lantern down, which Jenna did. He signaled to continue through the main rooms and up the grand staircase. Hand in hand, they kept going higher. They were pushed to the right once on the landing, into the Sewing Room, which, according to the framed picture of the small family, was the living quarters of the Cabets. Then they were directed towards the narrow stairs to the sixth room. They ran into Mr. Cabet as he was coming off the last step.

"Hello James. Lookin' for these?" Jonas asked, holding the burlap sack. Mr. Cabet looked at the sack, his eyes red from crying. The front of his green overalls was stained a dark color now. He seemed confused as he looked at Will, then Jenna, their hands entwined. Squinting through his glasses, his face suddenly cleared.

"My Amelie? It's you! You're all right!" Mr. Cabet whispered, smiling oddly.

Jenna looked around, hoping he was talking to someone else. Desperately she shook her head. She and Will started to back up the only way they could go, stumbling into a large trunk, towards the far wall, near the open window. The portal window. Both tried to shy away but the path was blocked. Jenna didn't understand why Mr. Cabet would think she was his daughter when he obviously knew Amelie was dead upstairs.

"Amelie, come here to your pa!" Mr. Cabet called out sternly. He held his arms out toward her, still holding his gun. His hands were bloody from trying to revive his daughter upstairs. He seemed unconcerned with the gun that Jonas was pointing at him. He pushed away the rocking chair next to him with his free hand—leaving an ugly red smudge—and kept moving. Jonas was just as baffled, now a spectator. He didn't understand why his gun didn't hold the threat that it just had. He wiped the blood out of his eye with his arm, blinking to focus.

Jenna was now stuck, her back up against the side of the window with nowhere to go, shaking her head back and forth. Her eyes never left Mr. Cabet. Will couldn't find a way out either. They were trapped with two demented men. Mr. Cabet rushed over to Jenna, his firearm raised in his fist. Will attempted to move in front to protect her, but Mr. Cabet pulled the gun on him, forcing him to back down.

"I'm not Amelie!" Jenna whimpered, wincing as he got closer.

Mr. Cabet was upon her now, a crazed disregard in his eyes. "You're standing no more'n a foot from me, plain as day. I fretted something fierce thinking you were dead. It was that magic trickery again. I warned you not to get involved with your mother's sorcery. This time it took years off my life! You're not ever to do that to me again, 'hear?" he ranted. The butt of the gun swung forward, whipping Jenna, knocking her head hard into the window frame. Will was able to pull her to him just as he heard a deafening roar.

A bullet whizzed past their heads, smashing the glass lamp on the table on the other side of the window and lodging into the framework. Mrs. Cabet was standing in the doorway, still in the shooting stance, smoke rising up from the large gun shaking in her arms. The hair on the left side of her head was matted with dried blood. Her shoulder was bleeding from a deep gash.

"Stop it!" she screeched hysterically. Mr. Cabet and Jonas didn't move, their faces sharing matching disbelief.

"Sylvie!" Mr. Cabet exclaimed. He recovered and smiled, relieved, and dropped his hands as he turned towards his wife.

Jonas regained himself to try to control the situation, setting his diamond bag carefully on a nearby table. He stepped toward the door, pointing the gun at Mrs. Cabet. Will used the distraction to lower a stunned Jenna to the floor in a sitting position, pulling under her arms to move her away from everyone. Welts from an abrasion on her temple from scraping across the wooden frame were beginning to seep blood.

"There will be no more!" Mrs. Cabet yelled, moving closer, hysterical now. She reloaded the gun proficiently while keeping her head in position and her eyes on Jonas to keep him in her sights. But Jonas moved quicker. He used his free arm to grab Mr. Cabet and spun him in front of himself and stepped away just as Mrs. Cabet fired the gun. Mr. Cabet tried to move backwards to get out of the line of fire, but was blown back by the immense force of the gunshot, his face frozen in a silent scream. His gun dropped with a clatter, and he tripped over Jonas, silently falling out of the open window. A dull thud could be heard a second later. The recoil from the gun was enough to force Mrs. Cabet back a foot. It took a few seconds for her to steady herself, and half that for her body to buckle under the weight of what had happened in front of her.

Crouched down, away from the window, Will flinched, his arms protectively over Jenna who was still not coherent and didn't even flinch. Will pulled her behind a small table, his hands feeling along her head for other injuries. He felt only a goose egg forming near her ear from the gun. Until she came to, all he could do was hold her and wait.

"You killed your husband, Mrs. Cabet," Jonas cooed calmly, picking up the orphaned gun without breaking eye contact with her. He distractedly rubbed his oozing head with the crook of his forearm. Mrs. Cabet was on her knees, stunned. The gun hung limply at her side as realization caught up with her.

"What will the good people of Orchard Creek say now? I've heard folks talk. You never attend church services. The Reverend's never been invited 'round for supper. It's not lookin' good fer ya. They's thought you was a witch already, what with your worshippin' away from town with your own kin. What will they do once they hear you've murdered your own husband and one of your tenants? Your dead daughter can't save you, neither. You might as well have killed her, too. She'll never be able to say that I done it. You're going out of your mind right now. By the time you're able to fetch the sheriff I'll be miles gone where no one will ever find me."

Mrs. Cabet was now shaking harder, a guttural rumble rising from deep inside her as she began to rise.

"You'd like to kill me here, wouldn't you? What will that prove?" Jonas teased, staggering towards her. Both guns were raised now and trained on the petite woman. Jonas knew he had the upper hand with point blank range and three rounds in the chamber. His gun would fire when he pulled the trigger. Mrs. Cabet had used her shot. The gun would need to be reloaded before she'd become a threat. She was no better off if she stood there without a weapon at all.

Feeling like a caged animal, she knew she was stuck. "You're evil!" she screeched hoarsely. As Jonas neared, she retreated, but it was a sideways move so he couldn't cut her off. Unable to get back to the door, she started whimpering. The window was getting closer. Will pulled Jenna farther away still, fumbling over furniture, his arms like shields around her, trying to keep them both out of the way. Despite the small number of people in the room, they had been overlooked.

"Your life is over now. There are no good Christians who kill their family, a-yuh. Join your husband. The window's yonder. You'll go insane otherwise from the misery, missus. The nightmares will haunt you terrible. You'll relive shootin' your husband, seeing your daughter's blood spilt on the floor. You'll hear her call out for you in the dark of night." His bottomless eyes bored into hers and a sinister look crossed his face. "You shoot me, I'll find a way to come back just for you, that's a promise. I don't have nightmares when I kill. I sleep just fine." Jonas laughed heartily. His voice was thick and he was now slurring his words and having difficulty standing upright. Blood was now flowing freely from his head where he rubbed it, and his sleeve was saturated and dripping.

Sylvia was too distraught to notice. Her world had caved in and her thoughts were like shattered chards of glass inside her. Everything in her mind hurt. Maybe it was all another dream like she had a fortnight ago. It was very much like this. How she wished it were so. She knew if she didn't take control of herself soon she was as good as gone, like her whole family. No! She wouldn't think of that now. She needed to concentrate. Looking at the window, she weighed her options. She started to walk away.

JONAS DRIFTED BACK to the table to retrieve his loot. His body was no longer moving under his complete control; his eyes were opening and closing, but it seemed he could no longer focus. He slid James's gun across the table and grabbed the bag, but lost his grip and the burlap unfolded. Diamonds fell and scattered on the floor.

At first it didn't register that there were shiny raw diamonds on the floor. Finally, Sylvia's mind cleared and she saw the good fortune before her, as if a sign. She stared at Jonas for a moment, then the floor, knowing she wouldn't have long to act. Jonas was now trying to steady himself on a chair. Hesitantly, knowing it was useless anyway, she put the gun down and scooped up as many stones as she could. Her hands shook as she started to purposely set them back on the floor around her.

Will leaned forward, watching intently now, anticipating and hoping. What were the odds? He shook Jenna one last time, this one bringing her back to reality. She started to say something, but he put his hand over her mouth. She turned toward Mrs. Cabet where Will was focused and watched.

Mrs. Cabet reached into her bloodied apron and pulled out a knife from a rawhide sheath. It was small with a modest crooked wooden handle. It fit perfectly in her hand. The black metal blade had a fine point and was only about four inches long. It trembled in her grasp.

"She's going to stab herself, Will!" Jenna hissed, clawing at his arms to get out of his hold.

"No, she's not. I think that's her athame."

"Her what? The knife thing? Like your mom had?" Jenna asked, exasperated.

"Watch what she's doing."

Sylvia knew her life was balanced on the head of a pin. Jonas was not long for this world, but she had to act fast if she was to have any chance at all. She turned to her right, trying hard not to think about her husband disappearing through that wicked window, and raised the blade out in front of herself. "Air, come," she spoke quickly. She closed her eyes as if to pray and turned abruptly, her back to her enemy. The hems of her skirts spun with the momentum. "To me now, fire," she uttered, her hand raised to the west as if conducting an orchestra. She continued to move clockwise, Jonas now on her right, rubbing his eyes once more.

"Yes. She's raising a circle. A protective circle."

"Water, join me. Earth, I ask for your company."

"I don't understand."

"She Pagan, Jenna. She's a witch."

"She's a…witch? Like, hocus pocus spells and a broom?" Jenna was starting to lose touch; it didn't seem real.

"Spells! That makes sense. Those picture from my house. She was in a few of them, and they were of this building."

"The pictures vibrated and burnt my hands, Will."

His face cleared as the pieces fell together. "Trigger objects. Oh, Goddess, they were trigger objects."

"We fell into the pictures. We—"

"Because of today's date. She must have done it. That's powerful spell work." Will could tell by Jenna's expression she was completely lost. He didn't have the luxury of time. "Sylvia was the one who put the spell on the pictures. I'll explain later. I don't want her to stop what she's doing."

Jonas was yelling and mumbling. Sometimes it was crystal clear threats, other times it was incoherent sounds. Somehow, his hand still owned his gun, though, and that was the biggest danger. It stayed trained on Mrs. Cabet. At times, it somehow found Will and Jenna. Will was very sure Jonas wasn't faking his actions, his face was pale and his head was a bloody mess. They watched Sylvia put the last of the diamonds on the floor around her.

"Ok, a witch. And she's making a, um, circle with the diamonds?"

"Yes, I think that will help us get out of here," Will whispered, a relieved smile on his face.

"How?" Jenna rushed. She was shaking her head, confused and overwhelmed.

Will sighed. He turned his head towards Jenna, but his eyes never left Mrs. Cabet.

"I promise I'll tell you everything. If we can get into her circle, maybe we can get back home that way. Trust me, Jenna, I think we'll be okay."

Mrs. Cabet was consumed within herself, focused on the task at hand. At the moment, she was not distracted by anyone else in the room. Jonas was leaning heavily into the chair now, drifting in and out of consciousness. Every few seconds he'd lurch forward, his eyes sharp, his gun pointing dead on his target. Sylvia hardly flinched. At other times, the gun swung at his side as if forgotten, his eyes unfocused and drooping. So much blood had accumulated on the floor the room was thick with the sickly, rusty smell.

"I have no choice. I'm free to do this. He's gone now, and there is no other way," Sylvia muttered to herself, quaking, as she held the knife out in front of her and closed her eyes.

As Mrs. Cabet chanted, she walked clockwise, holding the knife out in much the same way Will's mother had earlier that evening. Sylvia's long skirt swished, only skimming the stones around her from years of experience.

Will was now pulling Jenna up to her feet and inching them both towards the circle, chanting as well under his breath. Jenna's head was still foggy. What was Will saying? It was different from what Mrs. Cabet was saying. She continued to recite as she used the athame as a pen to write '10-01' in the air. From where Jenna was hiding, she could see the numbers haze into view like silky smoke, lingering just long enough to recognize. They dissipated just as quickly. The stones on the floor seemed to shimmer. Jenna's mouth hung open, slack-jawed in amazement.

"Mark this date, avenge those who have done wrong. Relive to undo the evil here. Put it to rest. For when the year reaches the first day of the tenth month, today and hereafter, the wheel of life will halt to allow..." She didn't have a chance to finish. She had again turned her back on Jonas. This time was just long enough for him to make one last move, his blood loss and wound now about to claim his life. He lunged at the landlord, pushing her out of the circle before she was done, one hand firmly around her throat as he was raising the gun. She had just seconds to get her hands up to intervene.

For once, the short woman was stronger, and she struggled awkwardly to turn the gun around while Jonas tried to counter her moves. Although Mrs. Cabet stood bug-eyed with Jonas's large, dirty hands around her throat, she stared at him, determined. Her face was a puce color now. Jonas appeared to be staring her down as well. They continued to struggle. Her hands were tangled in front of her with Jonas's other hand, the gun, and the knife. There was a thunderous blast as a final gunshot rang out.

From behind the table, Jenna screamed and threw her hands over her ears. For an instant, no one moved. There was blood, so much blood. It was impossible to tell whose it was. With eyes wide, Jonas glared at Mrs. Cabet, grimaced and opened his mouth as if to speak. Instead of words, a stream of blood poured out. His grin faded and his grip loosened as he looked down at the blood gushing from his chest. His time had run out. Jonas slowly collapsed and fell to the floor.

"Set it in motion, so mote it be," Sylvia grunted. She moaned as she staggered outside the circle and dropped the gun. It was the best she could do. She reached for her stomach where the hilt of her athame jutted out. It was then that Will and Jenna realized the diamonds on the floor were beginning to emit a faint glow. Preoccupied with her back turned, Will pulled Jenna into the circle with him. The room started to spin, getting darker, but not before they saw Mrs. Cabet pull the knife. It came out with a nasty suction sound. She stashed it in her apron and lifted her head towards the door as if she heard someone downstairs.

"This must be dealt with first," she gasped. With one hand, she clutched the oozing gash, with the other she grabbed Jonas's shirt, struggling to drag his body to the door.

Fourteen

ENNA HIT THE floor with a thud once again. She knew her eyes were closed and she just didn't have the energy to open them. There were shouts and loud voices surrounding her. Time passed while she lay there, unable to even form words, let alone clear her thoughts. Then she was being shaken by someone, her heavy arms picked up. Her body was weighted.

Finally, she smelled it, Sulis's perfume. She was still weak but the heavy feeling began to subside. She felt someone move to her side and a candle shown a shadow of light on her surroundings as she opened her eyes. There was nothing she wanted more than to find Will, if only she could move on her own. She could barely see around the others kneeling beside her, but could tell he remained motionless on the floor not too far from her.

"Jenna! Thank God you're back! What happened?" her dad

asked, pulling her up to a sitting position, hugging her limp body tightly. She moaned as her father embraced her.

"Is Will okay? Is he awake?" Jenna whispered. She felt so tired and sore, feeling the goose egg on the left side of her head around her father's grip. Sulis reached over and squeezed her hand.

"He's all right," she reassured her. Jenna could see Will as he began to sit up on his own. He looked over at Jenna, his face relaxing.

"I fell into the picture. We never left here. It was awful," Jenna began, her voice cracking. Several people gasped. Mr. Levy was the loudest.

"What?"

"It's true. We saw the woman in the pictures, Sylvia Cabet."

"Will, those pictures must have been taken…"

"Yeah, we know, a hundred and fifty years ago."

"What happened?" asked Toby.

"Dad, there's an upstairs to the upstairs. We were there. It's the missing staircase, Mr. Jacobs."

"Here." Tina pushed a red plastic cup of water at her before she went and did the same to Will. Jenna took a huge gulp before being helped up by the men. Will waved them off, sitting with one arm around his knees, drinking the whole cup.

"Thanks," Jenna said, sitting at the table with her dad. "There were two guys arguing because they shot and killed Sylvia's daughter, Amelie. She was the one we connected with in the Ouija board. She told us then she was killed by a man with a gun. Then the men took off—"

"They went into the basement and Sylvia came down with a gun," Will added, finally getting up and sitting at the table next to his mother. "There was a scuffle. Sylvia was knocked out and one of the men was killed."

Jenna frowned, remembering the men had been digging for the diamonds. Will skipped over that part. When he put his cup down, she picked up the story.

"That was when Sylvia's husband came in. His name was James. He thought the men were going to bury his family right there. The bad guy, Jonas, was a tenant here when it was a boarding house. Then, he realized we were there."

"James took off, and Jonas held us hostage. He made us walk upstairs. This whole place looked so differently. It wasn't a museum or a mill, people lived here. Sylvia and her family's quarters were in the Sewing Room. Anyway, James must have found his dead daughter—"

"Ooh," Jenna interrupted. "I bet that was her bedroom."

"It must have been," Will agreed. "Anyway, when we saw him again, he had been crying and he had blood on him. Then it got confusing. He mistook Jenna for his daughter, and I guess he thought he had been seeing things. He yelled at her. You know how you get when you think something bad has happened to your kid, and then you're so relieved they're okay you get mad because they scared you so much?" All the parents shook their heads in agreement.

"Like the time I thought you waded into the water at Sylvan beach and we had the whole park make a human chain in the water only to find you at the swing sets? Yes, I understand," Mr. Jacobs said, briefly looking over at Toby.

"Well, I don't think he meant to really hurt her, only punish her—Amelie that is—but it was really Jenna." Will got up and walked around next to Jenna. "He whacked her with the butt of his gun. It hit her on this side of her head," he pointed, "and she hit the window frame on that side. It was the Sewing Room's window."

Everyone reacted to this. His mother just listened carefully, but her eyes betrayed her. She was startled, too.

"I don't remember a lot after that," Jenna admitted.

"You were stunned and out of it awhile. I pulled you behind some furniture until you came around. Then Sylvia showed up with her own gun and she was hysterical. She meant to shoot Jonas, except he did a bait and switch thing, and she ended up killing her husband. There wasn't much distance between the two of them, and the force of it blew him backwards. He fell out the window. *That* window. Jonas laughed and goaded Sylvia to jump. He even said if she did manage to kill him, he'd come back for her." Will looked around at the faces staring at him, weighing his thoughts. Jenna had wandered towards the main room, but he got up and sat down next to his mother. He now understood why he needed to be true to who he was. "When he said that, I felt it. Worse than ever before. It was like stepping into a walk-in freezer." He took a breath. "And as an empath, I felt it within my very being."

"Right now, my only concern is how you got back?" Mr. Stevens asked, glancing over at Jenna.

"I think Jonas had been shot in the head while in the basement and it was just a matter of time before he died. Sylvia made a circle and we were lucky enough to jump in."

"That doesn't make sense!" Mr. Levy exclaimed, pounding his fist on the table. Everything jiggled.

"None of this makes any sense," Tina admitted, picking up a few of the stones that bounced near her.

"Jenna, sit down, you're hurt."

"I'm okay, dad. I just need to walk some of this off." She went towards the front door, needing the reassurance of something modern. She was captivated by the change in scenery once again as her eyes scanned the row of cars outside, illuminated by the floodlights. She could vaguely make out the outlines of all the tombstones from the vast cemetery in front of her. There were too many houses and tall trees to see Rodger's Pike Road from here now. She turned back facing the others as Will continued to talk.

"Mom, what happened here? Could you follow it through the board?" he asked. He looked at the Ouija board in front of his mother as if it might start moving on its own.

"Bits and pieces. There were many voices trying to speak with us, and it got confusing. You're saying this Jonas promised he would come back?" Sulis inquired.

"Yes. He said he would haunt Mrs. Cabet. Sylvia. She's a witch and must have cast a spell inside here for a way to return to undo the murders."

Mr. Levy spoke up, a suspicious expression on his face. "Come on, now. A witch? A spell? Are you both pulling our leg? Is this all some sort of illusion?"

"I saw two people disappear and then reappear within seconds right next to me," Toby answered, his face sober. He looked from Will to Jenna, concerned.

"So did I," Mr. Stevens added. Sulis looked at her son knowingly.

"Will?"

"We might as well," he answered, nodding.

"We are Pagan, Mr. Levy, just like Mrs. Cabet. Witches," Sulis continued, indicating herself and Will. She knew she needed to plow through the basics before anyone made any more assumptions. "History and fiction have made it nearly impossible to break free from the myths. We honor nature and the elements and use their energy, protective properties, and forces they hold to help us. When we put our energies into the stones, gems and our athames, and surround ourselves with them, they become more powerful."

"Like the diamonds we saw," Jenna's voice came from across the room.

"Ah, that's the connection. Yes, if that is what Mrs. Cabet used. We have some of our own gems on the table with the Ouija for just that reason."

"She raised a circle, and it was possible for us to get into it. That's how we got back home," Will stated. "But the circle was broken, and it looked like she was stabbed pretty badly. The last thing we saw as I pushed us into the circle was Mrs. Cabet trying to drag Jonas's body out of the room. There are things I still don't understand." Slowly, those who were still standing started to take their seats, except Jenna who had her arms around herself while she looked out the window.

"I've never heard of the ability to do what she did. It appears she had a good portion of the spell done, but not enough if it brought those who entered the past to the point after her daughter was shot. That cannot be undone, and I'm sure she knew that," Sulis offered.

"This is getting too personal. We need to stop right now," Mr. Levy ordered.

"No! We need to keep going. We need to find a way to permanently end this. Don't you see? This will keep repeating otherwise. Every October first we are in danger! The pictures become a doorway to this building's past, and not only could we fall in, like Will and Jenna have, something from the past could cross over here to our present. Whatever or whoever is over there on the other side—whatever you want to call it— is now cognizant of that. It's a new entryway that right now cannot be closed," Sulis warned.

"Yeah, okay, but how do we shut *this* window?" Mr. Jacobs asked, rubbing his hand through his hair.

"There are way too many windows here," Toby commented nervously.

"That's the problem," Sulis stated, frustrated. "These layers overlap and keep building."

"So, what do we do now? Send someone back over a hundred years where there are crazy people waving guns?" Tina questioned. The room was silent for a moment.

"That won't be necessary. I'm already here, and I'll put it all to right." The voice came from somewhere hidden in the darkness of the staircase, behind Jenna. His hearty laugh gave him away. Jonas was with them in the room, now visible as he walked into the cast of the candle's light. His clothes, brown and filthy, shook with his delight as he held a small sharp, black-bladed athame in his spotted hand. The handle was indistinguishable in his large grasp.

The dead man's face was full of stubble, and his short hair was concealed under his decomposing cap until he turned his head. The whole right side of his temple down past his neck looked black. The color of his face was off too, that was evident even in the dim glow from the candles. Deep circles under his eyes made them appear sunken and sallow. In the middle of his shirt was a patch of black as if he had spilled tar down his front. One of his suspenders was missing. The other held only by threads. Everyone froze, shocked, trying to accept this change in reality.

"Jonas," Will whispered to himself. Sulis's eyes were drawn to the athame, and she found Will's hand under the table and squeezed it.

Jonas leered at the group before his face morphed into a smug smile. He confidently turned around towards the great room, his arms out to his sides the way one would stand before a duel. Only this showdown involved a knife, not a gun. "Hello again, Amelie."

Jenna gasped, horrified, as she realized she was now stuck and unable to get back to the others. She squealed and bolted away from him, self-preservation kicking in. She disappeared in the darkness and was up the stairs before she was able to realize that was the worst place to go.

Tension was high at the table. Up until this point the men had their hands on the backs of their chairs and the table, adrenaline readying their muscles. With Jenna's screams, Mr. Stevens was unable to process what he had just seen, but knew his daughter was in danger. He jumped up without thinking, the instinct to protect was his only concern.

"Jenna, no!"

"Hang on, Jack!" Mr. Levy pushed a shrieking Tina away from the area and into Sulis's outstretched arms. Will was already grabbing a chair for her to sit down. "I'm coming!"

Mr. Jacobs frantically looked around the table for something to use as a weapon. He grabbed the silver candlestick and gripped it tightly in his hand. "There's nothing good here to use," he yelled. "Toby, look for something in the office."

"The Mag flashlight is on the file cabinet!" Toby yelled, disappeared into the darkness. Without waiting, the men advanced. None expect what followed.

Jonas ignored Jenna for the moment, and casually turned towards the oncoming men. With one snarl and an incredibly fast move, he stood in their way. His face contorted into a million crinkles with his smile; it had the sound of tissue paper ripping. It seemed one small breeze could make his petrified skin crack and fall off altogether.

Amid shouts from the men on how to take him down, he exhaled forcefully, a simple gesture that was almost laughable. But his mouth, toothless and gaping, emitted a thick stench that made all the men fall back, including Toby who had rounded out of the office and into the invisible barrier. Immediately, everyone doubled over, their hands on their knees, gagging involuntarily. The chalice and flashlight fell to the wooden floor, bouncing with a clank and a thump. Jonas breathed at them again—Mr. Stevens in particular—and hooted. "No one's goin' nowheres."

Jonas was back in control. He spun around and flew to the staircase faster than anyone thought possible. His voice was crystal clear, carrying farther than his silhouette, which was now barely visible as he climbed the stairs.

"That's right. Upstairs is where it all started. It's your turn fer the window. I killed you once, and Missus will love that I'm going to do it again. She can't save you twice!" he shouted as he took the stairs two at a time. His voice was not winded at all.

Mr. Stevens gasped, unable to regain control. "Got to-save-Jenna."

"I'm-trying," Mr. Jacobs choked out, bent over but inching towards the staircase.

Will had watched this from a safer distance and wasn't affected. He looked to his mother with urgency. "Mom, if we go after Jenna and get Jonas instead, I'm afraid we'll get sucked back into that portal."

"We're lucky you both got back at all! I've never seen anything in our Book of Spells that would prepare us for this. We have no way to protect ourselves."

"I'm pretty sure we could get back to our time if we had a picture of the place. Or, maybe have an athame."

"You realize this is way beyond what we're safely capable of doing, Will."

"We've never experienced this, I know, but we've got to get Jenna. Jonas is going to try to stop us. I got that through the Ouija. We need to figure out a way to send him back, too. I think Sylvia may have used the pictures as trigger objects. Couldn't some of these photos be entryways?"

He could see the wheels turning. "They could. We can try

it." Will frantically started pushing pictures out of the frames. His face may not have shown fear, but his hands were shaking. "There are a few protective spells that might help. You'll need both a picture and the black tourmaline stones." Sulis started moving things about on the table.

Will looked up at Mr. Jacobs who was no longer advancing, trying to drag in a clean breath. Mr. Levy's eyes were tearing faster than he could wipe them. A coughing fit had slowed Toby down but he was still pushing on. Mr. Stevens was attempting to move forward, breathing with his arm up to his mouth.

"If you don't have an athame or a picture, how will you come back if you fall in?" Will yelled. For a second, everyone froze. They were unsure what to do.

Mr. Stevens was still not able to stand upright, having received the brunt of Jonas's foul toxins. He was powerless. "My-daughter!" he forced out weakly.

"We will save her Mr. Stevens, but we must do this first," Will said, trying to keep his voice even. "I think I know a way I can get us back if we fall in again."

"Please trust us. No one go up just yet. I don't want Jonas to get stupid and rash." Everyone else in the room had the same expression.

"Of course the dead man from the past is going to be stupid and rash!" they heard Tina cry.

"Need-to go-now!" Mr. Stevens was shouting, although it was little more than his normal speaking voice. Whatever poison Jonas spewed, it was debilitating.

"Jack-hold-on," Mr. Levy breathed in between heaving. It seized his whole body. "What if they have a better plan?"

"Dammit, that's my daughter, Mark!" his voice was barely above a whisper. He attempted to push his way past the barrier. It was slow going.

Will and Sulis had ignored the words around them, putting their energy into their work. They moved swiftly, in sync, with few words spoken. Will picked up specific stones from the table and shoved them in his pocket. He gingerly folded the pictures in half, then quarters and put them in another pocket. His mother grabbed his arm and shook her head.

"Here. I won't be able to move like you." She passed her sheathed athame to him, and after the slightest hesitation, he slid it in his waistband. From upstairs, they heard doors slamming and Jenna's frantic voice.

"Yeah, someone needs to take the knife," Toby managed to say in between coughing. That used up too much of his air and he had to grab ahold of a chair until the dizziness passed. Waving his arms, he tried to clear the festering smell away. It was inch by inch.

"It's an athame," Sulis corrected calmly, not looking up. She knew Tina—by now clinging to her chair, crying and hyper-ventilating behind her—had passed the point of self-control and would need help to calm down. "And that's not what we will use this for. It's a weapon in the wrong hands, yes, but also a tool that Will can use."

Mr. Stevens finally managed to take a few productive steps. As if running in slow motion, he started for the staircase. "Let's move. I'm coming Jenna!"

"Go, Will, now! You need to be up there with these," Sulis urged.

Drawing his hair away from his face with his hand, he made one detour around to the office, flicking on the main power panel for the whole building before bolting for the stairs. His chocolate brown hair flew behind him as he lithely bounded toward the Sewing Room. In the stark brightness from the light, the evening felt almost dreamlike. Then they could hear things tipping over, and a man's booming laugh.

"HELP ME!!" Jenna's voice exploded from above as the men reached the stairs. "What do we do if he lets loose another stink bomb?" Mr. Levy asked. "Is there anything else we should do?" They looked back for a leader to direct them on what to do next. There was no one. Sulis had already sat back down. She had taken a deep breath and closed her eyes, her hand back on the planchette, the blue sapphire shining in the artificial light.

WILL REACHED THE landing, his momentum already in the direction of the Sewing Room, knowing that room in particular needed monitoring. Suddenly he caught movement from the corner of his eye in the Display Room. He hesitated for just an instant hoping Mr. Stevens had gone on ahead of him, but didn't have time to find out. Right behind him were the other men and Toby. It hit him quickly what had to be done right away.

"All the old pictures here must be tipped over and covered right now! Who knows what's coming out of them at this moment, and there are pictures all over the place," Will yelled.

"There are quite a few in the office, too!" Mr. Jacobs hollered to no one in particular. He hesitated. No one wanted to turn around and leave.

"For the love of all that's Holy, everyone must go! Toby, I

need someone who can move fast. Go ahead of me and see if Jenna's okay." Will looked around, taking inventory. "Mr. Levy, we need the doors and windows locked. This needs to remain inside the building or it could get much worse."

"I can go downstairs if we're sure you'll be able to get Jenna okay," Mr. Jacobs offered, halfheartedly. His eyes were scanning the landing above, his face wrinkled with worry. It was obvious he was anxious to go upstairs with everyone else.

"We will. That would be great if you could watch the basement and the orchard. Overturn any picture you come across on your way. This whole area is unsafe now, and I'm not sure if anyone will try to get in. Anything out of the ordinary, we need to coordinate, so we stay in control."

Everyone was scattering. Will yelled louder. "The pictures must be covered! Tell Tina to turn them over downstairs on the wall. I need a liaison to advise me on what my mother is getting from the board that can help us," Will ordered. It was easy how his knowledge from his family's cleansings was meshing with improvisation as his natural leadership kicked in. In a brief instant, everyone was gone. Another scream from Jenna pierced through Will's heart, and he automatically ran into the Sewing Room, forgetting everything else.

Will was immediately caught off guard. Two men had Jenna pinned against the corner wall opposite the window, and one had Toby backed up behind the door. Will only recognized Jonas. He was against one wall with Jenna's neck in his hands. Jonas was indeed wearing the same clothes as when they saw him from the past, except now they were weathered very badly. In the fluorescent light, his face was a hideous brown color and something about his eyes was off.

The man next to him was just as ghastly. He was filthy with plain overall clothes. It looked as though at one time he had dirty blonde hair, cut short roughly and parted down the middle, but now it was just thick tufts. He was the same sickening color as Jonas and had a deep slash down his neck. Jenna's wide-eyed stare was petrified as she made eye contact with Will. He started toward her, dodging the sewing machines and antique table with a large poster board of how the old machines worked.

"Will, your back!" Toby shouted. Will had been too focused on Jenna to remember he had seen someone out of the corner of his eye by the Display Room when he was coming up the stairs. It obviously wasn't Mr. Stevens, who was nowhere to be seen. He swallowed hard, knowing he was cornered. Too many things were flying in his head. He needed time or a distraction until a plan came to him.

"Jonas!" Will called, ignoring the stranger closing in behind him. Jonas turned his head and stared at him, puzzled, then smiled easily. A muffled squeak made Will's eyes dart to Jenna. She was still against the wall, but was now being lifted off the floor by Jonas, her arms flailing about, her sneakers trying to make purchase with the floor. Will instinctively dove for her attacker just as he heard Toby yell.

"No, Will, don't!"

Will's forearms and head glided through his target and hit the wall with a smack that left him stunned. He blinked, trying to clear the purple dots from his vision, not sure what had happened.

"It's one way! We can't touch them like they can us. Trust

me, I've been trying," Toby said through gritted teeth. His assailant was just as dirty but wearing more proper clothes of black pants and vest. His eyes were vacant and his mouth lopsided in an evil grin. It seemed he was wearing a tie, but on second look it was the trail of dried blood from the large hole in his neck that extended through and down his back.

The ghost behind Will laughed a deep, expansive laugh as he closed in on him. His tattered navy-blue clothes and matted hair stunk of the deep earth. Part of his head was missing, but luckily the details were covered by the rest of his black, curly hair filling it in as if it were a pothole. Something slimy crawled through his thick, black beard. It was much worse with the modern lights illuminating their features. It was almost painful to look at.

Toby was trying to slide along the wall closer to Jenna, ducking when the figures got too close. The ghost covering him didn't seem to mind a little challenge. His brown mottled hands hovered, savoring the chase. Jenna sputtered and gasped, her lips turning ashen.

"What can we hurt them with?" Will asked desperately. He was trying to sit up and make his brain work, to think of a plan 'B,' when he hadn't even thought of a plan 'A' yet. He was surprised at how his fists were aching for contact with these forms who were hurting the girl he had grown so fond of in such a short time.

"I don't know if there is anything," Toby said, darting to Jenna's legs to support her.

"Yes…there… is," Jenna struggled to say. She exhaled, went limp and Jonas released his grip. She toppled listlessly over

Toby's arms, her head just missing the floor. Her long hair hid her face and cascaded around her, reminding Will of Amelie. Toby scooted her over his shoulders and stood up easily. He had been benching way more than she weighed.

"What're you going to do now, runaway?" Jonas teased Will. Jonas and the blonde guy laughed menacingly. Will was prodded over to the wall with his friends.

"Where is my dad? Everyone else?" whispered Toby.

"There were a lot of pictures in the Display Room. I'm pretty sure that's where these guys came from. I bet Mr. Stevens has his hands full right now," Will answered quietly.

"Hush!" Jonas ordered, the smile vanishing. The three of them were trapped now. Their one chance at touching these guys and getting away was resting with Jenna, who had passed out cold from lack of oxygen before saying how.

"Jonas, what now?" asked Divot Head, the one in front of Will.

"We round them all up, see, and out the window they go," Jonas laughed, waving his hand in that direction. The window was once again open. "Then this place is ours. We can finally collect up everything that's here. Norman, you, Bernie, and Eli, go get the others. Amelie here won't give us no more trouble, and I can handle the rest just fine," Jonas ordered as he eyed Toby and Will.

The ghost men got up and went for the door, their shoes making a soft, scuffing sound in the otherwise quiet room. From inside the building they heard men's angry voices yelling, and the occasional slamming of a door. Jonas started for the door himself to make sure they did what they were told, but didn't go far. He paced in front of the door, but seemed preoccupied with something on his shirt.

"I hope my mother can see this in the board," Will whispered.

"What's the plan, Will?" Toby asked under his breath. He eased Jenna down onto his knee and lightly tapped her face. She was still out, but at least she was the right color now, and her breathing was more even.

"I think I would have been able to get us back here if we went through the picture again. It's a different story now that they're here with us. Toby, you've done this before. What did you do?" Will asked. Apparently, there were no hard feelings now that it was clear that Jenna and Toby had no interest in each other.

"I don't know. The last time others came and took them away. All I know is that we can't touch them," Toby said.

"Wait a minute," Will said, his mind racing. "Where did those others come from?"

"Here. The window, I guess," Toby answered, understanding dawning on his face.

"Jonas wants *us* out the window." Will paused. "We need to send them all back that way, or maybe through the pictures, but either way we need to close that damn window before we have a whole graveyard full of these guys."

"You say something, boy?" Jonas asked, his uneven eyes glaring at him.

"No sir, Jonas," Will answered. Jonas smiled and looked back at his chest. Will was trying to gauge the distance from Jonas to the window when he heard Jenna breathe heavier as she began to rouse. Her eyes fluttered open and she squinted, reaching her hand to her forehead.

"Ooh, headache. Ouch," Jenna mumbled. Toby brushed her hair away from her face, noticing for the first time a dark, wet spot under her arm. The blouse had a jagged tear on the side just above where her elbow rested on it. Toby's eyes met Will's, concern coloring both their faces. She was bleeding.

"Jenna, don't move. Let me see how bad it is," Will said quietly. Jonas hadn't heard Jenna waken. He now stood in the doorway facing the stairs. His head was down and his arm was bent and moving as if he was trying to brush something off the front of his shirt.

"Jenna, what happened?" Toby whispered.

Jenna looked around blankly for a second before everything caught up with her. She sat up, but too quickly, and reached out to them both to steady herself. "I dodged the knife thing," she said, grimacing as she put her hand around to her side.

"It doesn't look as though you dodged it completely," Will remarked, gently prying her hand off the area. He was able to peer inside the rough opening and relaxed a little. "I don't think it's too deep. The bleeding has just about stopped."

Toby was still concerned about Jenna. "How would you know?"

"I've taken community first aid classes. I needed it for my job back home." Toby nodded once, satisfied.

Jenna wiped her hand on her jeans to get the blood off. Her eyes met Will's and she smiled a little. "I got him, too. Caught him off guard. That's the way I found to touch them. I grabbed the, uh, "thamie" with him when he tried to cut me, and it kinda bounced off me and got him on his side. But it only cut his shirt. I don't think I hurt him."

"I don't think he can get hurt anymore. At least not bleed. I couldn't touch him. You were able to cut something physical on him? I wonder if you were able to do that, would it be possible to do more? He's been very interested in his shirt. That must be why he's so distracted," Toby surmised. Jonas was now just outside the door, his hand on the door jamb, looking out over the landing, yelling to his men below. The noise from downstairs was getting louder. From far away Tina's scream reached them.

"Tell me again how you made contact with him," Will asked urgently.

"I had my hand on the, um, ath-mee knife the whole time," Jenna offered, trying to remember the name of it.

"We can only touch them when they're trying to hurt us?" Toby suggested.

"No, because I couldn't grab anything when he had me by the neck," Jenna corrected, rubbing her hands over her neck, remembering. She swallowed and grimaced. "Ugh. My throat hurts, too."

"Our hand has to be on the weapon at the same time theirs is? I wonder if it's the athame. I'm almost positive the one he has was Mrs. Cabet's. Everyone's is different and unique, and that one really looks like hers. I wish I knew if there was something special about that particular athame, or just an athame itself. There's only one way to find out for sure, and we've run out of time for anything else. I've got my mom's athame so let's cross our fingers. We need to lead him to the window."

Will rose slowly, taking the athame out of the sheath. The three cringed when the ceiling light bounced off the blade and shot a beam of light across the room. Luckily, Jonas was still out on the landing. Will's eyes were fixed on Jonas, his face set with determination. If this hadn't been happening right in front of her, Jenna would have sworn it looked like it came right out of a movie. She stood up, took a deep shaky breath, and moved away from the wall she had been leaning against. Straightening the end of her blouse down over the waist of her jeans, she walked toward the window.

"I have an idea. I can get Jonas back in here." She looked toward the door and spoke louder. "Sylvia sent me back for you, Jonas. Amelie Cabet came back for you," Jenna improvised. She once again reached around, holding her side for a moment. She leaned forward, her footsteps uneven. Will and Toby watched her take the lead nervously. Jonas moved back into the room and swung his head around, perplexed. Jenna noted the athame was Mrs. Cabet's. The short, crooked, wooden handle was tucked into Jonas's belt. She feigned losing her footing and staggered backward toward the window, holding her hands up to Jonas so that the smears of blood were visible.

His jaw tightened. "Too easy," he drawled, "after waiting so long. Funny how coming back was all Sylvia's doing. We just had to wait until someone found those blasted photographs. She stopped us the first time from taking our loot and blowin' town. I woulda had everything I ever wanted. So's I took away everything she wanted, most of all you. And now," his grin widened into a sneer, the wrinkled skin stretching to its limit and beyond, "this is just fine. Here I am, getting it all: the diamonds, and destroying you. Knowing I'm gonna kill you again, it makes me hungry." He licked his dry lips—it reminded Jenna of sandpaper— with a blackened tongue, his eyes locked on hers. Moving swiftly towards her, he avoided each sewing machine without looking.

Jenna's eyes quickly darted to Will and Toby, to see if they caught on. She stopped by the window, keeling over slightly.

"I'm hurt bad, Jonas, but I'm not going without a fight, y'hear?" she breathed.

"There's nowheres you can run, Amelie. You deserve a hundred deaths for what that witch of a mother did to me." He stopped just short of the three of them, looking at Toby and eyeing Will suspiciously. He relaxed and smiled a malicious smile, his rotten mouth flooding the room with stench before turning his full attention back to Jenna. The fingers of his hands, the nails a greenish hue, were outstretched into the shape of a claw.

Will held his breath at the last second, but Toby didn't and made a long retching sound. He forced himself to stop before he became incapacitated. He and Will just stood there, watching and waiting, their eyes darting from Jonas to Jenna.

Jenna quickly looked over to her friends once more. "Jonas…" she moaned and tipped over onto the floor.

Jonas lunged at her but missed as Toby, anticipating his move, rushed forward and pushed her off to the side in much the same way he did in football practice with the pop up dummies. He stood and started to turn around to help Will who had taken the athame out from behind his back and ran it into Jonas stomach. Will hoped he didn't plow through Jonas and stab Toby by accident. The athame made contact, stopping suddenly into the foreign being. It took Jonas by surprise. Letting out a startled yell, Jonas whipped his fist around, hitting Toby square in the eye. Will thrashed with him, forcing himself to stay connected. His loose hand automatically went to grab Jonas's shoulder for support, but passed right through it. An achy chill ran up his whole arm. Jonas was flailing now, trying to get free. With effort, Will managed to get both hands on the athame. He was pushing hard with all his strength to get Jonas to the window.

"Get him out! I can't see out of my eye!" Toby hollered, his hands covering his face. Jenna got up off the floor, pushing Toby out of the way.

"Good, Jenna! Try to get the athame!" Will yelled. Jenna grabbed at Jonas as he squirmed. Her arm went through him several times as if he wasn't there before making contact with the athame Jonas had secured in his belt. She pulled it out and stepped back. Will twisted his athame farther into Jonas. Jonas hadn't felt pain in over a hundred and fifty years and was stunned enough that he wasn't paying attention to anything else. Jenna tried to help Will as he hustled Jonas to the window jamb, maneuvering him awkwardly by only the handle in his stomach. Her hands met no resistance as she tried to push Jonas. It would've been an easy job if they could have just touched him.

Sixteen

"No, you don't!" Jonas yelled, regaining some control. He tried to push Will backwards, his hands touching him without difficulty. Will had his feet apart, planted firmly and hardly budged. Toby was swinging at air with one hand, covering his rapidly swelling eye with the other. He tried to get around Jenna, who stood there looking at the dried blood on the black blade. She knew the only way to help was by the athame in her hand. She turned the athame upside down to invert it, her hand squeezing the handle. She looked up and almost didn't have time to help. Jonas had Toby around the middle pulling him in as Will was pushing Jonas against the window ledge.

"Hold on to something Toby!" Jenna yelled. Toby grunted, bending forward as much as he was able to, clutching the window frame as Jenna rammed the athame into Jonas's right breastbone. With a shriek, Jonas straightened, his hold on Toby eased enough for Toby to pull himself free. In the midst of sweat and corpse rot, Will and Jenna pushed Jonas farther into the window. They seemed to be stuck, Jonas writhing in anger and surprise, Will and Jenna both exerted almost to capacity.

"I can't push anymore!" Will warned. Jenna knew it was now or never. If Jonas regained full control, all three of them would be out the window. She reached her right arm around to her left, reinforcing the athame and pushed with all her might.

Jonas looked wildly at the two of them, still surprised at his vulnerability before gravity took him backwards out the window. He reached one last time, gathering the neckline of Jenna's blouse in his fist, attempting to pull her with him. She could feel herself start to go. All her weight was against him, and her hands were still cemented to the athame in his chest. As her body passed through the window frame, the color started to fade around her and a loud whooshing noise grew louder. Whispering voices surrounded her head. Then, all at once, her feet no longer touched the floor. She was flying backwards, pulled by strong hands around her middle, disconnecting her from Jonas. She landed on top of Toby face up with a groan, his large arms still locked around her waist. A sharp bang came from in front of her as Will slammed the window down hard.

"Sorry, did I hurt you?" Toby asked, panting and coughing. Jenna rolled over to a sitting position.

"No, I'm fine," Jenna replied. She frowned at her friend's purple and swollen face. "Ooh Toby, your eye."

"I'll manage." He smiled weakly. "How's your side?"

"'S'okay. Will?" Jenna asked.

"I'm okay, but I'd feel better if you let go of the death grip on the athame. You're scaring me a little," Will replied, bent over with his hands above his knees, trying to catch his breath. Jenna needed to concentrate to purposely peel her fingers from the handle, they had trouble moving on their own. The hilt was dry, no trace of blood at all. She gingerly handed it to Will as if it were hot. He righted the blade, deep in thought. His brow furrowed as his gaze shifted from the athame and the window next to him. He regarded Toby with his shiner and Jenna with her bloodied shirt and bump on her head. All at once he inverted the athame, his knuckles growing white, and drove it into the double hung sash creating a lock of its own. He shook his head.

"I'm sure we could probably use this better against the others, but we need to permanently close the window. I think Sylvia's athame will be more potent. It's only logical," Will admitted softly, brushing his hair away from his face.

Their victory was short lived as they heard chaos downstairs. Will secured his mother's athame in his waistband and reached into his pocket. He took out the folded pictures, handing one to each of them. "Here, take these. If we come across any more of Jonas's friends, we'll need to try to get them into the picture."

"How do we do that?" Toby asked, focusing through one good eye.

"Well, I don't know. If they run at you, hold it up towards them so they'll touch it. Sorry, we're going on a trial basis here. You have any better ideas other than luring them all up here to this window?"

Toby blew out a gust of air. "Nope. Pictures sound good to me. Come on, we gotta go."

They headed out the door cautiously. All was quiet when they searched the other rooms upstairs. One of the fathers must have been there. All the pictures on the wall were overturned. They stopped on the landing overlooking the great room to survey the scene. No one was down at the table anymore, but there was evidence of struggles everywhere: overturned chairs, the veil covering the table was askew and wet from the spilled soup, picture frames and stones scattered on the floor. The Ouija board was folded and abandoned, as if the players had tired of the game. Jenna made a mental note that the planchette was nowhere to be seen. They quietly went downstairs. It was empty.

"Where is everyone?" Jenna asked.

"I don't know. It makes me nervous. We need to stay together so no one gets lost," Toby said. He and Jenna went toward the rooms adjacent to the office. Those doors were open, the areas deserted. Will went to the windows to see if they needed damage control outside. He cupped his hands around his face to see through the darkness, then nodded and gave a thumbs-up sign as he met them at the door to the office. The voices inside gave them hope that they were all there. Slowly they opened the door—just a crack—unsure what they would find.

Apparently, no one had heard the trio come downstairs. The first thing they saw was Sulis standing in front of Tina who was against the wall. Tina was nervously holding a photograph, her well-kept hair pulled from its barrette and scattered around her flushed face. Sulis was poised with her arm raised as if ready to strike, something shiny in her grasp glinting off the lights. In the middle of the small room were Mr. Stevens and Mr. Jacobs.

The fathers had been circling a ghost like a lion tamer. It was the one in the black suit.

As soon as the door opened, Mr. Jacobs and the apparition looked over. In an instant, Mr. Stevens took advantage of the opportunity and swung his hands holding the loose picture on top of the ghost. Like some warped computer graphics from a movie, the ghost seemed to be sucked into the picture, initially too big but fitting anyway. It defied reality and all reason. Mr. Stevens scrambled to fold the picture on top of itself, his blond wavy hair askew, his chest heaving from all the exertion. Mr. Jacobs smiled at seeing his son, his face a mix of sweat and dirt, his clothes ripped and filthy. He then turned back to Mr. Stevens. They worked together to lift up a metal file cabinet and stuck the folded picture underneath. They looked incredulously at each other for a second before running to their children.

Sulis came over on shaky legs and hugged Will. "Are you all right?" Will nodded.

"Where's Mark? Was he with you?" Mr. Jacobs asked Jenna as her father scooped her up in his arms. "He and I started downstairs together, but we got split up."

Jenna looked at Tina, still up against the wall. Her eyes were huge behind her glasses, and her expression was beyond anxious. "No, we didn't see him."

"We need to go find him," Toby stated.

"Wait a second. The pictures worked for you?" Will asked Mr. Jacobs.

"We weren't sure at first. When you're face to face with

one of those spirits, though, you'll try anything," Mr. Jacobs admitted, shaking his head.

Jenna tried to respond to that, but her father had her in a bear hug and hadn't let go. All that could be heard was a muffled response and everyone smiled, the thick tension from their encounters breaking briefly. Jenna pried herself away from her father long enough to explain how each of the athames linked them and the ghosts to their advantage in touching them. "I'm really surprised the pictures work, too. We hadn't had a chance to try it out."

"Sulis is pretty clever. One of those ghouls tried to sneak up on us, and she used the board piece as a makeshift weapon. It gave us enough time for me to get my picture open," Tina added, grinning slightly. She held her folded picture up, but it shook so hard from her nerves she lowered her hand.

"It seems there are only a few ways to make contact with them," Sulis surmised, opening her hand. She was still clutching the Ouija planchette. "This worked quite well, actually."

"Okay, now we know what works. We need to do a head count. There were several of these guys upstairs with us. We put Jonas back out the window. How many did you guys get rid of?" Will asked.

"Two for me," said Mr. Stevens.

"I had one," Mr. Jacobs added.

Sulis pushed her glasses up on her nose. "Tina and I did as well."

"Well, that means more than we saw," Toby summed up.

"So, we need to look for Mr. Levy and the rest of Jonas's posse," Mr. Jacobs finished, heading for the door.

Tina moved slowly away from the wall. "I've never been so scared in my whole life and now my dad is missing. Can we go?"

"Please, let's all stay together this time," Sulis asked, readjusting her glasses. She put her arm around Tina's shoulder to comfort her. It also steadied her shaking frame. Tina looked one step away from losing it altogether.

Quietly, Mr. Jacobs opened the door and looked around tentatively. He saw no one and motioned for everyone to file out.

"The upstairs is secure. Which way did Mr. Levy go?" Will asked Mr. Jacobs as they stood in the corridor.

"I'm not sure anymore."

"We looked out the window and didn't see anything." The expression on Mr. Jacob's face indicated he didn't understand Will's comment. "Remember, we didn't just have pictures of this building. We had ones of the cemetery and orchard, too."

"That's the best we're gonna get for now. We need to find Mark," Mr. Stevens said.

They went through the remaining rooms on the main floor. It was a peculiar sight: seven odd, dirty, disheveled, and injured adults carrying folded black and white photos to defend themselves against ghosts.

"Where is he? Where's my dad?" Tina whispered when they came up empty. Toby hugged her tightly. Sulis and Will looked at each other silently, uneasily wondering if Mr. Levy had not been able to fight them off or worse yet, if he went into a picture instead of his perpetrator.

"If he fell into a picture, what would happen?" Tina asked,

her thoughts going in the same direction. They approached the stairs to the basement and stopped. Mr. Jacobs and Mr. Stevens were debating with Will on the best way to go forward.

"I'm not going to sugarcoat anything. He would go into that past. I don't think it would be possible for us to know which picture or which past," Sulis answered as she gently rubbed Tina's back.

"What if we couldn't get him back tonight? What would happen then?" Tina asked, her voice barely audible. She was fidgeting with her sleeve, her head down. "It's almost eleven o'clock now."

"The window would close for now. I'm not confident of what would happen after that. This is the most unusual experience I've had, but I don't think we could try to get him back until the next 10-01."

"Uh oh," Will said, stopping in mid-sentence. He turned towards Tina as if she had called him. He broke away from the men and started to weave through the group, trying to get to her.

"We can't leave him in there for a whole year!" Tina cried, panicking. The trauma of the night finally caught up to her. She started shaking against Toby. He tried to steady her while Sulis rubbed her back, but it was fast going beyond control. Her breathing became erratic and her face paled. She looked down at her hands. "I can't feel my fingers! Oh my word, I'm going to die!"

Will scooted past his mother who touched his arm. A silent exchange took place.

"I know. I'm on it." He shifted to step in front of Tina, face to face, and calmly took hold of her arms.

"Tina, look at me. Look me right in my eyes and breathe." His hands moved to her shoulders, running down her arms in a soothing way with the same rhythm as his breathing. It was the same technique Jenna had observed in her dream.

"I, I ca-can't stop!"

"You're doing great, Tina. You've got to watch me." It took a few tries for her to calm down enough to retain eye contact and get her breathing to mimic his. "Breathe in and breathe out. Don't look away." Her breathing slowed and her face took on a little color. "We still need to go downstairs. That's where a lot of the incidents took place. In the cellar. There are enough of us to protect ourselves and to help your dad if he's in trouble down there. We need you to have positive energy now, okay?" Will spoke softly, his full concentration on Tina. She took one huge breath, her shoulders relaxing. "Good. Now, imagine yourself surrounded by a protective, warm, white light where nothing can get in to hurt you. That energy force will follow where you go. It's there waiting to give you what you need to do this." She had regained control, her eyes taking in her surroundings. She was still too shaken to answer other than nodding. They turned to the door just as the men had decided.

"…our best bet. This door is going to squeak anyway. Let's just rush them," Mr. Jacobs suggested. Mr. Stevens agreed and took a deep breath. Single file behind them were the others. The door whined, and they all rushed down the steep stairs as quickly as they could. It was a good thing they hadn't tried the ambush approach, as it was impossible to go down that staircase without making noise.

"Déjà vu," Jenna whispered. She was once again following Will, descending into the darkness in the basement, not sure what she would find when she got there.

"Yeah, really. Same stairs, same day, different century," Will replied sarcastically. His hand found Jenna's shoulder and held it firmly.

In the dim glow from the overhead bare bulbs, it was mass confusion. It took a while for the men to figure out if Mr. Levy was down there at all. By the time Tina reached the bottom with Sulis, they were all standing in the small space with the last four ghosts.

"Whoa, there are a lot of them here," Toby muttered under his breath. "Where'd they all come from?"

"There are a lot of those pictures in this building. Maybe once Jonas and his friends passed over, others found they could too. I didn't realize he had such a following."

These ghosts were much bigger and sturdier than the ones Jonas had been ordering around. They looked like their jobs had been manual labor and had died just as hard as they had lived. One wore a beaver hat, had a wool overcoat over his wide shoulders, and wore tan leather chaps that extended from his knees to his thick black boots. His face was turned away from the stairs. The smell was concentrated in the windowless area. It alone, was enough to convince anyone the dead had come back to life.

Watching the procession down the stairs was a large specter. He may have been African American while alive as his skin was a mixture of a ghoulish green and black. His thin shirt had the sleeves rolled up revealing pock-marked skin with burn scars everywhere. He had on a short blacksmith apron and brown pants. Almost all his features and details were overshadowed by the gaping hole in the middle of his forehead. When he moved, the hole allowed what was behind him to be seen. He held a large piece of broken wood that looked like the handle of a modern shovel and waved it back and forth. His toothless grin was confident any confrontation would be to his benefit. He looked over to his comrades and grunted a laugh.

The remaining two dropped their tools and stepped away from the muddy mound they had been digging. All the water had conveniently loosened the floor. They wore union suits that fit them poorly except in the biceps where it molded to their muscles. There were no visible gashes or other obvious cause of death. Their exposed skin was a grotesque greenish-brown, and their faces were sunken and taut despite their evil grimaces.

The basement was torn apart; items that were lying around had become instruments used to dig the dirt floor. Mr. Levy's body was slumped in a heap off to the side. Toby saw him before Tina. Swearing under his breath, he tried to turn her to get her back up the stairs, but it was too late.

Seventeen

"Noooo!" Tina screamed. The control she had just achieved was gone in an instant. The ghosts responded, moving in closer, lunging, taunting, and laughing with no hint of concern. Loose tools, water soaked mallets, and broken ladder rungs from the flood just a day ago were waved at them menacingly. Toby helped Sulis get Tina upstairs where her sobs could still be heard. Sulis's muffled voice filled the spaces when Tina's went silent. Toby's footsteps sounded again on the stairs as he came back down.

"They're cocky. Remember, they don't know what we know," Mr. Stevens said in an undertone.

"Here, take this." Will handed Mr. Stevens the athame. "Jenna and I will be defense; you and Mr. Jacobs, offense. You know what defense is, right Jenna?" His brushed his long hair away from his face with his free hand, glancing back at Jenna.

"Yes, I do. Okay, I'm ready," Jenna murmured.

"I'm set here with the indicator thing," Toby added, his deep voice joining the group.

"Okay, left to right, starting with me," Mr. Stevens ordered, his voice getting louder. The ghosts had been lining up in front of them, waiting to be rushed.

Mr. Stevens hollered loudly, spooking them all. As he hit his mark, the first ghoul shrieked, shattering the carefree stance of the others. Suddenly everyone was in play. They all knew what they had to do, stay out of the way of being grabbed, and get the pictures over them as soon as they could, or hit them with the planchette or athame. Even so, mistakes were made. The compacted, sodden floor was still slippery, and the tight space made it difficult to stay out of each other's way. The small drop-down light bulbs were accidentally hit, some swaying and casting eerie shadows everywhere. Some shattered, causing blackouts.

Time seemed to stand still as the fight continued. The small area, thick with decomposition, carried the sounds of grunts, groans, and hollers. Only when sirens were heard in the not too far distance did the action start to slow. The last ghost went down with both Toby and Mr. Stevens on top of him.

"Let go of him! Get back! You can't be touching him when I hit him with this! I'm not taking the chance you'll go with him!" Jenna yelled. The men wrestled to each side, still connected to the ghost by their crude weapons of the planchette and athame, crunching in the broken glass fragments from the lights.

"One, two, three!" They each pulled their hands back, the sharp item that fused them to the ghouls no longer touching. The men scrambled away as best as they could to avoid re-touching.

Together, Jenna and Will pulled the dog-eared picture open and hastily slammed it down over the specter's head, following it all the way to the ground just to be sure. Despite the many times they had done it, it was still mind-bending to witness.

They had learned going over the ghost's head was the safest if two people held the picture open above the ghost, set it on the top of its head and pulled down. It seemed to be the hardest for them to see coming. There was a very small window of opportunity where they could surprise them. When Mr. Stevens took the first apparition down, everyone was running at each other, and none of the ghosts saw what he had done. By the time the second ghost was put away, the two remaining were just figuring out they could be touched. By that point it was irrelevant; their advantage was gone. Only in the end did they realize just what the pictures were doing to them. Even though they put up quite a fight, at that point they were grossly outnumbered.

The last ghost disappeared, and Will and Jenna collapsed on the floor, panting and gasping. They looked over at the fathers who had gone over to Mr. Levy as soon as they were able.

"He's still alive," Mr. Jacobs called out. The sirens had now stopped directly above them. Mr. Levy was unconscious, but seemed to be breathing on his own okay. Not wanting to hurt the injured man further, they wiped blood off his bruised face and tried to maneuver the old tar bucket out from under him. "I can't believe we used this bucket earlier today to collect water from the flood. It feels like a lifetime ago."

"Yeah, what about all of this? Look at us. We can't go telling people we were fighting off ghosts. We'd get our own suite at the local psych unit," Mr. Stevens mused, looking at what was once a light blue shirt. It was now totally ruined, stained with mud and dots of blood that continued down his arm.

"Maybe they'll think we were all sharing the same hallucination," Toby suggested.

"That's not even funny, Tobe," his dad replied, wiping his face with the bottom of his shirt. The knuckles on his right hand were swollen to twice their size.

"The ladder is broken. We're filthy. We could have been digging and working in here, and somehow Mr. Levy fell," Will offered.

"You're too quick, kid. It might work though," Mr. Stevens admitted.

"Thank you. I just hope he's okay," Will started to say as the paramedics came downstairs.

"What happened, you guys have a sewer leak? It's awful down here," asked the first EMT, wrinkling up his nose. He was stocky, with a friendly face and graying hair.

"Yeah, you could say we're having a lot of difficulty with all our systems right about now," Mr. Jacobs retorted, motioning them towards his friend.

The second EMT, a tall, lanky man in his twenties, stepped off the last stair and gasped. "Yikes. I thought the girl upstairs looked bad. No wonder the lady told us to come down here first." He looked over at the four strange bloodied people in front of him, then to his partner. "Dave, we're gonna need more help. I'm calling in to get another unit here a-sap. Is this her dad?" Everyone nodded.

"Mike, Unit Two can probably assist."

The two workers went right over to Mr. Levy, one stopping

long enough to say something low and indiscernible into his walkie-talkie. A female's voice responded in the affirmative, and the line went silent again.

It took a while before Mr. Levy was stable enough to transfer. He was still unconscious after they had him on the stretcher, and his arm sat in an awkward position. Oxygen was being given to him through tubes in his nose and more tubing with an IV was attached to him by a clean spot on his wrist. Monitors and lights were beeping and flashing everywhere. The rest of him was covered too much to see any more damage.

More sirens grew louder, then stopped overhead. With the walkie talkies clicking on and off it was almost possible to believe none of the evening's events had just transpired. Mr. Jacobs and Mr. Stevens went with Mr. Levy, helping the paramedics get the stretcher up the stairs. Toby followed them carrying their medical box. Will and Jenna hung behind until the traffic cleared.

"What do you think they were digging for, more diamonds?" Jenna asked. She looked around at the holes the ghosts had managed to dig.

"I don't know, but they said there was more here," Will replied.

"That's something worth looking into," Jenna said. She reached up to fix one of the pulls on the light and lost her balance, her eyes fluttering to stay open. Will was surprised by how fast he reacted, considering the night they had just had. He caught her at waist height, his arms cradling her back, her hair swaying behind her. She reached up and held him by his upper arms which were more muscular than they looked. Jenna exhaled slightly when she realized she was face to face with Will. This time there was no danger, no threat, and no rush. She saw him through the grime and fatigue. Despite their lives being threatened on multiple occasions tonight, his eyes were now fearful. Her heart did that knowing flip, her stomach full of butterflies in full force. She knew that didn't have anything to do with her balance.

"Sorry, just a little dizzy still, I guess. My equilibrium is off."

"I know of something else worth looking into," Will said softly, his brow quivering. He had not pulled her up from his arms. His deep brown eyes were searching for confirmation. "But you really do need your head looked at. You took a beating tonight."

"I'm pretty strong you know. It's just another day here at the museum." Jenna tried to make light, her nervousness now making her feel funny. She started trembling. Will now looked concerned. He held her tighter.

"What's wrong? Are you okay?" His face was now panicked.

"Fine. Just scared, a little. It'll go away, I think, if you kiss me."

Will's faced relaxed for a brief second as her words sunk in. Smiling slowly, he shook his head unbelievingly. Hesitantly, he opened himself to her feelings and found a curious anticipation. And it floored him to realize it was for him. He bent down to kiss her, and she reached up to meet him. A hint of his cologne lingered, and she sighed. His lips were warm and sure on hers, and a calmness spread through her whole body.

Despite the summersaults in her stomach, her trembling did stop.

"Oh. Oh, sorry." Dave, the older paramedic had come back down to check on them, stopping short on the last step, feeling awkward. His clean, wrinkle-free uniform was a blatant contrast to Jenna's and Will's muddied clothes. He cleared his throat uneasily. Will righted Jenna. She swayed and blinked twice heavily. Will kept his hand on the small of her back just in case.

"Still a little dizzy, but that was nice."

"It looks like everyone here needs to be checked out. You two are the last. I don't even think I want to know what happened here tonight." He mumbled the last part to no one in particular. He looked around the room shaking his head. "God, it really stinks, though. Smells like something died down here."

Jenna started to giggle, and Will nudged her along upstairs, hopefully, for the last time.

The stark brightness from the lights upstairs made Jenna and Will wince. They scanned the room. Tina and Mr. Levy were gone. The table had been cleaned of the gems and goblet of soup. The Ouija board was no longer there. Mr. Jacobs was sitting in a chair, his right hand wrapped in gauze. He was talking quietly with Mr. Stevens, who was having his left arm worked on. The paramedic attending to him peered over his glasses. He was dropping pieces of glass into a small jar with his tweezers. Mr. Stevens's arm was brown and wet from the sterile solution. Everyone looked up as Jenna and Will passed, now hand in hand. Her father's face held the slightest bit of confusion, before he sighed, resigned, and smiled weakly.

"You're okay, Will. Thank you for saving my Jenna tonight," he said quietly.

"My pleasure, sir. I'm sorry it got to be such a mess. I know I'm responsible for a lot of it, and I've been taught to own up. I truly am sorry," Will replied.

Mr. Stevens's smile became sincere. Jenna leaned over to give her dad a delicate hug. The change in direction made her woozy, and she fell into him a bit more than intended.

"I'm okay," her dad reassured her, misinterpreting her fall as concern. "I must have rolled into some of the glass, but that's all. Mitch here tells me I may need a few stitches at the most." The paramedic looked up at both of them trying to figure out the whole story, and becoming all the more perplexed with each new piece of information. He put the lid on the cup and went to get a clean dressing from his case.

Sulis walked over. She was the only one of the group who wasn't disheveled and didn't smell. Her patchouli perfume was somehow refreshing despite it being heavy and earthy. The same could be said of the non-beings, except this smell was welcoming and relaxing. She stepped between Jenna and Will and huddled them toward Mr. Jacobs and Mr. Stevens. Toby came over with an ice pack on his eye.

"We're very limited on time, folks. I know it seems like this is all over, but next year it will replay itself unless we do something straight away to close that window for good. Now, I know we never had a chance tonight to catch up on what happened with each of us, and we still don't have time. However, I was able to sit back down with the board and was able to get in contact with Sylvia. I got enough from her that makes me believe I can do a circle that might close it permanently, but I'm going to need your bodies there. Mr. Levy is on his way to the hospital, and once they got Tina calmed down, she went with him. I know that some of us really do need medical attention, but the hour is drawing to a close, and I'm afraid we really cannot spare even a minute."

"I'm not hurt," Will stated.

"I'm still standing," Jenna commented.

"Barely," Will said, under his breath. He squeezed her hand.

"How long do you think we have?" Mr. Jacobs inquired.

"It's a quarter to midnight, but I think it's enough time. How do we get these gentlemen to leave?" Sulis asked. They all looked over at Dave who was walking towards them with his duffle. He stopped and frowned, looking back over his shoulder. Of course nothing was there.

"Who's next?" he asked apprehensively.

"Are you okay, Jenna?" her dad asked her very softly. "This can be done without you, I think, if they really needed to. I don't know what happened all those times we were separated. You need to tell me." He studied her face looking for answers.

"I'm good."

"I think we're all set here," Mr. Stevens announced to the paramedic. "Anyway, we're all going to follow up with our doctors tomorrow."

"You're refusing to be assessed?"

"Yes, I think that's what we're saying," Mr. Jacobs said. Mike joined them from outside. The walkie-talkie in his hand spluttered to life, static reverberating through the room. A muffled voice wanted updates. Dave didn't seem convinced and whispered to his partner. His finger pointed to the basement several times as he talked, and then up towards his own head. Shaking his head from side to side, he shot a sidelong nod toward Jenna.

"She really needs to be seen."

"Can I go on my own?" Jenna blurted out. "I don't really want to go in an ambulance."

"I'll take my daughter myself. I'll be maybe fifteen minutes behind you," Mr. Stevens stated.

"There are some papers to sign if you're going to do that. They're in the rig."

Mr. Stevens got up, but motioned for everyone to carry on. Mr. Jacobs stood up and put both hands on his son's shoulders. The bandages were almost as big as Toby's head.

"It's a good thing your mother is busy selling pottery this weekend or I'd have more hell to pay. Where to?"

"Upstairs, of course." Sulis answered. They all made their way up the staircase to the Sewing Room. Will's arm remained around Jenna's waist protectively as they went. As Jenna passed through the doors, she thought how it felt like the evening would never end. Suddenly, she was very tired.

Sulis wasted no time and began pulling stones out of the small velvet purse around her wrist. She started laying them on the floor in an arc. The gems were smaller and less discernible than the ones Mrs. Cabet had put down. Their colors seemed to be nonexistent from more than a foot away. Will kissed the top of Jenna's head and stepped forward. He took the gems that he'd put in his pocket when Jonas appeared in the great room, adding them to make a large circle. He called everyone to stand inside. Jenna was lost in thought, her eyes heavy. She heard her name and looked up to see Will smiling at her, his arm outstretched for her to take his hand. She took it briefly to stand in the small area with her friends. She tried to stay out of their way as Sulis and Will used Sulis's athame together to call the four elements for help and protection, both focused and proficient in their actions.

Sulis began chanting as Will started to unfold one of the pictures. "I call upon the elements to banish the spirits and close the portal so that they may not return…"

"We've got two minutes left by my watch," Mr. Jacobs warned. Jenna was now feeling very heavy and was starting to shake again. She needed to lie down. All her thoughts became weighted and thick as sludge. Her body felt tingly, and she could no longer feel her legs hold her up. Things seemed to go in slow motion. She couldn't tell if it was in her head or if the circle was creating some strange time warp. Her father came into the room, and she watched through a fog as Sulis made a rainbow motion and her dad jumped through it into the circle at the last minute. By then all the words Sulis was saying were running together. Colors blended from Sulis's burgundy robe into Will's brown stained shirt and Toby's dirty green one, even her blue jeans. Sometimes it felt like the lights were on, then they were off. She felt heat warming her hands and face. Then she heard one thing very clearly.

"So mote it be!"

"Are we done yet? Are we done? Uh oh, oh no," she heard herself say. She couldn't remember seeing anything at this point and thought about how far away her own voice was and how it sounded so urgent. She wondered if she should be worried about that. Unable to keep her eyes open any longer and too tired to try, the lights went off and stayed off for a long time.

Eighteen

"S OMETIMES WE'RE ABLE to keep up on adrenaline, maybe the fight or flight reflex has kicked in which can last for a while, but eventually, the energy stores are depleted, and that's when this happens."

Jenna thought about the words she heard, but they didn't make any sense to her. She didn't even think they applied to her. Slowly she became aware of all the white things around her.

"I'm back in the hospital," she said aloud.

"Oh good, you're awake." Will's gentle voice was next to her. She looked over to where it came from. He picked his head up from the corner of her bed and smiled weakly at her. He was still dirty and smelled, so she knew she hadn't been there too long. He looked really tired.

Her father's head popped through the curtain surrounding

her bed, his anxious expression being replaced with relief. He must have had gone home to change as he was wearing blue jeans and a clean, plaid flannel shirt that covered his arms. No one was home to bring him new clothes. Her brother was at his best friend's house and her mom was still in Pennsylvania. He smiled, relaxing when he saw Jenna. "Oh, thank God, you're awake," he said, rushing over to her side. He smoothed her snarly hair and kissed her cheek.

"How are you feeling?" the doctor asked, appearing from behind the curtain.

"Okay."

He nodded approvingly, stepping closer. He picked up a clipboard and gave it a cursory glance.

"I've got a headache. I'm still so tired, but I feel like I slept really soundly. Not like the last time I was here," Jenna answered.

Her dad visibly relaxed, his shoulders smoothing out from the tension they held. "Good. The doctor said you were okay, but I was concerned because you weren't waking up."

"The lab work came back fine, and all the tests regarding the hematoma—the bump on your head—were within normal parameters." He looked over from Jenna to her father. "I'll get the nurse to get another set of vitals, and if she feels good enough to leave, I don't see why she should stay." He scribbled something on the clipboard and put it back on the end of the bed before disappearing behind the generic, geometrical-designed curtain.

Jenna looked herself over. Her favorite top was gone, a drab shapeless gown with a triangular pattern was in its place. There was a small piece of tape in the crook of her arm and she felt a tight bandage on her side. "Someone tell me what's going on. How long have I been here?"

"It's nine-thirty in the morning. Sunday morning." Will yawned as he looked at the clock on the wall behind Jenna. He brushed his hair away from his face with one hand, and for once, it stuck awkwardly in that position.

"It's kind of funny. You came in the ambulance anyway. They did wait," her father began. "Those guys have a sixth sense, I swear. They said they were talking about what they should do because they didn't feel comfortable leaving, even though I signed a paper saying I would be responsible. By the time I came back up to the Sewing Room, Sulis was just about done anyway."

"What happened with the circle?"

"I don't remember the exact words she used, but Sulis said some things and used her ceremonial knife to write the date in the air. That part was amazing. After she did that, I swear we could see the numbers. I don't know if it was the power of suggestion, or what. They hung there for only a second or two, and I had to strain to really see them since they were thin and white like a spider's web. And then they disappeared. Something changed from that point, although I can't put my finger on it. It just felt different in there, calmer. I'm not sure how to describe it really. She thinks it went well, the dates on the pictures disappeared. It wasn't obvious like last time, no strange noises or people.

"And just as soon as she was done you started mumbling and clawing at us to steady yourself like you had been holding on for her to finish," her dad continued. "You weren't the right color. Your eyes were open, but you weren't there, and then you were out cold. It's a good thing Will has quick reflexes." He stopped a moment to accept the boyfriend was faster than he was. "The EMTs had actually come back in to check one last time just as I was running downstairs to call for them.

"What did you tell them?" Jenna asked hesitantly.

"Will had a good idea. The floor was still wet from the flood, and there were so many broken tools. It really did look like we had been trying to find and fix a leak. We told everyone who asked that you got hit in the head with the back of the shovel handle that Mr. Levy was using. When he lost his balance on the ladder, the light broke, and we all fell down trying to support him. Flimsy, yes, but it seemed to pacify everyone who asked. None of us wanted to file any reports, and since the doctors didn't know anything differently, it was a non-issue," he answered quietly.

Jenna tenderly touched the spot over her ear. "What happened to me?"

"The doctor says exhaustion and trauma. You had been banged up pretty badly, but not enough for it to be anything worse. He said that you'd wake up when you were ready. I've been pretty impatient. It's been one of the longest nights of my life," he added after a moment.

Jenna took that all in. She thought about everything. "How are Mr. Levy and everyone else?"

"Mark is going to be okay. We thought he looked pretty bad off when they brought him in, but when they cleaned him up, cast his arm for a broken collarbone, and stitched his head, he looked better. We were hoping to get hold of him before the doctors started grilling him so he knew what our story was. Luckily he thought fast and told them he was working there. Our stories jived."

"And Mr. Jacobs?"

"Tom? He has a sprained wrist, and his knuckles look like raw meat. Toby got off with just the black eye. It didn't damage his vision at all. They both left for home a few hours ago. Tina needed some help to relax. I think they gave her a sleeping pill to help for tonight. She's a pretty anxious kid."

The curtains rustled in front of them before parting. "Oh, good timing," Sulis said, sweeping over to the bed with a handful of flowers. She must have showered; the red streaks in her auburn hair were now gone. She was simply dressed in an oversized white t-shirt and black pants under her jacket but still wore her jewelry. The fresh scent of the carnations and sunflowers, clean and sweet, mixed with Sulis's signature patchouli and washed over the bed. Jenna smiled, inhaling the pleasant smell deeply. She hadn't been able to get the funk of the ghosts out of her nose.

"Thank you. I'll take them to go."

"Wonderful! I think everyone needs some time to recoup. Will, it looks like your vigil has ended, and you are free to come home now, shower, and sleep," Sulis ordered firmly. Will yawned once again, nodding.

The words bounced around in Jenna's head. "How long have you been here, Will?"

"Since you came in."

A faint smile grew on Jenna's lips. She shook her head as if not able to believe everything herself. "Wow."

"That was an interesting experience, Jenna," Sulis stated. "Of all the things I've done over the years, this one takes the cake. Mr. Stevens, do you think Mr. Jacobs would object if we were to stop over at the museum later today and pick up the Ouija board and help clean up?"

"I guess not. It's Sunday, already. I'm not sure if he is going to open Monday, but it does need to be cleaned up. You're sure it's safe?" he asked.

"Fairly so, yes. I did as Sylvia instructed. The dates disappeared, and there were no more visitors from the past. You should probably discuss that stubborn window. Will told me he used Sylvia's athame to try to lock it. Knowing how that affected the ghosts in the first place gives a good probability of closing it for good. It would be prudent to check that room first, and see if it's still intact," Sulis suggested. Mr. Stevens shook his head and sighed.

"It needs to be done anyway. I'm just glad it's October second and we're on our way out of here. My wife left Pennsylvania this morning and should be home in a few hours. Everyone needs to get some sleep, too. How about five tonight?"

"We'll be there, if sleeping beauty here wakes up by then," Sulis replied, motioning over at Will. He had put his head back down on the bed and fallen asleep. She shook him gently, and he got up slowly as if achy. They said their goodbyes and left.

"I'm sorry I left you for a few minutes, kiddo. You were still sleeping and they reassured me you would be okay. And, of course, Will was here." He sighed heavily as if that would take some getting used to. He scratched his blond, wavy hair to buy himself a second. "I went home just long enough to shower and change. I think your mom will be less stressed if we look half-way normal. It will be easier to convince her we're both okay to go back to the museum tonight."

Jenna's stomach became tight when she thought about going back. Her nerves were frayed. Even so, she needed to feel safe there again. There was a lot to clean up. She hoped Toby and Mr. Jacobs would come, too. It would probably be best if they all were there.

Jenna slept much of the day after she got home, and convinced her mom to stop worrying about her. She thought it was going to be harder to get back to the museum this time around. The last time she had been in the hospital from an "accident" at the museum, her parents had forbidden her from returning for a while. This time she was surprised to see that her dad had not only already paved the way for her, he also planned on going.

"I figured there would be no way to talk you out of going, with all you've been through there. I need to know the building is safe before you go back alone, anyway." He hesitated briefly. "And I think I'll just have to get used to the fact that wherever Will is going to be is where you might want to be, too," he said, unable to look his daughter in the eyes just yet.

"I guess so, Dad. I'm glad you understand."

"It's a work in progress, Jenna. I wasn't prepared for this. Any of this," he admitted.

"That makes two of us, then." She met his smile halfway. It

was good they were still bonding. It was just weird that it was in such an unconventional way.

IT WAS LATER that evening when Mr. Jacobs hesitantly unlocked the door to the museum. Will, Sulis, and Toby were behind him, with Mr. Sevens and Jenna bringing up the rear. Mr. Jacobs's boots clicked on the floor as he quickly walked toward the office to turn on the main power switch. The lights went on slowly, as usual, and they all stepped inside, closing the door behind them.

Nothing seemed to have changed since last night's events, at least as far as they could tell. It was quiet. It was not an innocent quiet like some buildings felt. It was a secretive quiet; this place had seen too much for anything else. The walls had been battered with bloodshed and bullets and interventions, both good and bad, but nothing walked the floors, except them.

"Should we start to clean up down here or check the Sewing Room first?" Mr. Jacobs asked, nervously swinging his keys around the keychain on his finger.

"Someone should go up to the Sewing Room before we decide to go anywhere else but here," Sulis suggested.

"I need to go," Jenna found herself volunteering. Her stomach fluttered.

"We all should," suggested Mr. Stevens as they all started up the stairs.

"This is promising, the door is still closed," Will said, stopping in front of the Sewing Room door. He leaned his head in to listen. There were no sounds. "That's a good sign. This door has been opening on its own for the last week. Are we ready?" He looked around to make sure everyone was paying attention, and opened the door slowly. No gust of wind or snow hit them this time. There was some disarray from their scuffles, but the window remained closed and locked in place. The athame stood stoically in the middle.

Once it was obvious the room was empty, in every sense, Toby and Sulis went back downstairs to upright the chairs and clean off the table. It seemed like each room was going to be a project of its own.

"Tell me what happened when we got separated, dad. I never did get the whole story," Jenna encouraged as she picked up the rest of the used tar buckets.

"Well, we were split up to begin with. I went into the Display Room looking for you. Of course it wasn't you I heard in there. I was cornered by those creatures, and they were everywhere, materializing out of the pictures on the wall. That was one of the scariest things I've ever seen. The majority of them left the room—and I can't tell you how thankful I was for that. I was chomping at the bit to find you, Jenna, and I couldn't get out of the room. I had to fight the one guy left for me. I was up against the display wall with nowhere to go. I ended up sticking him in one of the pictures I pulled down from above me at the last minute. It was close. I still couldn't find you after that, and somehow I was downstairs," her father remembered. He picked up the last of the pieces of loose wood and set them in a trash pile.

"Mark, er, Mr. Levy, tried to keep Sulis and Tina away from the fighting by putting them in the office," Mr. Jacobs said, picking up a broom. "By then the ghouls were after us, somehow herding us in different directions. I wound up in the second room off the main floor, you know, the old kitchen. I was sure you were still in the Sewing Room, but I couldn't get anywhere near there. The weird guy with the slit throat and I went at it for a while. It was like wrestling with air but being pinned by a vice. No one told me you couldn't touch these guys, y'know? It wasn't easy, and I'm out of shape for someone, well, someone my age. I think I'm going to have to start going to the gym with Toby. Anyway, I had the picture, so I won," he finished in a rush. He stopped sweeping the broken glass in front of him. The memories were too fresh to not get worked up.

"I couldn't stay connected through the board, although I tried for a while. Sylvia came back, trying to help, but she was fighting on her end, too. The planchette was all over the place. And then I needed to close out because the ghosts were here, and it wasn't safe anymore, even with protection spells," Sulis stated, packing her belongings into the plastic tote.

"Yeah, what does…what exactly…I mean, everything was so crazy last night… you did say you both were witches, right?" Mr. Jacobs stammered. His face was getting red and Jenna was surprised how much he and Toby looked like each other.

"Yes, we are," Will said, speaking up. His face took on a little color itself.

"Huh," Toby commented, nonplussed. "What's that all about?"

"Toby!"

"I'm not being mean, dad. I think they're both pretty cool. I'd just like to know."

"No, it's okay, Mr. Jacobs. This can get very confusing because there are many different distinctions. We are Pagan which can be described as an umbrella term for those whose faith is earth-based. And most Pagan are witches. We identify as Wiccan, which is our religion. A commonality of all is that we consider ourselves naturalists," Sulis explained. When the men's faces reflected confusion, Will jumped in.

"We respect nature and all living things. We don't believe in hell or the devil. For the most part, we live our lives and practice our beliefs like most other people." He looked over at Jenna, clearly worried. She grinned back at him. Buoyed, he let his guard down. He wanted the room to know they weren't without a sense of humor. "And, of course, we use our powers for good."

"Powers for good," Mr. Stevens parroted, shaking his head while looking heavenward.

"I am confused on one thing," Jenna admitted. She picked up the sheath of Sulis's athame. "Sylvia had her knife the whole time and didn't use it on anyone?"

"An athame is never meant to be used as a weapon, even in self-defense," Will stated. "It seems as though she never even thought of that herself."

"Oh. But I used it..." Jenna put her head down, remembering how she had stabbed Jonas with Sylvia's athame.

"Jenna, that's completely different. We used the athames as a means to connect with them," Will clarified, knowing what she was thinking. She thought it over for a moment and nodded, relieved.

"Do you, y'know, use spells all the time?" Toby asked, addressing Sulis.

"Sure. It's a way we ask for our prayers to be heard. We give thanks the same way, and ask for protection from things that can harm us. Actually, we ask for protection for others, too. Our golden rule is very similar to every other religion out there. Treating others respectfully is how we would like to be treated. How we treat others comes back to us threefold, so we try to keep it positive."

"So, no worshipping Satan or anything like that?" Mr. Stevens asked, wanting confirmation.

"No, but that's not to say there aren't those out there who don't, and there's power in numbers. There are no hard and fast rules in Paganism. Most everyone follows what resonates with them. We don't participate in curses or use spells that wish ill will on others, but again, there are a lot who do."

With the room put to right, Sulis started towards the basement. Everyone followed. Will and Jenna put their hands out towards each other at the same moment, and smiled.

"We all choose our path and how to achieve our goals. What we use our caldrons, wands, and blades for can be very different from the way others use them. I think that's important to keep in mind."

Nineteen

A S THEY STARTED to take the steps downstairs to the basement, the atmosphere became thick with the thoughts of Mr. Levy being by himself and hurt worse than anyone.

"Speaking of misuse, take Jonas. I'm very sure he found a way to manipulate Sylvia's magic to try and get what he wanted," Will suggested.

"He was strong just by himself," Jenna added. Will squeezed her hand tightly.

"Stronger with those buddies of his," Toby confessed. "They're much harder to take down when you're ganged up on."

"That's the truth," Mr. Jacobs agreed, putting his hand on his son's shoulder. They all looked over the mess in front of them. He and Toby grabbed shovels and started in to make the floor level again.

"Look at this place," Mr. Stevens said, walking over to a tar bucket and moving it towards the broken tools. Jenna and Sulis began collecting the pieces as he retrieved what was left of the ladder. "I'm taking this back upstairs, right Tom?"

"Yes, thanks. If you could find another broom up there for all this glass that would be great."

"What were those guys looking for, anyway?" Toby asked. He threw the remaining dirt from a mound into one of the holes, and stepped on it to tamp it down. "Why would anyone dig holes in the basement? They're everywhere down here."

"For that, I have no answer," Sulis admitted.

"Maybe they did a lot of digging back in their day and it was familiar to them," Mr. Jacobs suggested, uninterested. He grimaced and wiped his nose. "Who knows and who cares? Right now, I'll be happy once this place is aired out and I don't have to worry about the walking dead."

Jenna picked up the last large piece of broken wood, listening to everyone talk around her. She caught Will's eye as he glanced up at her and winked. She had mentioned Sylvia using diamonds to cast her circle, and Toby had been upstairs when Jonas talked about a diamond, but no one else knew the whole story. It was still a secret shared between only them, and they wanted it to remain that way. They each knew there was boundless time to search knowing there was treasure here somewhere. All they had to do was dig.

THINGS FINALLY DID calm down. Just to be safe, they kept the museum closed until Tuesday. The window had remained sealed albeit with the help of the athame jutting out in the middle of it. Inconveniently, it was the beginning of October and their monthly Historical Association meeting was at the end of the week. Frustration was high, and no one could agree on what they would say or do. After two days of listening to arguments and squabbling in the museum, Will spoke to his mother about needing to intervene beforehand. At 8:30 p.m. on Thursday, the nine of them squeezed into the back booths in Mandy's Place, a favorite coffee shop in town.

"This caramel macchiato is one of the best I've ever had," Sulis said, sitting in a chair that had been pulled up in front of the two booths to accommodate them all.

Mandy smiled her gratitude as she placed a large tray with assorted pastries on the table. "I just can't believe how grown up these three are," she gushed, indicating Jenna, Tina, and Toby. "I figured I'd see them in my shop a time or two, but not for a business meeting."

"Thanks Mandy, but I don't work *there*," Tina stated, emphasizing the place implied. Her mood was as sour as her father's had been.

"Well, you know what I mean, hon. Holler if you need anything else. I've got to get back to the others in the front."

"That was rude, Tina," Jenna whispered across the booth. Tina pursed her lips and crossed her arms as she slumped back into the molded seat, leaning her head against the wall.

"Yeah, don't take it out on Mandy."

"Shut up, Toby!"

The bickering began again, and Mr. Levy frowned. "Let's get to it Sulis, we closed the museum early for this." He was sitting in the chair next to Sulis so he could better manage the sling his arm was in. He was the only one who hadn't placed an order.

"Mr. Levy, it's only a half an hour," an exasperated Jenna exclaimed.

Sulis put her hand up and the chattering stopped. "I think before we can talk about the Association meeting, we should talk about what happened on Saturday." Some of the expressions she was met with prompted her to clarify. "I don't believe this is the type of relationship all of you have had with each other. A lot happened that night and it would be healthy to talk about it. And yes, I have seen this before," she said, glancing over at Mr. Levy as he opened his mouth to speak. "This reaction is also not that uncommon."

There were a lot of eyes looking at each other but nothing was said. Will, sitting directly across from Jenna, had been studying a spot on the table, and took a breath. "I'll start. It's hard to wrap one's head around what happened, but it did happen."

"I thought it would've been easier to deal with since we went through it before," Mr. Stevens admitted, "but it hasn't. Why?"

"You're not alone, if that gives you some comfort. It's a prickly feeling to have to question everything you've ever believed, especially when you experience something that contradicts those beliefs. It's a psychological concept called cognitive dissonance."

Everyone looked at Sulis, confused. "One might be able to rationalize an isolated incident, but not when it keeps occurring. We're called back quite often after doing a cleansing or intervention for this exact reason. It's a crossroads where the status quo is questioned. Everything you've ever counted on must be seen through a new lens."

"I've been doing that myself. I've been wondering what else will change," Mr. Jacobs said in between bites of a cheese danish.

Sulis nodded and looked over at Mr. Levy. "What's weighing on your mind?"

"I feel I'm not on solid ground anymore," Mr. Levy eventually mumbled.

"And how does that make you feel?" Sulis prompted, dabbing her lip with a napkin.

"I'm angry."

"Almost like I've been manipulated," Tina added, sipping an iced tea. "And I can't share this with my family or friends at church."

"That is the most difficult, I'm afraid," Sulis said gently. "Those firm in their own faith have a hard time making peace with what they've grown to believe."

"Grown to trust. Most of the Levy family have held positions in the church. In a way, I feel I've been disloyal, participating in that. In my mind, those who are able to work magic are evil."

"Clergy prefer to use the term 'miracle' instead of 'magic'. Your religion canonizes those who have performed miracles. They become saints and are revered. How is this any different?"

Mr. Levy's frustrated expression remained, but now it

seemed for different reasons. It was apparent the wheels in his brain were turning as he reflected. Sulis was right and he had difficulty finding fault with this logic. "I never thought of it that way."

"It may take a while to weave this into what makes you, you, and that's okay. Everyone here experienced this, so there is some part of you that is open to encountering the paranormal. None of this has happened to any of the guests, right?" Sulis asked. Heads shaking back and forth confirmed this. "Then it's isolated itself to the seven of you. There's something there that's special."

"My father had some, uh, ability, and Jenna certainly does. I thought it might have skipped over me, but probably not, huh?"

"No, I don't believe it did. What about you, Tom?"

"I don't have anything."

"Neither do we," Mr. Levy interjected. His anger had fizzled, and now his face reflected the tiredness he felt.

"That you know of. Not many discuss this sort of thing, but clearly, it's too much to process by oneself. There are two types of people in the world: those who do the type of work Will and I do, who respect the realms and keep them sacred, and those who end up on the front page of a tabloid. Fate has a funny way of keeping things in check, so those who blatantly announce the existence of magic like this usually find themselves exploited with an untrustworthy reputation. And that is the crux of why we're here tonight. Now, going forward with the Association's meeting. I'm assuming no one will bring this up either?"

"Of course we won't!" Mr. Levy looked aghast.

"It would make it easier, though." Mr. Jacobs gave a little laugh. "I don't like to lie, especially to the president, Mr. Robertson. He's been around long enough to hear the stories from the last go-round, and maybe the one before that. I think some of those other members are only on the board for the title. They wouldn't understand."

"That's true. They've never contributed to the minutes at the meetings I've gone to," Jenna added.

"Some only go to the minimum number required."

"Mr. Robertson would be the only one who wouldn't laugh in our face, actually," added Jenna.

"Then tell him," Sulis suggested.

"You just told them not to," Toby stated, confused. A little powder from his donut remained in the corner of his mouth.

"No, I said not to share with those who would make a big deal out of it. It sounds like the president already has knowledge of what the building is capable of."

"I think it's a good idea even if I'm not a member of the Association," Tina agreed, taking a piece of baklava Jenna offered.

"At this point, I don't think it matters who's on the board, just who survived last Saturday." Mr. Levy gingerly raised his arm for emphasis. With his other hand, he pulled off a piece of the dessert his daughter gingerly held in between two fingers.

"I feel awful you got hurt."

"I know, Jenna. I'll be okay."

"That'd make me feel better. What about you, son?"

"Sure," Toby answered. "I don't like us yelling at each other."

Sulis put down her half-empty coffee cup. "I agree."

"What will we do about the Sewing Room window?" Will wanted to know. He had been watching Jenna more than anything, but was keeping up with the conversation.

Mr. Levy sighed heavily. "Honestly, I wish the thing was boarded up permanently. All of our problems seem to start there."

"That's true, Mark. I want to be assured of our safety, but I also don't want the integrity of the museum compromised," admitted Mr. Jacobs. "We agreed when we started working together that we would put safety first. The last time the window stayed closed it was because some force closed it for us. This time Will closed it with the…help me here Sulis—"

"Athame."

"Thank you. Athame. It's stayed shut since last week. Maybe we could give it a trial run or something. I'm willing to rethink our plan if it starts opening again."

Mr. Levy took his glasses off and attempted to wipe them on his shirt. "We wouldn't be able to explain it to the board if we bricked the thing up anyway."

"It's also a huge part of the building." Jenna set down her latte. "It's important, even if it has had a remarkably negative role in its history."

"I swear you will always defend that place," Tina admitted, shaking her head as if her friend was a lost cause.

"Yeah. It's what I do. Anyway, I refer to that window on every tour."

"You know what I think?" Mr. Stevens asked after a moment's silence. "I think all of us should be members of the board."

"That would be great, Jack." Mr. Jacobs face lit up. "New memberships are taken at the start of the fiscal year. That's only in a few weeks! I can bring over the paperwork. Sulis? What about you and Will?" They looked at each other and nodded.

"We would be honored to be members," Sulis replied. Will smiled.

"Hell, yeah!"

"Toby, watch your language."

"Sorry, dad."

"I think I'll pass," Tina said, talking over the others. She had trouble looking up from the edge of the counter.

"But Teen, you don't have to—" Toby began.

"Toby, it's okay if she doesn't want to. No one is being forced." Sulis took a deep breath. "So, does everyone feel more comfortable where everything stands?"

"Not entirely," Mr. Levy stated. "I don't want the Sewing Room opened to the public. And I'm on the fence about having the place open on Halloween. There's too much liability."

"But Mr. Levy—"

"This," he said, indicating his head, "has not caught up. "This," he pointed to his arm, "is a vivid reminder of the violence I endured a week ago. I take pain medicine every eight hours. This is all telling me it's too soon. I'm still sore. I don't want to entertain thoughts that the building might come back to life again in another few weeks. Anyway, with all the leaks and blown fixtures we're behind. The new displays aren't done, and arrangements for the party have been neglected or overlooked. We're not prepared. For anything."

"But I've had people, friends and teachers, come to me asking about the party already." There was an urgency in Jenna's voice neither Will or Sulis had heard before.

"I understand, but Mark…. it's one of the few times of the year everyone in town comes together. They enjoy the museum and the holiday." Mr. Jacobs moved his attention from his partner to Sulis. "As each year passes, word of mouth gathers more and more out of towners to the festivities. It's hard to deny the revenue we'd lose if we cancelled. It's the largest part of our yearly income." He turned back to Mr. Levy. "You know our budget is planned around the fact that, other than the tourist season in the summer, Halloween is the biggest day for business."

"The town knows nothing about last week," Toby interjected.

"I know we can do it. Will and I can. I'll work overtime without pay if I need to…"

Will leaned over to the aisle to see Mr. Levy clearly. "I'm happy to help in any way."

"The first party lacked a lot and it was successful. The college is on board for food just like every year, and the school already has their volunteer list. We know what we have to do," Mr. Jacobs ticked off on his fingers. "We've done enough to get by."

Even though there were other customers in the shop, it seemed like the room held its breath. "If you truly believe we'll be safe, then okay," Mr. Levy acquiesced. "I want a backup plan and concessions in case we need to close and lock the Sewing Room door. Maybe something on a sign that says 'under construction.' I want the whole room out of play if it starts to get squirrelly."

"Done."

Twenty

*J*ENNA AND WILL could only keep their curiosity of
the basement contents to themselves for a few days
before being consumed by the mystery. They were
both grounded for a week for the Ouija fiasco so they couldn't
see each other outside of work and school. And they shared no
class other than lunch, so Will had started sitting with Jenna at
her table. Sometimes Tina and Toby would join them. Talking
about the museum was tricky, even with their friends there.
Toby had been there when Jonas had said more was buried,
but Toby didn't know what Jonas was talking about, and Tina
didn't know a thing about the basement mystery. Even alone it
was difficult to talk because the small table was always full with
their classmates. They took up carpooling to school each day.
Being completely alone, they could talk without reservation.

"Two weeks ago, they had a good foot dug, if not more.
I wish I could have somehow marked all the spots we'd seen

them dig when we fell in the picture, so we don't waste time in the wrong place," Will lamented for the second time that afternoon. He was driving today, and school had just let out. It was one of the few days they didn't have to work, so they decided to walk around the local mall. Their plans to enjoy the fall foliage at a local nature center had to be changed. It was too wet to do anything outside.

They were going at a snail's pace because it was pouring sideways, another typical autumn day in upstate New York. The windshield wiper blades swished in rhythm to the spattering sound of heavy rain as it hit the body of Will's car.

Jenna reached her hand over to take his, and he relaxed and smiled at her. They had fallen into an easy relationship that had been intensified by the bond forged during those harrowing events the first week of the month. It still surprised her. She never thought she would find someone who understood her and her weird obsession with the museum, and there sat Will, who knew exactly, and wanted her still.

They hit a big pothole, and the car bounced. "Ah, we're almost done with road construction season and are fast approaching pot hole and snow plow season," Will sighed.

"Well, it's not like the basement is humongous. It's more a matter of finding time by ourselves to look. I'm glad Mr. Jacobs postponed you working my opposite days until after Halloween so we can get the annual party planned.

"And we're working together."

"Yes, especially that." There was a moment of comfortable silence. Jenna frowned. "I hate that my mom put a time limit on our phone calls at night. We just got off being grounded; we only want to catch up."

There was so much to learn about Will and time got away from her. There was schoolwork and chores on their days off. What time they did spend together at the museum wasn't time to socialize. Since they had become so inseparable every moment they could, Jenna's parents had instituted a rule that every other weekend was family time with their respective families. Not that Jenna and her family did much, but Will was always busy. He and Sulis were working very hard on renovating their house. He liked to kid that he was lucky he had access to shower and clean clothes. He was also adamant that Jenna not visit until they were done, so she could properly appreciate that he didn't grow up in a barn, or something like that.

"That's okay. I think my mom was on the verge of limiting me, too. I guess three hours a night could be thought of as a lot." He smiled again, the left side of his lip higher than his right. It was the same way Sulis's was, Jenna thought to herself.

"So, I never had a chance to ask before. Your mom's real name is Rebekah, right? Why does she go by Sulis?"

"Sulis is her craft name. She prefers it over her given name, and uses it everywhere except at work. Actually, she's in the process of changing it legally. I hear all the grumbles. It's a pain in the neck to change everything."

"Huh. What does it mean? Why did she change it?" Jenna had been intrigued from the moment she met her and had never gotten around to asking.

"It means 'healing goddess'. We're dysfunctional, just like everyone else, and she has always been unconventional.

'Captivated by earthly alternatives' is how she likes to put it. So, I was named after her last name to keep it going, which no one does. I'm glad she decided on just Will, though. I cannot imagine the heckling I'd be getting if she named me Willowby. Albireo is bad enough. How many guys do you know who were named after a constellation star?"

Will was tapping his thumbs on the steering wheel as he waited for two cars to pass by. The traffic cleared on both sides, and he took the turn toward the mall, the rain now coming from behind them. "Anyway, she always leaned in that direction. Then, after my dad died, it was really hard for her. I wasn't quite two years old yet, and she was on her own with me. She searched around for answers, was drawn to Wicca, and she settled down there."

He found a spot close to the entrance and turned the ignition off. They stayed there a moment bracing for the weather. With their hoods up tightly, they rushed out of the car and ran to the main doors. Splashing through puddles, they made it inside, soaked and laughing. Will scrunched Jenna to his side and squeezed her. The mall was empty for the time being except for an elderly mall walker. The high schoolers were the first to be dismissed. Within a few hours, it would be crawling with 'tweeners. For now, it was desolate.

"Why Wicca? What did she find?" Jenna asked. Her sneakers squeaked in time to Will's on the polished floors.

"Mom had a lot of anger. She was mad at everything: the unfairness of losing my dad, of being a single parent, of being by herself. It was eating her up. When I asked her about all of this a few years ago, she said she needed to find something hopeful for the moment she was in. Now, neither of us have any complaints about other religions. She's always considered herself an unrepentive Christian anyway. It's just most of them talk about the past and what will be at the end. For her, Christianity put followers at the mercy of God instead of being empowered, with control over your own life.

"She needed something to get her out of the rut of grief she was living in, and Wicca did that for her. It fit her personality and temperament. It celebrates nature and beauty, and accepts that all creation is respected and sacred. She started looking at things from a new perspective, and found peace in the mark my dad made on her life, and in the world. And that he was still around in a tangible way other than me. She changed her lifestyle and adopted a new name that described what she was and what she wanted. Sulis also means 'mother goddess,' so she worked on having positive energy." His arm found the middle of her back. Wafts of citrus and sandalwood floated over to Jenna.

"That still sounds kinda hard with the death of someone so close."

"I guess she was concentrating on the Wiccan Rede. It's like the golden rule of the religion. It pretty much says you can do anything as long as you do no harm to yourself or anyone else. The goodness that you do will come back to you threefold."

"That's cool."

"Now, the flip side is whatever harm you have done will also come back to hurt you threefold. She's always tried to be a positive person, so she wanted to share the wealth—so to speak—surround herself with happy people, and hope that good things would find her again."

They had stopped in front of a little coffee shop and went inside. After a few minutes, they were tucked into a booth sharing a hot cocoa.

"Do you think she's happy now?" Jenna asked between sips, warming up from the dampness of the day.

"Yeah, I do," Will replied thoughtfully. "It brought her family closer together. I have four older aunts who live about an hour outside Libertyvale where we used to live. Actually, we live closer to them now here in Orchard Creek. Everyone had been doing there own thing, living their own life. After my dad died, she got back in touch with them on a regular basis, and they became interested in Wicca also. A coven was born."

"What exactly is a coven? Because I'm sure it's different from how movies portray one."

Will reached across the table and took Jenna's hand. In a way, it was to comfort himself. He still wasn't completely at ease divulging everything about the religion he practiced, despite being proud and committed to Wicca. There was always the fear there would be one detail too many for Jenna, and she'd turn away from him.

"It's our word for congregation. It's a group of witches who get together to worship. We have eight main sabbats on the Wheel of the Year."

Jenna's eyes searched his, wanting to understand. Will thought a moment, then rolled her sleeve up to expose her forearm. He turned her hand over and held it. With his other hand, he drew a circle on the inside of her wrist with his finger. "The Wheel of the Year is our calendar. We recognize the four seasons, or Solar Festivals, because the sun causes those seasonal changes."

From Jenna's perspective, he drew two lines, each on opposite sides of the circle. "Say these represent the directions of west and east. We pay tribute to the summer and winter solstice. Solstice actually means the sun stands still, so these are either the longest day of the year or the shortest day of the year." He brushed his finger to mark the north and south ends of the circle. "And we honor the spring and autumn equinoxes, when we have equal hours of light and darkness."

Will's finger made smaller marks in the spaces between these invisible lines. "These cross-quarter days are Fire Festivals which refer to agricultural events like first harvest. Remember, this religion and practice dates back to times when our ability to harvest good crops equated to our continued existence. Crops were dependent upon enough sun and rainfall, and mild winters helped us get through lean times."

He dared to raise his eyes to Jenna. She studied her wrist a moment before looking up at him. Even in the brightness of the shop's lights, her eyes seemed darker. He let his wall down to feel her mood. It was calm and curious.

"Where does Halloween fall in this?"

"It's our highest holy day, our new year. It signifies many things. It's the third and final harvest; the end of summer. We remember and honor our ancestors and loved ones, sort of like the Mexican Day of the Dead. It's when we make preparations for winter and dry herbs and store foods."

A smile played at Jenna's lips.

"Yes, my mom actually does that. Our kitchen usually

smells like basil or rosemary or whatever we've just walked by and kicked up in the air. Obviously, we didn't put in a garden, but we've bought produce from farmers' markets and canned things. I especially like making blueberry jam."

Jenna paused a moment. "Do all your aunts do this, too?"

Will laughed. "They'd kill each other if they were all in a kitchen together. Aunt Whitty and Aunt Lee are good cooks. Aunt Diane is more of our herb lady, she makes great herbal tea blends. Aunt Mina is impartial to the culinary world. As long as she eats when she's hungry, she doesn't much care what it is. When we're together as family we're just family, I guess. But when we're together as a coven, we're all business. We support each other and push ourselves to continue learning. It's been a positive influence on all of us."

Will noticed the tiny goosebumps that had broken out on Jenna skin, but didn't think it was particularly from the cold. He kissed her hand as he stood. He slid out of his jacket and hung it on the hook on the corner of their booth.

"That sounds nice." Jenna was not sure what else to say. She really didn't know anyone else who was affected by spirituality in such a way. It wasn't necessarily a big part of her family's life.

"It sounds that way, but it hasn't been so easy. Like I've said before, there are many misconceptions. People don't under-stand. I've been taught to revere all living things. I'm a pacifist for crying out loud." He paused a moment. "Well, that didn't count when we were fighting off Jonas and all those non-living entities, but we don't sacrifice animals, and we certainly don't drink blood.

"We've been ostracized a lot. I've been bullied and teased

at school. Once we had nasty things written on the side of our shed." He hesitated again, his eyes dropping to his hands in his lap and began again quieter. "The worst was when we received a newsletter every month for a year from a local church. We were clueless as to why we were getting them, and contacting the minister directly did not stop them from coming. He was pleasant and very nice every time we called, and assured us we weren't on their mailing list." Will stopped, only continuing when Jenna reached out to touch his arm.

"It took a whole year before we finally found out who it was. We used to eat every Wednesday at the local diner. It was a small, family owned place, and their chicken and dumplings were wonderful. One day the waitress behind the counter started laughing with her coworker and pointing in our direction. She had the whole staff laughing. When it was time for the check she brought over the bill. On the tray underneath, was a sticker for the same church. She could barely get out if there was anything *else* she could do for us, without breaking into hysterics. It was then that we noticed the large crucifix necklace and cross earrings. She must have worked in the church office," Will finished, subdued. Jenna felt her face redden with anger.

"It was mortifying," Will whispered, his smooth voice edged with irritation. "I've never told anyone about that. Until now." Jenna got up and slid into the booth next to him. She put her arms around him and hugged him tightly. After a second, he did the same and when she moved away, his usually confident face was for once vulnerable, his brown eyes etched with the pain he'd been through.

"That's awful. I'm so sorry. I can see how you might not feel comfortable trusting people."

"Trust is scary."

Jenna laughed once and studied him, his expression now low and tired. "You are so not right. With everything we've experienced you think trust is scary?" Things were getting too heavy, and she didn't like how sad he looked. She pulled the mug over to where she sat as she continued. "Are you happy now?"

"Most definitely," he replied without hesitation. His pained expression brightened, then changed to one of concentration as his gaze met hers, and she was once again lost in his eyes. His intense look wandered and settled on her lips. Her stomach fluttered again as he leaned in and kissed her softly.

"You can trust me, you know," Jenna whispered, breathing in the mixture of cologne and Will. "I'm here for you."

They sat for a while with their heads together, just enjoying the connection.

THERE WAS HARDLY a free moment between the two of them at work that week, let alone together, to sneak downstairs on their own. They would both volunteer if supplies needed to be brought up, or something needed to be taken down. But, just as soon as they started to go, someone would interrupt them, or Mr. Jacobs would walk by. Time passed quickly as they scrambled to finalize for Halloween.

"We are never going to get down there," Jenna said, exasperated. She shook her head and blew her bangs out of her eyes. It was October fifteenth. They had just confirmed a DJ last minute and were taking Mrs. Forrester's Victrola out from the corner. The unofficial tradition at the party would continue with a DJ early in the evening, and then some older period records played the last half. Jenna had explained it was a quiet reminder and tribute to Mrs. Forrester. They were arranging and cleaning. Jenna became pensive as she handled the antique with care.

"She was really special to you, huh?" Will asked, observing her mood change.

"She was a spitfire, like having a grandmother, mentor, and co-conspirator all rolled up into one. She really experienced the past, in a tangible way, whereas I've only been able to dream about it. When she would take out her handkerchief, for example, or pictures of herself when she was a toddler, it was real. She had been there. She knew about this place, Will. At first, she protected it for all the wrong reasons. But she believed us when we confided in her, and I don't know of anyone who would trust a bunch of twelve-year olds. And then she protected this place for all the right ones. She deserved so much in return that I couldn't give her. She would have loved to have seen those diamonds," she remarked.

Will brushed his long hair out of his eyes and grinned his crooked grin at Jenna. Her stomach never failed to do somersaults every time he smiled at her like that.

"We'll get down there, too. We just need to bide our time," he advised, his eyebrows flirting with his devilish grin. He had also been thinking of different ways they could get down there, and was excited that Jenna was chomping at the bit just as much as he was.

Will continued to work, his thoughts racing. He wanted to dig down there in a big way. He also wondered if the museum would be safe on Halloween, or if anything else would come out of the woodwork. He wasn't anxious to meet any of the ghosts again, but the possibility of finding a lost treasure was too enticing.

There was a comfortable silence between them as they cleaned the dust off the unprotected antiques on the shelves. Jenna didn't feel the need to talk just for the sake of it. They both seemed to understand each other in a way Jenna had never felt, even with her girlfriends. She had kidded herself for thinking she had feelings for her first boyfriend, Alan. Compared to what she now felt with Will, it was like black and white versus technicolor.

As her thoughts wandered, she smiled as she thought of how close Will and Toby had become as well. They joked with each other like old friends every chance they got. Toby was around the museum quite a bit these days, mostly helping with the heavy manual labor. He had bulked up the last few years and preferred to do real work than go to the gym. It was great to see the two guys she loved the most—for different reasons, of course—truly enjoy each other's company. It was good for Will, too.

With her cloth gloves on, she began taking the more delicate items down to clean. Her smile faded when she thought about her best friend, Tina. She had hardly seen her since their meeting at Mandy's Diner. At first, Jenna thought it was just Tina's anxiety over the museum because Tina still called her and was friendly. Lately, though, Tina had been hanging around the band room, even when her boyfriend Rob wasn't there. The loss, even though it wasn't actually acknowledged, stung.

"Hey, you ok?" Will called from the other end of the room. Jenna turned around to see concern on his face. She shook her head to clear her thoughts.

"Yeah. Yeah, I am."

He walked over, restocking a bunch of their maps on the tiny shelf under the podium, and grabbed his leftover grape soda he had stashed there from their break. "I'm here if you want to talk."

Usually Jenna dismissed these offers, but now she studied him, remembering one of her dreams. "Grape has always been your favorite, huh?"

Will smiled at her in agreement, but the smile quickly dimmed. "Wait. This is the first time I've brought any grape drink to work. I don't believe I've shared that tidbit with you."

"Well, um, I saw it in one of my dreams." Her face heated up. She never really talked to anyone about her special talent. And amazingly, it had never really come up with Will.

"What?"

"It's kinda what I can do. When I'm not connecting to ghosts, that is."

Will looked at her pointedly, but his face was still amused. "Trust, remember?"

"Yeah." She blew out a breath and with more confidence, continued. "I can walk dreams."

That got his attention.

"I've been able to for as long as I can remember. I've

connected with Toby, the cashier at the grocery store, Mrs. Mercer from English Lit—that one was bizarre—the librarian in town, and probably a handful of other people. I connected to you in your dreams right after you started working here."

Will's crooked smile returned. "Okay. Impress me."

Jenna looked out into the darkness of the evening and the tiny white snowflakes that swirled under the floodlight. It looked threatening, but the white dusting would be gone by sunrise. It didn't seem like they'd be too busy tonight with tourists. "Okay," she repeated, raising her chin and taking up the challenge. "You and your mom, and I think your aunts, were all at an outdoor concert. You were trying to find certain emotions of the other concertgoers with your eyes closed. You had grape juice afterwards. You said it was your favorite flavor."

Will was indeed impressed. "Wow. I believe that was at Onondaga Parkway. How do you do it? Do you go into a meditative state?"

"I'm not even sure I know what that is," Jenna admitted, gathering a few cleaned items in her arm. "If there is a pattern at all, it's that I'm led to strong emotions. Mostly, they just happen. Sometimes I know I've connected to the other person in their dream, but not always."

"So, it's not astral traveling," Will mumbled to himself. "And you could actually get into Elizabeth's dreams, too?" He held the ladder while Jenna started up.

"I guess." Jenna admitted, placing the dusted artifacts back on the shelf.

"And across the veil as well. You are amazing. It's like what my mom can do but she does it without the dream part."

"I'm only really able to get what's already happened. Everyone is usually much younger. I told Toby about the times linked to him and he confirmed they were things that happened in the past."

"Mom usually gets things that are going to happen. You truly are talented."

"Thank you." Jenna came back down to ground level and took off her gloves. "What I want to know about is how you can pick up emotions of others." Will at once looked uncertain.

"Oh no you don't," Jenna scolded with a grin. "Trust. Now dish."

Twenty-one

ILL HESITATED.

"COME on, Will. You can pick up on what I'm feeling. You just did it again a few minutes ago. You also said something about being an "impath" a couple weeks ago, but we were too distracted with Sylvia and Jonas to focus on it. And we didn't have the chance to talk about it afterwards. That's what you were doing in the dream I got into, right? You can do something more than just connect to people through the Ouija board."

"Yes. I'm an empath, but so are a lot of people."

Jenna's faced clearly showed her confusion but her openness to learn more about him.

"Empaths are those who are affected by the emotions around them. We are highly attuned to what others are feeling, even if we don't want to. Others' emotional baggage can be absorbed by an empath if they're not careful, and it's exhausting.

So is being "open" to all those feelings out there. It's incredibly overwhelming."

"How did you know what that was?"

"My family figured out I was an empath when I was really little, around the same time they learned I could bridge the realm between our world and the one beyond. So, mom and my aunts helped me not only with control, but how to manipulate it. I'm able to decipher quite a few different emotions from several people all at the same time. They taught me how to block it out, or open myself to it, if I wished."

Jenna watched Will turn the flour sifter over and over in his hands as he talked. By now he should have been able to write out from memory the complete schematic on how it worked.

"I'm a little different from most because I can do the opposite as well. Not only can I feel the emotions of others, I can project emotions onto others."

"Have you done that around us?" Jenna asked hesitantly. Will looked unsettled.

"A little. I did use it on Tina when we found Mr. Levy in the basement." He set the sifter down and picked up his soda can. "It's a useful tool, another way to gauge a situation. I apologize for the few times I've slipped up. I guess I'm just more in tuned to you, because I try very hard not to let that wall down. It seems invasive otherwise."

Jenna could tell Will was on his way to shutting down and she didn't want that to happen. She wanted all lines of communication to stay open between them. "Well, I guess that's okay. That's different from seeing what color undergarments we're wearing."

It was so far from what Will was expecting, he sprayed a little of his remaining soda out of his mouth. "That's not in my skillset! You know, you are a complete goof."

"Takes one to know one. We're all abnormal here. Welcome to the club."

"We sure are. But can you imagine what we'd be like with all our talents working together at the same time?"

It was a hypothetical question she was sure, but it made the hairs on the back of Jenna's neck stand up. "Yeah."

ON SUNDAY, OCTOBER sixteenth, the weather was gorgeous, and Will and Jenna needed sunglasses on their way to Beaver Lake Nature Center in Baldwinsville. They had worked five consecutive nights preparing for the Halloween party, and were getting a well-deserved weekend off. Sunny skies made the colors of the trees pop, a drastic difference from when the weather was wet, which made them seem dull and faded. The nature center had over a dozen mulch-lined foot trails, broken up by the type of area it encompassed and named accordingly. A few went through a very deep part of the woods, some surrounded swamp land, and one went the perimeter of a small lake, giving the best viewing of the spectacular oranges and yellows. The largest trails were a few miles long with some taking an hour to walk. Several were smaller and less than a mile each.

"Let's do the Pine Trail first. You'll love this one," Jenna suggested, pointing to the rustic sign over the rough path.

"This is great. I'm so fortunate to have my very own guide to accompany me."

"This goes down deep into the woods and is lined with pines the whole way. It smells awesome. Good thing you brought your jacket, the mosquitoes are monsters here." They walked under the sign, the path taking them away from the two other trails next to it. Immediately it got dark, the sunlight blocked by the tree canopy. The smell, fresh and woodsy, was clean and invigorating.

"Speaking of guides and cool places around here, have you ever been to the mines?" Will asked. His thoughts did not stray far from the buried treasure at the museum. The mulch and moss under their feet was soft and muffled their footfalls.

"Herkimer? Yeah, I haven't been there in years, though. It's a great place to visit. You get to watch a short video before you go pick. They're not real diamonds, but they are almost as hard as real ones. They look like a diamond and naturally have, uh, six sides I think, whereas a real diamond needs to be cut by man to get those facets. They look real, and the good ones are beautiful. It's hard manual labor to try to get to the diamonds, though. That's a good example of not judging a book by its cover. What looks like an ugly rock on the outside could hold a beautiful diamond on the inside. It's pretty therapeutic to hit the rocks with pickaxes and hammers, too. I've come out with a few about the size of a pea, but nothing bigger. There are some in their showcases from ages ago that are worth a pretty penny now, like the ones Jonas had. Those are whoppers."

"Do you think that's what's buried downstairs in the museum? Those guys seemed very determined to get down there and get their lot." Will slowed and swat at a sweat fly buzzing his head.

Jenna shrugged. She fished out a hair tie from her pocket and pulled her long hair back into a ponytail, securing it. "It must be. We don't have anything else around here of value. We don't have rubies or tourmalines. I saw a program on television about those once. The small ones are worth more than our small Herkimers. No one ever gets big diamonds out of there anymore."

"I bet the ones Jonas buried are huge. They'd be worth a lot if you're saying the mines don't have many big ones left anymore. What would you do with a bunch of diamonds?" Will's soft-spoken tone took on a seductive quality, that, mixed with the dim atmosphere, made Jenna's stomach flip flop.

"I've never given it too much thought other than being excited to find it," Jenna replied brightly, trying to ignore the fact that they were alone in the woods. "Who doesn't dream of finding and digging up a buried treasure?"

"The security of that much money is enticing," he teased.

Jenna stopped abruptly as a chipmunk scurried across in front of her and jumped into the nearest tree. "Sure it is," she answered. After a moment, she continued. "You know I've always felt differently from everyone else in the way I feel about that building. I've been thinking about what you guys had to deal with. Your mom seems pretty secure with herself."

"She is who she is and proud of it. She feels people will accept her—or not—for who she is on the inside, not based on anything else. That's how it should be, anyway."

Jenna nodded. "I know it was harder for you. As soon

as I figured out who your mom was, the day the window got broken, I could tell you were nervous. Your face went completely blank."

They walked up an incline reaching a clearing where the elms parted, and the sun made them squint. The temperature was noticeably warmer. A few red raspberries remained on a bush next to the trail. A mischievous smirk played at Jenna's lips as she looked around quickly. Seeing no one near them, she waded into the thick grasses and pulled some berries off their stems. She scrutinized them first for any tiny bugs, then popped them into her mouth. When she climbed back to the trail, she handed a few to Will who took them without question. A few feet farther the pines closed in on them again, lined and spaced orderly like oversized vertical Lincoln Logs.

"It's a hard habit to break. You wouldn't believe how many friends I've had drift away after seeing my real life. That evening at the museum scared me silly. I wanted to know you better, but I was apprehensive. You intrigued me like no one else ever has. I had never met anyone who was so unique, so involved with a community interest. All the girls I've ever known were cut from the same mold, superficial and interested only in what they looked like, or the clothes they wore. It was rare to find one who didn't work in the mall.

"And to learn that you were so close to being like me, having dealt with the supernatural. I grew up with it, it's all I've ever known, but you were thrust into it. It's not normal at all, but you seemed okay with what you've experienced. If anything, you were more concerned about others not being taken by surprise. It didn't seem to intimidate you. It felt too good to be true." Will bent down and picked up a small stick, fiddling with it absentmindedly.

"I wanted to go slow and take my time to try to ease you into who I really was. Then I screwed up by breaking that stupid window, and then Mom showed up. The illusion of control that I had was slipping through my fingers like water. When my mom walked through that door, it seemed my new life here would shatter. I figured you'd run away like everyone else has in my life. I thought I was used to it, but then I didn't realize how quickly I had fallen for you..." Will found the words tumble out of his mouth again for the second time that month. It was difficult to rein in his thoughts with Jenna. He wanted to stop leaving himself so exposed, but it was hard to stop. It was too easy to talk to her.

Jenna's stomach did another flip, and she caught her breath before it tried to get away from her.

Will shook his head, internally chastising himself and stopped walking. He broke the stick in half to smell it, and smiled. He offered it to Jenna.

"See, it smells like lemon verbena. I admit I went a little nuts when I thought you and Toby had a thing. I thought if I had been that close, to not have scared you off, and have a shot at being happy here...and then for you to already be with someone else...It was like rubbing salt in an open wound."

Jenna sidled up alongside Will and bumped him with her hip. "Toby has always been like family and always will. I wish I had known that was what was bothering you, I was so confused. I would never flirt with anyone if I was already involved elsewhere, trust me."

"Right, trust." He bumped her back and smiled. He was willing to trust if it meant spending more time with Jenna.

THE WEATHER TOOK a turn for the worse less than a week later. Torrential downpours and high winds lasted days, reminding everyone of the impending rough New York winter ahead. It caused an unanticipated delay in setting up for the Halloween party as there was another minor flood in the basement.

"I know its October twenty-sixth, Mark! I'm well aware of the time crunch. This place is becoming more high maintenance than my wife," Mr. Jacobs muttered. He paused a minute, flinching. "You didn't hear that, Toby, understand? Anyway, it seems like we just had a flood down there," he added, trying to get away from his blunder.

Toby was moving the display cases to the sides of the room to accommodate the tables and chairs that would soon be brought in. He grinned and rolled his eyes, but didn't reply.

"We did. About four weeks ago," Mr. Levy answered sourly. Jenna and Will, who were sitting at a small desk in the room off the great room, going over the order sheets for refreshments and food, looked at each other quickly.

"If it would be helpful, Jenna and I can try to clean up as much as we can ourselves," Will offered in his usual soft-spoken tone. "It would be hard for you to do this by yourself, Mr. Jacobs. I know Mr. Levy is still out of commission for a while with his arm." It was impossible not to hear the urgency Jenna knew he felt inside with this golden opportunity.

"We really could have used a wet-vac a few weeks ago. I was going to buy one but didn't because I thought it was an isolated incident, and the new sump pump would take care of everything. After I'm done with this stuff here, I'm going to pick one up if you can wait. It'll make it easier to clean up down there."

"Jenna and I can start working on it right now, and if we still need the wet-vac, we can use it when you get back. We're just about done with our bookings anyway," Will announced.

"Yeah, I guess. At least you were down there the first time and know what needs to be done. Jenna, are you okay with that?" Mr. Jacobs asked tiredly. "It's going to be a messy job."

"Oh, yeah, I'm okay. I keep a pair of old jeans here, no big deal," Jenna tried to say nonchalantly. Her eyes were wide, and she had started tapping her foot on the floor. Will reached over and took her arm and held it firmly. She understood and stopped moving.

"I know Toby is busy with the display stands, and he has an exam tomorrow which I'm sure he needs to study for. I wouldn't want to slow him down on his work. If we need help, I'll yell. Or we can wait until we have the wet-vac," Will once again offered quietly. Toby shot him a disgruntled look for having his exam date thrown out in the open, but he wasn't really mad. He went back to concentrating again and grunted as he picked up the corner of the counter he was moving.

Jenna and Will finally made it downstairs alone. There was still roughly two inches of freestanding water over much of the floor. Even the lumpy ground from where the ghouls had been digging a few weeks ago was hard to find. Will retrieved the pickaxe and shovels they had previously brought down. Jenna looked over to the corner where Jonas had dug up the huge diamond.

"I wonder where all the diamonds from the burlap went. What do you think?" Jenna asked. She scanned the room, thinking of other possible locations. She tried to remember what the room had looked like when they were down here after falling through the picture. The only real landmark was the bearing wall in the middle of the room and the storm cellar door.

"That's a good question. Jonas had the pouch up in the Sewing Room and Mrs. Cabet used the small ones to make the circle. I'm sure she saw the big one. Well, we should probably start where Jonas left off. It was right about here, I think. The water needs to go anyway. Why don't you start skimming the water with the shovel and I'll try to get through a foot or two. I know I won't forget the feel of metal on that burlap," Will admitted, sliding over a large empty bucket.

Jenna took the deepest shovel they had and started scooping the water. She emptied each measly shovelful into the bucket while Will struck the floor with the shovel. Even though it was a sod floor, it was just as hard as concrete to unearth. The flood had loosened up about the first inch, but not much more. After five slowly balanced passes, she had collected less than an inch. The water level didn't seem to go down and Will wasn't making better progress. Using his foot to push his shovel into the sod, he unearthed only small chunks at a time. The water immediately filled in the spaces before Will could get more cleared. Cold and dirty water sloshed and dripped as they tried to move quickly. At first Will thought it would be an impossible task, but he found his rhythm. It just took much longer than he expected. They stopped a few times whenever it sounded like someone was close by, and they worried they would get caught. An hour later, they had slowed considerably from their exertion. The water was almost gone and a small, modest area had been dug up. Sweaty and covered with muddy splatters, they had gotten no farther in finding more diamonds.

"Mr. Jacobs just got back from the hardware store. I told him we were done and didn't need the wet-vac. Are you sure you heard them right, Will? I thought Jonas had only taken part of what he had buried. Remember he said it would have to do for now? Do you really think Jonas had more down here?" Jenna panted. She had just returned from dumping the bucket of water outside. She picked up her thick hair to fan the back of her sweaty neck and let it fall back down. Her shoulders slumped in defeat.

"Both he and James said they had a stash," Will replied. "It would make sense they would hide it here where no one would stumble on it. With boarders coming and going, where else would be safe? Anyway, we've seen both Jonas down here as well as the ghouls. I'm sure that's where Jonas told his friends to start. Don't be frustrated, it's just a minor setback. There's lots more room down here," he finished, reading Jenna's body language. Together they smoothed over the holes he had made in the damp floor.

Twenty-two

TWO DAYS LATER, the rains made their way upstairs. Mr. Jacobs exhaled heavily. He and Mr. Levy had been bickering repeatedly with all the pressure and unanticipated setbacks.

"Then I'll do it. We can't let this cause more damage by ignoring it," Mr. Jacobs said curtly. He pulled over a ladder from near the staircase, and set it up in the corner of the landing near the front of the Sewing Room door. A tear-stained leak had been trickling for almost an hour, and he felt he needed to assess the damage before calling in a roofing guy. The leak hadn't been found right away, so there was also a mess on the floor. Jenna was almost up to the second story. She was carrying old towels to soak up the puddle and had stopped short on the stairs. When Mr. Levy and Mr. Jacobs argued, it made her very uncomfortable.

Coming up behind her with a bucket, Will sensed her

unease and rubbed her shoulder. Jenna knew he was an empath but sometimes she wondered if he could read her mind. She sighed and walked around the ladder.

"Toby, we could use a hand here!" Mr. Levy yelled downstairs as he was bracing the ladder. "Grab a flashlight. I'm not sure what we going to find. Maybe another bucket, too, just in case."

"I've already got it covered," Toby said, turning the corner of the staircase with an empty plastic bucket and a toolbox full of flashlights and screwdrivers in the crook of his large arm. He took the stairs two at a time and was clicking on a flashlight before his father had climbed up to the ceiling.

"Damn. The corner is crumbling already, and this leak just started showing. This is doing more damage than I thought. Some spots are soft," Mr. Jacobs said, tentatively pushing in on the top of the wall. He shook his head. He rested his hand against a dry part of the corner wall to stabilize himself as he reached for the flashlight in Toby's hand. He no sooner grabbed the light when his other hand broke through the wall leaving a hole in the shape of his hand.

The black opening gaped at them while sheetrock pieces and paint chippings rained down. Toby lowered his head into his arm and rubbed the fragments off his face. Mr. Jacobs began to lose his balance and swayed precariously. Five arms from the men below reached up, grabbed his legs and steadied the ladder.

"Whoa. What the hell? Why…?" He stopped mid-sentence and swung the brightness into the newly formed hole.

He pulled himself up higher to see inside the fist-sized gap, his concern for ladder safety temporarily forgotten.

"What is it? How bad?" Mr. Levy asked impatiently. He looked at Toby who shrugged his shoulders. Will was studying his work boots absentmindedly as he held the ladder.

"There's another room up here. It's been boarded up all these years," Mr. Jacobs's muted voice answered. For a brief instant, there was no movement. Suddenly, Jenna cocked her head to one side and gasped. A confused look crossed her face as if she were trying to remember something just under the surface of her thoughts.

"That's the sixth room. I forgot about it. That's the one picture I couldn't figure out. Remember Mr. Jacobs, the one with the unknown staircase? And the other picture, the one of the Sewing Room, looked different because the ceiling was higher. I think it was Amelie's room." Jenna now knew this for certain. So much had gone on that night, they had forgotten.

Will thought it through for a moment while Mr. Levy asked Mr. Jacobs to come down so he could look. While the men were switching places, Jenna went to the Display Room, scanning the wall for the photograph she needed. When she returned with the photo in hand, Toby was leaning in closer to the conversation.

"Who would have boarded it up? Why?" Toby questioned.

"Sylvia?" Jenna heard herself say.

"Sylvia was hurt really bad, Jenna. We saw her. Could she have done this?" Will wondered aloud.

"Do you think this has something to do with the date that was on those pictures?" Mr. Jacobs asked Jenna.

"It better not," Mr. Levy's voice came from above them. "That stuff is over, I'm telling you right now. I'm done being ghost-chow." Highlighting his point, he accidentally banged his cast on the ladder as he was coming back down, now grumbling under his breath.

"I don't necessarily think this is connected to the dated photos. But the pictures reflect the Sewing Room being bigger, see?" Jenna showed everyone the picture. "And there is the staircase I couldn't place."

"What did you guys see up there? I don't understand," Toby asked, confused.

Mr. Levy motioned with his good arm for Toby to go up. "Apparently, our ceiling is the floor of another room, like an attic. From what I could see, it's a decent-sized room. It looks like it was added after the original building was built. From the picture, the high ceilings in the Sewing Room show what that room looked like before this room was built. Afterward, the ceilings were obviously shorter to accommodate the space taken above."

"So, the room was boarded up after the pictures?" Toby asked. A section of the metal ladder suddenly became illuminated as his LED came to life, shining on a concentrated point. He twirled the tiny light in his hand as he scaled the ladder.

"That had to be after Amelie was killed, anyway. The room was there when we fell into the picture. It must have been her room," Will agreed. "We didn't know it at the time, it was hard to tell. It's weird we never thought about the room itself," Will added a moment later.

Toby was now up the ladder, trying to peek through the

fragile layers. Chunks were coming down quickly, needing no help. His father yelled for him to stop, but the ceiling was coming down on itself now due to the water weight from the leak. Toby climbed back down and refolded the ladder. They all backed away as best they could, pulling the ladder behind them as the ceiling and corner of the wall crumbled. The dust cleared amidst coughing and sneezes.

"It's not really screwing up the integrity of the building, Dad. It was a pre-existing room that we just help uncover," Toby offered. His dad rolled his eyes briefly before turning his attention to this new addition. They all looked up into the room that had not been seen by human eyes in over a hundred and fifty years. A good-sized hole that could easily be crawled into from the ladder remained.

Toby and Will opened the ladder once again and started up before Mr. Levy could stop them. "What if this room is like the Sewing Room's window? What if we disturb something that is supposed to be left alone? At least keep to the beams so you don't fall through. There had to be a reason it was boarded up in the first place," he began. No one seemed to listen or care. Will, Toby, and Mr. Jacobs were through the hole before he was done speaking.

"There's only one way to find out for sure, Mr. Levy," Jenna answered as she grabbed a flashlight and climbed the ladder, squeezing herself into the opening.

Mr. Levy drew in a deep breath and shook his head. He had tried to convince himself the theatrics were over. He had seen and heard too much to ignore as much as he wanted to. Now he was becoming bitter because the supernatural was taking up more of his life. Even after time to absorb the existence of the paranormal—something he had witnessed not only once, but twice now—he still didn't like it.

"Crap. Here we go again," he muttered as he one-handedly ascended the ladder.

They were all standing on the solid surface of a loft room, the air thick and pungent from years of being boarded up. Other than the small area of the floor, the ceiling from the level below that had disintegrated, there was no other damage to the floor. No visible leak could be found above the wall that crumbled either. It was almost as if the hole opened to make the room known.

"Oh crap, here we go again!" Mr. Levy repeated, this time louder.

Toby's flashlight waved forward now across the room. It roamed quickly, trying to take in its whole surroundings in a moment's time.

Jenna felt her stomach start to sour as her eyes adjusted to the familiarity of Amelie's room. From where she was in the far corner, she shone her light and squinted to see the spot where she knew Amelie's body had laid. She exhaled loudly when she saw nothing. She walked across the room slowly, ignoring Mr. Levy's advice to stay put. Her footsteps stopped abruptly and her breath caught when she reached the exact spot where Amelie died. About three feet of the flooring was darker than the rest, visible even through the layers of dirt.

Jenna looked over once when the men said a few things to each other quietly, and Mr. Jacobs nodded and climbed back down the hole onto the ladder. Jenna noted she could barely see the tiny opening in the floor he disappeared through, and was too preoccupied to recall what they said.

The space was barren. The wardrobe screen which had been to the right when she and Will found themselves here was gone, as was the short bed that had been in the corner directly across from them. A few large spider webs filled the top angle of both walls. The room was an odd space, narrow width, with no windows. To Jenna, it was about the size of a very large bedroom or a small living room. The wooden walls were different from the rest of the building. These were wide planks that reminded Jenna of railroad ties, except they were not as thick. Even in the weak light, they looked gray rather than brown due to the dust that had accumulated in the grooves of the unfinished wood.

There was a small doorway across from Jenna that didn't have a doorknob. The door behind her had a handle, as well as another door on the opposite side away from the guys.

Jenna continued walking to the wall in front of her. She searched, unable to stop herself until she found what she knew would be there. In the dim light provided by the flashlight, Jenna was able to make out a small hole that remained in the wall, the only evidence of Amelie's death. She touched the rough wood, her finger feeling the tangible proof of the tragic past. A few seconds went by before Jenna realized Mr. Jacobs had come back and had handed out some larger tools. Everyone had split up to the doors. Mr. Jacobs and Will were trying to figure out how to open the door on the opposite wall. It was difficult to open even though it was the one with the handle.

"If my direction is right, it'll lead downstairs into the Sewing Room," Mr. Jacobs said. He was using a large flathead screwdriver to un-stick the jammed door and stopped to push up the sleeves of his shirt.

"There will be a small landing through the door, but yes, that's the door we went out of, and it brought us out onto the Sewing Room. Of course, back then it was the living area of the Cabets, I think, according to a small photograph we saw," Will replied.

Jenna started walking, needing the company of the others. The door popped open and creaked loudly. It was pitch black on the other side.

"Well, in our reality, the stairs lead to the Sewing Room's wall," Toby stated, his flashlight meeting Mr. Levy's. Both flashlights examined the area for a moment before starting towards the other door. Will and Mr. Jacobs had beaten them there, debating. They were trying to figure out how to gain leverage to open the handle-less door.

"We're in luck. I actually found this in the toolbox downstairs. Here, try the crowbar, Muscles." Mr. Jacobs offered it to Toby. Mr. Levy mumbled something that sounded like "right, lucky."

Mr. Levy held his flashlight with Jenna's even though she noticed a sour expression on his face. She knew how much this kind of thing bothered him. The three men worked at the small door for a while. The only sounds were their breathing as they toiled at the handle, the occasional suggestion, and words of encouragement. Jenna could no longer smell the musty thickness of the room, just the sweat from the exertion of the men in front of her. Finally, with a small splintered crack, the door swung loosely open as if well oiled. Jenna and Mr.

Levy were the first to lean in, their flashlights shining brightly. Tentatively, they all peered inside.

Will stood there with the others, trying to get his bearings. His mind still raced with why the ceiling was leaking water that had no source, and crumbled to make a hole just large enough to fit into.

Flashlight beams bounced off the ceiling and floor. The room was long and just as small as the room they came from. Rectangular in shape and coated with years of filth, it, too, was completely bare except for a small table in the middle.

"That's weird," Mr. Levy said, confused.

Will knew the table was too short and tiny to be used as anything practical. "I think I know what that is," he whispered, his voice wavering. He was the first to move forward through the doorway. He waved the flashlight at his feet, barely able to see the floor through the inch-thick dirt. His boots left prints where he walked, but no floorboards creaked. The closer he got to the lone podium the more his suspicion was confirmed.

"Well, what is it? It looks like a kid's table," Mr. Levy guessed.

"It's not a table at all. It's an altar."

"An altar? Like for church?" Jenna asked, wiping her forehead with the sleeve of her shirt.

Will looked at the items in front of him, but something didn't feel right. "No, for Pagan worshipping. It's set up with candles in the way a witch would use for ceremony."

"But these rooms have been boarded up and abandoned for well over a century," Mr. Levy countered.

"That doesn't matter. Our rituals haven't changed." He

frowned, noticing what didn't sit well in his stomach. Some of the items appeared clean, almost shiny.

The darkness, the moldy aroma, and the unknown that lurked within collected together. For a brief moment, Will's thoughts flashed to the many times his mom and aunts had set up makeshift altars in old homes to redirect unsettled spirits. Some of his most scary memories were of those interventions.

Jenna placed her hand on top of Will's arm. Despite the heat, her skin was cool with goose bumps. Her flashlight started shaking, glinting off the delicate diamonds that surrounded several candles on the altar.

"Sylvia," Jenna and Will said together.

"This isn't right," Mr. Jacobs said slowly, joining them. His brow furrowed. "Look at this. There should be a hundred and fifty years of grime on all of this, and it looks like these were just placed here."

"I don't like this," Mr. Levy complained.

"Will, what does this mean?" Toby's deep voice from behind startled everyone. He stepped up, using the end of his shirt to wipe his face off.

Will bent down. The objects on the ancient stand were covered by an obscured cloth. The raw diamonds were roughly the size of marbles and had only the slightest trace of dust on them that could have come from what they kicked up walking over. At each corner of the square table was a small, pudgy candle melted into a shapeless lump from years and years of hot summers. The stubs looked like they had held color at one time. In the middle of the altar were other candles, also without form, faded into gray due to the dirt. In the middle, dull but clean, was a large pillar candle. This was an uncommon shade of turquoise-green, well used, but had several weeks of purpose remaining.

"Turquoise?" Will murmured to himself. He strained his eyes and leaned in closer to look. The material under all of this was grotesquely decayed. What hung off the sides, about six inches in length, had weathered better and remained intact with a hand-sewn hem. The thick covering that marked the passage of time drew the mind to acknowledge that select pieces had just recently been placed on top. It was disturbing to the eye in a macabre sort of way.

"What about the turquoise candle, Will?"

"I know there's too much that looks clean on the altar, Mr. Jacobs, especially the turquoise candle. I've just never seen one used in a ceremony." He reached out to touch the candlewick on the pillar candle in question. It crumbled where it had burned; a fresh, dark smudge was left on his fingers. "This has been lit recently," he announced quietly.

Twenty-three

EVERYONE HESITANTLY TOOK a step closer to examine the details. No one could argue with the evidence. It almost was expected the area would smell badly. But despite the tangibly decomposing effects, the air surrounding it was not putrid. It was, however, very distinct.

"What the hell am I smelling?" Mr. Levy asked loudly. "I am at my wit's end dealing with all the work and stress this building has dumped on me."

Jenna's breathing sped up with nervousness and her hand tightened on Will's arm.

"Something fruity?" Will suggested. This was totally out of context for a hundred-and fifty-year-old deterioration.

"Apple, I think," Jenna decided after a moment. She was beginning to feel more restless the more they discovered.

"What does *this* mean?" Toby's voice reflected the exasperation most of them felt.

"I don't understand how we can be smelling apple in the middle of this huge building," admitted Mr. Jacobs.

"Could this table be from the beginning of the month when all those ghosts were running rampant?" Mr. Levy asked. It would have made sense, yet Jenna had a feeling it wasn't related. More questions were voiced with possible answers. No one knew for sure.

It was after nine that evening before Sulis made it over to evaluate the situation. Mr. Jacobs was the one to initiate the call and ask that she come over. He and Mr. Levy had tried to have a private conversation about what they should do, but their voices traveled easily, and tipped everyone off to the polar opinions each had. They both agreed this was beyond what a member of the Historical Association could comprehend. Even though both trusted Will, he was employed by them after all, Mr. Levy was all for leaving their discovery alone and patching the hole permanently. Only Mr. Jacobs felt compelled to find guidance from someone more knowledgeable. That knowledge rested with Sulis in that area. Pressured not only by his partner, but by knowing there were people in the next room anxious and waiting, Mr. Levy consented.

As they walked upstairs to the second floor to show Sulis the hole, Will and Jenna recapped their first experience of falling into the picture, selectively omitting anything to do with the diamonds. Jenna was now becoming uncomfortable leaving out this information. She was getting anxious that it was a bigger part of the puzzle that everyone needed to know about, and losing a stash of diamonds was worth the risk. The few times she had started to mention Jonas and what he and Henry were doing, Will had spoken over her, changing the topic. Jenna just stared at him.

Sulis eyed their odd behavior and repositioned her glasses, contemplating. "Well, something definitely feels intense here. It's muted, though, muddied. Almost as if there was an attempt to keep it covered up, which, obviously, doesn't bode well with the wall practically coming down on its own."

She put her hands on her hips as she looked up at the new entryway into what the group was starting to refer to as the Loft. Again, done up for the evening for three readings, she was dressed in her long gown and cloak. Her hair was spiked in purposefully arranged disarray with black streaks throughout. Her many bracelets clinked together as they shifted on her wrist.

"I'm sorry I'm not able to get my plus-size up there. I'm sure the rooms themselves are interesting, too."

"Will and I have agreed we think the first room was Amelie's. That's the room she was killed in and the room that looked most like a bedroom. We never went through that other door. We're all assuming it was James and Sylvia's room," Jenna informed her.

"If the Sewing Room was their living quarters and the room we came from was Amelie's, it makes sense it would be her parent's room," Will added.

Sulis nodded thoughtfully as they all headed back downstairs to a small table in the middle of room adjacent to the great room. They had wanted to leave everything untouched in the loft, but were aware it probably wasn't possible for Sulis to climb upstairs, not to mention walk on the possibly unstable floor. Will brought down the diamonds and the turquoise pillar candle separately. They were the only things that could be removed. They were able to manage maneuvering the altar through the small opening and kept it intact. It was helpful the other candles had melded into the rotted fabric, unable to be pried loose, which had then bonded to the altar itself. It had been necessary to tip it onto its side to clear the odd-shaped hole. It now stood next to the table for Sulis to see.

"No doubt she was practicing and these are all hers," Sulis began, as she sat down and picked up the diamonds. Will stood next to her. Everyone else remained standing while Jenna sat down in the chair in front of Sulis, put her legs up against the table and folded her arms across her chest. They covered up the body of the original black and white Mickey Mouse on her monochromatic sweatshirt, only leaving his head and his rail hat visible below the numbers nineteen twenty-eight. Sulis looked at her as Jenna stared at Will intently. His gaze was tightly controlled, looking only at the altar.

Sulis absentmindedly poured the jewels from cupped hand to cupped hand, thinking. "Hmm, it is fragrant," she noted, surprised. She brought the gems to her nose then scrutinized them closely. The smell of apples had lingered on the items that were placed on the table. It was vague in the Loft, but concentrated more so directly near the table.

Sulis sighed and set the diamonds down on the table, turning towards the small altar. The room was silent as she looked over every piece. After asking to borrow a flashlight, she pointed the beam directly onto each candle, leaning in closely.

"This table was set up as an altar. The arrangement suggests a circle for protection." Will nodded in agreement. She backed up for the others to see and started pointing, the chiming of her bracelets the only sound. "It had four candles at each corner representing the four elements and cardinal directions. Those candles were probably all primary colors at one time. I could see just a hint of color when I shone the flashlight up against them."

"And the other mounds of candles could have represented the God, Goddess, and the three aspects of the maiden, mother, and crone. They would have been black, white, and red," Will added. It had taken a while for him to feel comfortable with the others about these types of things. Now, his confidence of this knowledge was evident.

"She could have used them to create the spell cast on the pictures for all we know. I'm intrigued with the turquoise candle. Diamonds could be used for ceremonies, yet I have no clue as to what this candle was used for. I also doubt that she set this up when we contacted her through the Ouija. That wouldn't have been necessary, and she definitely would have known that. She was a very powerful witch to cast the spells she has and to still reach us in so many ways, including olfactory. To be honest, that is very advanced and on a level I've never managed or even understood well enough to try."

"You think Mrs. Cabet is making us smell apples?" Mr. Levy posed skeptically.

"Can you give a better explanation?" Sulis challenged calmly.

"Yes, there's a huge apple orchard right outside this building, and the bees that have been buzzing us for the last few weeks are telling us they're ripe."

"But can you usually smell them when you're in the museum?"

"No."

"What about when you're next to an open window?"

"Well, no, not very much."

"Then I'll surmise you wouldn't be able to smell apples this clearly inside a windowless room set in a larger room without windows. There must be something of great importance we have missed that she is trying to tell us. We are being bombarded with clues. What do you get out of this, Will?" Sulis asked.

"Turquoise candles are nothing that I'm familiar with. Could she be telling us about the orchard?" Will asked.

"What about the diamonds?" Mr. Levy asked.

"We found that big diamond a few weeks ago in the Sewing Room and now these," Mr. Jacobs agreed. "I know the Herkimer mines aren't that far away, but what do these stand for?"

Jenna shifted, looking down at her nails, fidgeting nervously. Will walked next to her and reached over to hold her hand. Sulis eyed them suspiciously for a brief moment, then thought of something else.

"Hmm, I did say there were shiny things here, too," she added. "I can only imagine that Sylvia would have used them for ceremony. But they are worth quite a bit when they're this size. Why wouldn't she try to sell them? I get the impression she was unhappy having boarders while her husband worked the land. They couldn't have made much money. These stones would have brought some welcome relief."

"She never struck me as a material girl," Jenna said evenly. She was sure her eyes would betray her, so she kept looking at her hand in Will's. She was torn between wanting to lay it all on the table and keeping it confidential. "And it still doesn't explain the turquoise pillar."

Will and Sulis delved into a deep discussion of Wiccan symbolism that the others couldn't keep up with. Mr. Levy, who had started pacing through the main rooms, began to sigh loudly and grumble under his breath. He was the one to finally bring the group back to the present.

"What do we do about the room?" he asked bluntly. He was in a foul mood, his patience stretched thin. The group all sat down to talk and gave mixed suggestions, mostly that they would return the altar to the room. They would leave it as is, but not allow anyone to go up to the new level. Will recommended the room be blocked off until after Halloween.

"That's all we need, the whole spirit world having séances in the attic while we try to have a Halloween party downstairs," Toby interjected to lighten the mood. His words fell on deaf ears, everyone was lost in thought.

"I just don't want any more dangerous situations," Mr. Levy explained. "We're talking a lot of completely ignorant people walking in and out of here in about a week. There are too many variables that we don't understand, let alone can control. Our liability will go through the roof. Can you imagine what kind of lawsuits could come of this?"

"Someone could get killed," Mr. Jacobs stated quietly. "I

think we've been really lucky so far. Are we willing to push it further? Maybe this building is too unsafe to have open next week."

"The museum would have to be shut down if we don't have that party next week!" Jenna cried. "I've had the spread sheets explained to me. We need the funds to make it through another year!"

"Yes, but at what cost to us personally? Are you willing for any of us to get hurt or worse?" Mr. Levy snapped. Sulis stood up abruptly, her hands out in front of her. The soft sound of metal on metal lasted only a moment as the long-tapered sleeves of her cloak swayed. The conversation stopped.

"For now, let's keep the altar upstairs where it was found. We need to take a break from this. It's late, and there are too many emotions flying around in here. Something will come to us. We still have some time."

Mr. Levy slid his chair back quickly. It made a screeching noise in the otherwise silent room. He turned and walked into the office before anyone said anything else.

"He's still in a lot of pain. You have to give him that," Mr. Jacobs said. "Mark just isn't big on the supernatural. I'm just as interested as you are, but we have to think responsibly, not just out of curiosity. We need to do this the right way, whatever that means." He got up slowly, heavy with indecision, and walked towards the office.

JENNA TOSSED IN her sleep. Her nose stung from the thick, suffocating smell. She was shivering, cold—almost to the point of numbness—despite the fitted fleece sweater she could feel she was wearing. Her jeans did nothing to hold her heat in either. It was dark as she walked in a foggy mist among the apple trees. Her shoes managed the mud and rough ground as she stepped on tree roots and small limbs that were indiscernible beneath her. There were nagging thoughts that she couldn't quite remember. Time seemed to stand still, and she walked aimlessly for she had no purpose. She felt the presence of others, briefly seeing Sulis's shadow and hearing Will yell once, as if in pain, off in the distance. Jenna worried that they needed help. Even though she stumbled towards their voices, she was unable to find them.

The dream morphed and the mill materialized in front of her. As always, it seemed to call her and she gravitated towards it, fumbling on the uneven ground. She tried to keep the building in her sights through the thick fog. Each time she tried to focus on it, it would blur as if it had disappeared. She was only able to see it in her peripheral vision, like stars in the sky at night. Finally, she reached the main entrance. She had just started up the steps when the door closed swiftly in front of her.

Jenna awoke abruptly with a start. It was still dark outside and the house was quiet. She groaned as she leaned over the bed to see her alarm clock. It was early, seven fifteen. Fortunately, it was Saturday and there was no school. It was also not a Will day. This was their family weekend day. Flopping onto her back and snuggling under the covers, she stretched, feeling both tired and somehow achy. Her thoughts returned to her dream.

It was common for her to dream every night, but not necessarily to remember all the particulars. It was rare that she could recall everything. This one was different; she remembered it in great detail. It had been windy. It seemed like moments ago she could feel the sting on her cheeks. Jenna touched her face and her cheeks. They were cold. Not that it meant anything special, her parents kept the house cool at night for sleeping. She knew the sweater she was wearing was the cream colored one that kept her warm even in the dead of winter. Deciding it must have been the apple orchard she dreamt about, her brow furrowed. There were no large root systems there that close to the surface. Maybe the winds had brought down the branches she had been tripping over. Her feet did ache though and she reached under the blankets to massage her foot.

Jenna thought back to the dreams she had in the very beginning of her time in Orchard Creek, the dreams of Elizabeth and needing to find the handkerchief. She wasn't sure if this was the same. She needed someone else's opinion. She wished it weren't so early. No one was up yet and Jenna really wanted to talk to Tina.

The chores her parents had planned started after breakfast and took up the whole day. Unfortunately, it only kept her body busy. Her thoughts were distracted. In between carrying the deck chairs to the shed and helping to take down the canopy and netting from the gazebo, her dream kept replaying over and over in her mind. What did it mean? She couldn't figure it out or why it wouldn't go away. There seemed to be no good time to talk to her dad about it, with her mom and brother there. They wouldn't understand and Jenna wasn't up to explaining everything. Toby slept in on Saturdays, then hit the gym. And Tina had private music lessons so Jenna would have to wait.

Tonight, she would find out if they would hold the Annual Halloween Ball. Since everyone would be there, she had made up her mind she was going to tell the others about the diamonds. That was another reason why she was glad it was family day. She didn't want to have too much time alone with Will. That topic would most likely come up, and Jenna didn't want to talk about it with him. Obviously, he wasn't budging. Just spilling it out in the open later would be her best bet. It would mean letting Will down. She was torn, ruminating about it the rest of the day, knowing how unhappy that would make him. With only an hour until work, the phone rang.

"Hey, it's Tina."

"Oh, I'm so glad it's you. I've wanted to talk to you before tonight because—"

"Jenna, I don't think I'll be able to make it."

"What? No!"

"They had a call-in at the store. I'm stuck here until the manager can either relieve me or find someone to close."

"Deb lives, like, twenty minutes away."

"Yeah, but she was visiting her mother-in-law in Mercy hospital out of town. She might get here in ten minutes, or an hour. No one else wants to come in on their weekend off. I've been by myself since noon already and it doesn't matter if the mall is dead. We get dinged if we pull the gate down before 9:30. Uh oh, I've got a customer. I'll talk to you later." The phone went dead, and Jenna's excitement fell. She ate her dinner with her family, barely tasting the food.

Jenna drove up at the same time as Toby. She waited for him to get out of his truck so they would go in together. He slammed the door shut, frowning when he looked at her.

"You look really tired, Jenna. Didn't you sleep at all last night?" he asked as they walked through the front door. Jenna smiled weakly and waved at Sulis who was already in the great room. Will was turned away from her.

"I had a really strange dream last night that I just can't shake. It's almost like when I was dreaming Elizabeth's thoughts all those years ago. It was cold, and it was hard to breathe. Sulis and Will were there, too. I could hear them." At this, Sulis's smile fell, and Will turned abruptly, his forehead wrinkled, his eyes wide. There was a large red scratch down his cheek.

"What?" Will whispered. She noticed for the first time how tired he looked as well. Her eyes moved again quickly to Sulis and saw the same weary expression.

"Mr. Jacobs, you might want to join us for this," Sulis called to the office. "Jenna, tell me about your dream last night," she ordered as they all sat at the large table. Jenna described wandering in the orchard and hearing Will cry out. She described tripping often over the uneven ground and then walking towards the museum where the door locked her out.

"Wow," was all Will could reply at first. "I woke up this morning with this scratch on my face. I assumed it was from a sharp nail or something while I was sleeping. I tossed and turned a lot last night with strange dreams of apple trees and wading through water. It got weird after I woke up, and Mom said she dreamt I cut my face on a tree branch in the orchard."

Jenna felt all the color drain from her face. "We were all dreaming the same dream?" she whispered.

"Not exactly which is more fascinating in its difference," Sulis replied after a moment. She looked completely different, average, wearing just plain jeans and a deep orange tunic shirt. Her auburn hair was spiked but had no color accents. "I dreamt I was roaming the orchard, except when I looked at the ground, it was glassy and smooth. A large candle was in my hands but the particulars of it were unclear. I sensed you were there, Jenna, even though I didn't actually see you. I seemed to be following Will. The underbrush got thick and he was grazed by a low hanging branch. The scratch on his face in my dream is in the same place as the scratch on his face when he woke up," Sulis explained. Mr. Jacobs was shifting uncomfortably in his chair.

"I was in the orchard in my dream too, except it was so incredibly windy. I heard my mom, but I was focused on trying to get to you Jenna. No matter how hard I tried, I couldn't catch up to you. It scared me to see you walking on all those bones."

Twenty-four

"BONES? OK, NOW I'm creeped out," Toby interjected. Mr. Jacobs shook his head, wincing. "Whatever is going down has left this building and is now festering in your heads while you're sleeping. We can't possibly have the museum open anymore. Maybe it should be closed down until…" he hesitated, trying to collect his thoughts. "I don't know when. It's not as clean cut as when we knew we had to shut the window. This is something totally different."

"I was walking on bones?" Jenna murmured dreamily. "I thought they were the roots of the trees." She was lost in thought. Without forewarning, the words tumbled out of her mouth. "Jonas and Henry have diamonds buried here somewhere. They tried to find them when they came through the pictures." She then realized what she had just said.

Will glared at her and then turned away. He looked

disgusted and angry as he mumbled under his breath. "Trust, sure."

Jenna's face reddened as she saw how angry Will was. The lump in her throat was painful. The future of the museum was uncertain, and no loyalty could save it. She didn't know where she stood with Will either.

"Finally, it comes out. I know you, Will. I can read you like no one's business," Sulis said. "You and Jenna have been acting strangely since this started back up again. The diamonds were the secret. Now we have an idea what they represent. The shiny things have a connection to Jonas and Sylvia at least. Let's start putting this together. I need some paper and pens."

"Why didn't you tell us this sooner?" Mr. Jacobs demanded. "That's twice both of you have been sneaky. It's not earning you any points as employees, if you catch my drift. This isn't some field day fun house. We seem to be pawns in a dangerous game. I would think you would respect all our safety more than… selfish desires." He paused, disappointed.

"I need to start canceling plans. I'm sure Mark will be only too willing to start. He's in the office right now already pulling his hair out I bet. This is really last minute. I guess we can say we have a major repair that will have to shut us down. We're going to have to let the radio and newspaper know as well, and the town's not going to be too happy about this. I know I'm not. I guess this is it for the museum; we can't run this place on air," he muttered, getting up. "Sulis, we have paper if you want to follow me."

"Jenna, where's Tina?" Toby asked with urgency.

"Stuck at work," Jenna answered automatically. Toby nodded.

"I think I'll give her a call. Excuse me." He went with Sulis into the office, which left Will and Jenna alone for the time being. Jenna was scared to look up. She felt sick to her stomach, although part of her was relieved to have the diamond matter out in the open. Will didn't say anything, and the seconds ticked by.

"I'm sorry, Will. Everyone needed to know this stuff so we can figure this out," Jenna whispered to her lap. She looked up cautiously through her bangs at Will. His mouth was set and his nostrils were flaring. Her expression changed, her hurt feelings fueling the anger that grew from how immature he was acting.

"Don't take the liberty of including me with your plans, Jenna," he said flatly. Jenna shied away from his words as if slapped. That caught her off guard. Her lip started to quiver and she bit down hard and tried to concentrate on how frustrated she had become to stop the emotions from spilling over. Will's dark, inviting eyes had become hard as he spoke to her. His eyebrows quirked down once like they did when he got upset, but it cleared too quickly for Jenna to be sure. What she did recognize was a look of shock before he got up and walked away from her, stopping to stare out the window. Sulis came back with paper and pens, slowing down when she saw Jenna, then looked over at Will, his back to them.

"This is much worse than just the problems here," Sulis commented. She sat down quietly, not sure when to start. "If you will write down all the details you can remember, we can try to match them up with our details," she asked Jenna. Her amber eyes locked on Jenna's brown ones, trying to read the damage and reassure at the same time. Sulis was still watching her when she called to her son. "Will, are you going to help here?" Jenna's expression changed slightly, and Sulis understood the complications.

"Yes, ma'am," Will replied obediently. He walked over and took a piece of paper and a pen. He sat down next to his mother and began writing.

Jenna had difficulty concentrating but managed to put everything down. She raised her paper to Sulis at the same time Will did. She looked up hopefully. Will did not make eye contact. Instead, he watched Toby head out the main door, while he folded his arms in front of himself, gripping the sides of his beige linen shirt.

Toby came back in a moment later with Tina who was removing her purse from across her chest, laughing loudly until she realized how quiet the room was. She made her way to Jenna, took her hand and squeezed it before taking a seat.

Mr. Jacobs walked back into the room about the time that Jenna's dad arrived. He had called Mr. Stevens to tell him to gear-up for another round. Sulis had several notes on the paper in front of her that included columns. She finished writing and put her pen down. Mr. Levy peered around the corner of the office door to see what was going on and ended up joining the group. He was in a slightly better mood now that the Halloween Ball was cancelled. They all sat down, trying to get up to speed. The tension was thick between Will and Jenna.

"First of all, Will and Jenna should come clean on what

they haven't been telling us before we go any further," Sulis suggested.

A dead silence filled the air. Jenna sighed shakily and started from the beginning, filling in the blanks they had left out. "Jonas had us dig in the basement until we found his bag. It had one huge diamond and several smaller ones. Apparently, he had some kind of deal with James. He and Henry had been to the Herkimer mines and what they had taken out didn't sound legal. Jonas even said they were wanted men. I'm pretty sure James was hiding them here in exchange for a cut of the profit. There was more buried here, although we don't know where. Even the ghosts that came back a few weeks ago couldn't find it. But it's here.

"Sylvia used the small diamonds from Jonas's bag to make the circle we used to get back that night. The big diamond was right in the room with her, too. I'm not sure how much is here, actually." Jenna never once looked up for fear of losing her composure and missed the impressed look that crossed Will's face briefly before it hardened back into a guarded mask.

Sulis scratched notes periodically. Will interjected a few details that Jenna hadn't seen or observed, but kept his words short and precise. Jenna was exhausted by the time they finished.

"I've been trying to find a common thread from all the details of the dreams Will, Jenna, and I shared. Or perhaps we should be looking at what wasn't common. I've made a few lists, including what already happened at the beginning of this month. Maybe we should try the Ouija board, too. I've got a lot of specifics but no motivation or goal. As far as I can tell, there is more to this museum than just the building itself.

There is something very important in the orchard next to us," Sulis finished.

"If it weren't for the doom and gloom we're in the middle of right now, a buried treasure would be kinda rad," Toby admitted.

Tina's eyes were as wide as saucers. She hadn't realized so much more had happened. Will continued to sit with his arms tight across himself, not looking at anyone. Mr. Stevens only seemed concerned by the complete look of dejectedness on his daughter's face. He noted she wasn't sitting near Will. He eyed the boyfriend coolly.

"Do you think Mrs. Cabet is trying to have us find the diamonds?" Mr. Levy asked. He took his glasses off and rubbed his eyes before putting them back on.

"Where? In the orchard? Why find them now? For what, though? I don't see a clear reason," Mr. Jacobs countered.

"No, it sounds like the candle has some significance," Tina offered.

Toby sat up straighter, folding his arms on the table. "We're not thinking of who this message is pertaining to. There's something that needs to be done by Jenna, Will, and Sulis."

"Yes, I believe that's true," Sulis agreed.

Jenna shook her head, perplexed. "The question is what we're supposed to do."

"Dig," Toby replied. It came out as both a question and a statement.

"And when? Halloween is two days away," Will added quietly for the first time, not looking up.

Everyone's faces confirmed they all understood what would happen from here. Mr. Levy groaned quietly and Tina wasn't the only one who looked nervous.

It was Sulis who said what was in everyone's thoughts. "I think we all should come back and meet tomorrow night. All I can surmise is that Sylvia will lead us. We should be on the lookout. There will be more."

The group dispersed and Sulis and Will left without saying anything further. Mr. Levy got up with an air of finality and headed straight for the office with Mr. Jacobs trailing behind him.

"I'll, uh, see you at home," was all Jenna's father said. She waved him away with a weak smile.

Tina rose slowly. "Good night, Mr. Stevens."

Jenna just sat at the table. Somewhere in the back of her mind she realized Toby must have called Tina for moral support, because there was no other reason for her to show up at the tail end of their meeting.

"Hey," her friend said gently, sitting back down at her side. Jenna held it together until Tina opened her arms out. They sat that way a few minutes while Tina allowed her friend to cry on her shoulder. When Jenna was more in control, Tina looked at her worriedly. "Toby gave me a quick re-cap before I walked in. What happened?"

"I betrayed Will's trust. It's something he's craved but never really had before. And I ruined it. He should have been able to trust me. But not telling everyone about the diamonds, now that we're somehow sharing dreams, is dangerous in this place. So now I've lost the museum and Will."

"Breathe, sister. This is a lot to process on a good day, and you're tired. Maybe getting a good night's sleep will help."

Jenna did as she was told. "But what if I run into Will in my dreams tonight? What if he tells me off for messing up our secret?" When Tina didn't say anything, she plowed on. "He told me not to include him in my plans. Either he doesn't want me to include him in my life," Jenna's breath caught, "or he doesn't want to be included in the problems here. Either way I lose."

"It looked like Will's been cooperating since I've been here."

"He did, but his mother asked him to. So that leaves our relationship. He hasn't spoken to me, dang, he hasn't even looked at me since then. That's not a good sign."

Tina started to put on her coat. "He did look really upset though. He's not shallow; I know that much about him. I doubt it's because of a lost opportunity. I have a hunch it isn't because he was tattled on."

Jenna's face became hopeful. "You think he feels bad because we're fighting?"

"Hurtful words tend to be tossed out in the heat of the moment."

"I really want to believe that. I don't know what I'd do if I irreparably damaged what we have."

"Hang in there, friend. I love you."

"Love you too."

Jenna was hoping she was too worn out to dream at all when she finally climbed into bed that night. Between working outside much of the day and the emotional tension that night she was wiped out. She replayed the events of the night and the conversation with Tina, over-analyzing every detail until, her eyes burning with overtiredness, she fell into a deep sleep. It was already two in the morning.

SHE WALKED QUICKLY but stumbled often. She was searching outside for something but the rough terrain made it nearly impossible. It was also pitch black. Holding a candle in front of her, the light did little to illuminate her surroundings; it only outlined the trees she was walking between. It was eerie. There were too many shadows bouncing off the remaining apples, too much depth behind the tall trees.

She was cold again and made a point to look down. Her old-fashioned, thin cotton dress was long sleeved, fitted at the wrists. It had a scoop neckline and gathered at her waist before extending down to her feet. She felt the heat from the flame on her chest and face, but was concerned that her long hair would catch on fire, the way the wind was whipping about. As she continued to walk, a gust hit her full on, but the flicker of light stayed steady. The air was crisp and had the distinct smell of decaying leaves. Gradually it became harder to breathe. She stopped walking and dragged in a ragged breath of air, gasping.

Suddenly, she sat up in bed, dizzy. The room settle around her. It was Sunday morning and the bleak, gray light of late fall filtered in from the bay window next to her bed. It wasn't the warm, buttery sunlight from the Indian summer a few weeks ago. It was cold-looking even from the cast it made on her hunter green comforter. Rolling over onto her side, she stared at the framed copy of Renoir she had on the wall without really seeing it. She could hear the wind start up. Random leaves hit the siding of her house like an autumn version of a snowstorm.

Downstairs, the microwave beeped and utensil drawers opened and slammed shut. That was Peter's signature weekend quietness. If he was already up it must be late, Jenna thought. Lifting her head just a little, she read the numbers on her clock. It was nine-thirty, later than she ever slept.

Last night's discussion led only to believe they needed to dig, but for what, they weren't sure. They didn't even know where. The orchard was pretty big when you thought about the size of a shovel. If they were to get anything accomplished before Halloween, they needed more information. If they needed to do anything on Halloween night, they were clueless. Her dream last night was disappointing. It didn't show her where she was, let alone what she needed to do. There had to be some significance to the candle and orchard. At least those things kept repeating. She was hoping things would be better at the museum tonight, and that Will and Sulis had better luck with their dreams.

Once again, she turned into the drive right behind Toby. He walked right over to the passenger side as she shut her car off. He didn't wait for an invitation but opened the door and sat down. A faint whiff of his Oleg Cassini cologne followed in after him.

"How are you holding up?" he asked. He shook his head when he saw the dark circles under her eyes. "Not so good, huh?" He reached into his pocket and handed her a chocolate bar. It was the kind that had caramel, nuts, and dried fruit. "I had a feeling you wouldn't be. Here, I stopped at the store before coming over."

Jenna shook her head and smiled as she took the bar. "This is my favorite."

"Yeah, I know. What can I say, I'm an observant guy."

"You're the best, thanks." Jenna face fell again and she stared at the package in her hand. "I don't know anything anymore. I hurt Will. Again. But I couldn't take it any longer. Was I right in speaking up, Tobe? I really think it goofed everything up with him."

He was thoughtful for a moment. "Well, you were just thinking of the bigger picture. What would you have done if you both found more diamonds, hoark them for yourselves? Cashed them in for pocket money?"

"Hoark?" Jenna laughed weakly.

"Yeah, my word. Hoark." Toby was always good for comic relief and it did lessen the nerves she was bound in. "But it doesn't fit. That doesn't sound like you, Jenna. You'd do anything for this place. You have, time and time again. Even I can see what you did wasn't out of malice. I hope Will weighs his options and sees the real gem he's going to lose if he's not careful."

Jenna blushed but smiled and popped a chunk of the candy bar into her mouth. She felt a little better. Of course, she was only thinking what was best for the museum.

"Neither one of us would've snuck off with diamonds or even money if we found any. Actually, we both talked about how cool it would be to present the diamonds to everyone and get that recognition. Apparently, it got out of hand. Maybe if I had spoken up sooner, we would have figured this out before we had to cancel the Ball and lose the place."

"Don't put all this on yourself. I don't think that's true," Toby replied. "This is more complicated than a quick fix. As much as I could blame you for all the problems at the museum, I really can't. It started because of you five years ago, but this stuff's been sitting there, concealed for years, just waiting for someone to set off the trip. You know, someone to put things in motion. That's been you. You're someone special. You've been the key each time. Come on, we gotta do this."

Twenty-five

THEY GOT OUT of the car, Jenna's hair whipping straight up in the wind. Toby put his hand on her shoulder and squeezed her hard. Jenna thought about those words as she and Toby walked up the main steps. It gave her some comfort to know, at least, that Toby had her back. He always had a different perspective on things.

The door opened before they reached it and Will walked out looking straight ahead. "Let's get this show on the road."

Mr. Levy was out next with a handful of framed pictures from the displays inside. Mr. Jacobs, Mr. Stevens, Tina, and Sulis followed after him holding flashlights. Sulis handed Jenna and Toby a flashlight as she came through. It was dusk, but still light enough to examine the grounds around the museum. The floodlights were on as well.

Jenna was watching Will when his eyes slowly met hers. Several emotions seemed to cross his face: anger, guilt, nervousness, sadness. Finally, he broke her gaze, but he never spoke. Obviously, not much had changed from last night, except he didn't seem as annoyed. No doubt his mom had talked to him.

The wind current caught in the sheltered alcove and whistled loudly forcing Sulis to talk louder to be heard. "Let's start around the perimeter of the building first before we make our way to the orchard. Let your intuition guide you. If something feels differently, speak up." Everyone followed her down the stairs. "I dreamt of wandering through apple trees again. I know I was searching for something, but not what. Nothing new happened. Will dreamt something similar. What about you, Jenna?"

"I'm sorry I don't have anything better. It was windy and I was carrying a candle."

Sulis prompted her for details. Jenna thought it over and mentioned her dress and the orchard. "I know it was here but the ground wasn't level. It was really rough and I almost fell a few times. The candle was thick but I don't remember it's color. The flames stayed lit the whole time which was weird, considering the wind was strong, like it is right now. But you know how dreams are. If you or Will were there, I can't remember it."

"That's okay, at least we have some details."

The group went on. The water wheel sat silent, as always, the wood faded and dried-out despite the remnants of the fall rainstorms. Old bird nests inside the corners of the long blade sections had long been abandoned. They all walked down to the creek, looking up and down where it wound through the thick woods behind them. They could just make out Toby's house from there.

"I still feel that cold, uncomfortable feeling here, just as I did the first time I walked the grounds," stated Sulis. "Brief flashes come to me: forceful water rushing in the creek, ice cold nights, being wet, uncertainty, hopelessness."

"Can you explain how you do that? What's it like? I don't get it," asked Tina.

"It's like after one looks at a bright light or the sun," Sulis replied. "The image stays after a while. However, nothing feels different here and I don't think this area holds any new information for us right now."

Jenna remembered, so long ago, the first time she met Tina. "There were rumors that Elizabeth Avery died by the millpond or drowned in the creek. Of course, that was after the Cabets were here and after the boarding house was turned into a mill."

"That is the history that generated the ghost stories in the first place," Mr. Jacobs added.

"Yes, I remember you telling me about the building's past, as well as Jenna's experiences here. What I pick up are overlapping layers. What thoughts surface, or visions that flash in my mind just come to me. Unfortunately, they don't date themselves in the feelings that have stayed behind. It's difficult to pick up the ones we're looking for. Nothing is specific enough for me to know it was related to Jonas or the Cabets," Sulis articulated as she walked.

She led the group around to the orchard. "Luckily the rains have let up. There is no way we can control the weather, but it looks as if it's a part of this message we're getting. I wish I knew the value of the wind," Sulis said. Her long black cloak billowed around her, blowing the hood up and down on the back of her head. Will was looking at the ground, kicking up small stones and looking at the arrangement of trees. He seemed to be searching for something but kept his thoughts to himself.

"If Jonas, James, and Henry had been burying diamonds out here, where would they go? How far away from the building?" Tina asked.

"Remember, the apple orchard wasn't here then," her father added, holding up one of the pictures found in Sulis's canning cellar.

"Should we just start digging randomly?" Toby asked. "Tomorrow is Halloween already."

"That doesn't feel right," Sulis admitted. "We'd be looking for a needle in a haystack that way. I have the Ouija board in the car. I'm getting nothing significant out here and time is precious." She looked over at Mr. Levy who had an irritated look on his face. "Let's meet inside again. Anyway, it's getting much too dark to see properly now."

Everyone else seemed receptive to the suggestion. It was their last chance to find the information they needed, and they were running out of time. After going back inside, they quietly started to set up. From the office, the men brought out the turquoise candle and diamonds from the altar. The alter itself was now tucked away in the loft. Sulis came in a short time later, carrying the Ouija board and a cloth bag with all the other items.

It was eerie, the sense of déjà vu that was felt in the room. Again, the candles threw the only light around the table. This time they lit the turquoise candle they'd found upstairs, hoping to get some inkling of what it was for.

As they all linked hands Sulis chanted quietly next to Jenna, her eyes closed in concentration. Jenna's mind began to wander, the words Sulis was saying blending together into a calm hum next to her. She was nervous once again, gun shy from the last experiences. She tentatively looked up at Will across from her. His eyes were closed as he mouthed the same words as his mother. She ached to hold his hand, to be reassured that they would be okay. He had fit so easily into her life. Now it felt like a part of her was missing. It surprised her how much the emptiness hurt. Unable to will them to stop, tears silently ran down her cheeks.

Sulis shook her from her thoughts, breaking her hand free to put hers on the indicator. Will did the same. When Jenna just sat there, Will finally glanced at her and did a double take. His face fell, his jaw tightened, but then softened. He nodded for her to put her hand on as well. She did so hesitantly, feeling the warmth of his hand run through her whole body. Everyone else at the table reconnected to those who were touching the indicator by putting their hand on an arm or shoulder.

All at once, Jenna's mind went blank, but she could smell apples. There was a rush of intake of breath from the others. The circle was completed with everyone feeling the thread of energy from each other and all around them. Will asked the Ouija the same questions to begin with as he did the first of the month, but before he could start asking any new questions the indicator started zooming across the board. It had an urgency that wasn't hard for the others to see. The candles, including the turquoise pillar, dimmed without any cause or manipulation.

Sulis's composure cracked first. Her shoulders slumped slightly, her mouth dropped slack-jawed and her eyes went blank. Shock and panic shot across Will's face as he watched his mother. Then he looked over at Jenna. Her face was flat, her wide-eyed stare fixed on the indicator as it spelled out its first message.

T-H-E-Y A-R-E A-L-L C-O-M-I-N-G

"Oh my word, I've got goose bumps," Tina whispered. She looked from Jenna to Will to Sulis, not reassured by their expressions. They looked like frozen zombies. It was as if they didn't inhabit their bodies anymore. The fine sheet of anxiety that was never very far from her started to close in and squeeze, heating the pit of her stomach uncomfortably. She tried to keep it at bay. She needed to stay strong for her friends this time.

"Who is coming?" Mr. Stevens asked, loudly. He didn't like the look on his daughter's face and was becoming more nervous each second.

Will responded automatically by asking who was speaking. The indicator spelled out S-Y-L-V-I-A.

Jenna couldn't seem to move. Flashes of scenes went off in her head. She was in the orchard, except there were no trees, yet she knew where the trees would be later as their images appeared and faded. She was holding the large, turquoise-green pillar candle.

"Who is coming?" Will asked flatly. The words came out slowly with effort and his nostrils flared. He had to concentrate just to speak and his eyes no longer seemed to blink. The indicator took off again, moving their hands to spell out the names they hoped not to see.

J-O-N-A-S...   H-E-N-R-Y...   N-O-R-M-A-N...
S-E-T-H...

The indicator started to continue but the last name caught everyone off guard.

"What?" asked Toby. "No way! How?"

Will once again asked Sylvia.

O-P-E-N-D-O-O-R.

Jenna was slowly coming back to the present. She was beginning to realize the overlapping included both pasts as well this time. "We never knew where Seth went," she said weakly.

"What is that? Like a backdoor? A loophole?" Mr. Jacobs asked, frantic. The Ouija indicator began moving again. Everyone's head followed it as it floated across the board, everyone except Sulis, who seemed to be focusing on a fine point on the board.

M-U-S-T-S-T-O-P.

"Shut it down! Shut it down!" urged Mr. Levy. His left hand was turning purple from his daughter's grip.

Mr. Jacobs shook his head vehemently. "No, Mark. I don't think that'll work. We need to find out what's going on so we can stop it the right way."

"Will, start asking her how to stop them instead of why they're coming back," urged Mr. Stevens. "There are no pictures linked to the present now to put them into this time. Obviously, the window didn't do it."

"Remember the beginning of the month and how hard it was to fight them," Mr. Levy added. "We're just inviting them in to do worse."

"We couldn't grab Seth five years ago!" Tina complained.

"I know! We can't touch the undead, let alone kill them. Sulis, we've got nothing to get rid of them with if they show up," Mr. Jacobs said. He felt cornered and desperate and Sulis was no longer responding.

At this point her head rolled back. She took in a jagged breath looking straight in front of her. "I can get rid of them. We need to dig up their bodies first and get them away. Amelie too. Light candle...outside in... the...orchard... candle... spell... gone," Sulis's voice faded in sound. She was now an awful shade of gray, her lips tinged blue. She struggled, her body shaking violently.

Everyone was too immobilized from shock to do anything but watch. Her eyes bulging, she fought to say more. It was too much. She collapsed, the side of her head landing on the table with a thud, her arms limp where they dropped. Her color started to come back almost at once, but she remained unconscious.

Just as the men started to move to check on her, they froze. Everyone froze. For a solid minute everyone became incapacitated, their minds preoccupied. Will and Jenna both snapped out of their reverie first. They held onto the indicator tightly and quickly yelled to the others to stay connected. Slowly the group seemed to thaw out. They all looked around the room, blinking, bewildered, and disoriented.

Concerned, Jenna nudged Sulis with her shoulder, afraid of moving her hands. "Sulis, can you hear me? Are you okay?"

Sulis's eyes remained closed, but she stirred slowly. "Mmm, need a minute." Her voice was raspy.

"Sylvia was coming at us at the same time. I got a good look at where we need to start digging," Will whispered, thinking only of his mother and himself. He watched her, still concerned.

"Yeah, the basement, the opposite side of the storm cellar," Toby said. His muscles flexed underneath his t-shirt as he squeezed the hands he was holding. Tina's mouth popped open, then her face winced in a delayed reaction. She agreed with Toby, the tiny rhinestones of her headband glinting in the candlelight. She looked around her—anxious just like everyone else—only able to keep herself in check by doing some deep breathing.

Mr. Jacobs frowned. "No, the orchard by the two trees that makes a 'V' formation," he corrected his son.

"What *was* that?" Mr. Stevens asked, exasperated. He paused. "I saw what Tom saw."

"No, it's the basement by the storm cellar," Mr. Levy said quietly. Confused, he looked at Will and Jenna.

"Yes, I saw the basement by the storm cellar as well," Will mumbled. "It seems Sylvia blasted everyone with information." It took a while for it to sink in.

"Wow. I saw us outside. I had the turquoise candle," Jenna said perplexed.

"Sylvia, how many bodies are we uncovering?" Will asked the Ouija. The indicator remained still in their hands. Will tried a few more times with no luck. Sulis had started to move by this time. She used her hands to push herself back up to a sitting position as Will closed their communication and took the planchette off the board.

"Mom, are you okay?"

"Just very tired. That was the most intensity thing I've ever experienced," she answered.

"What happened? What did you see?" asked Mr. Stevens. Everyone was sitting on the edge of their seats, now active participants themselves.

"I was outside in the orchard, holding the turquoise candle. I saw Sylvia in the orchard reunite with her daughter, Amelie. It was too dim to see clearly, but somehow I just knew that's who they were."

"Where in the orchard?" Mr. Jacobs demanded.

Sulis shook her head. "I don't know where. It was too dark to make out any landmarks because the image kept shifting from one in an open space to one with trees. I couldn't get acclimated."

"We have to find Amelie?" Jenna questioned.

"Yes. She was just as talented and had abilities that rivaled her mother's. Sylvia needs Amelie with her to complete this spell," Sulis hesitated, "the spell we are to finish. I'm very hesitant about carrying it out. Sylvia wasn't compatible sharing my body. She disengaged before I could learn all the details. There are gaps which mean I could make mistakes."

"Well, I'm totally onboard now whether I want to or not." Mr. Levy interjected. "Whatever we have to do must be important. This urge I have is strong."

"I never had flashes of white light in my mind like that. It wiped out every other thought. The image of the basement furthest from the storm cellar was so crystal clear, it almost felt as if I was there seeing it in person," Tina shared.

"That's exactly how it felt to me. I was out in the orchard and I could almost swear I smelled the fall air outside," agreed Mr. Jacobs.

"So, we have to find Amelie's body, and who else?" Mr. Levi pressed.

"I think it might be Jonas's. I'm almost certain there is more than one," Sulis replied.

Toby shook his head hard and fast. "We don't have time for that."

Mr. Levy and Mr. Jacobs looked at each other. "The Historical Association has records of burial grounds and there is a cemetery across from here. That might narrow things down," suggested Mr. Jacobs hopefully.

"No, I don't think that will help us. We're being told to dig here," Sulis countered.

"There are bodies here?" Tina's face paled.

"Okay, right, we gotta dig. Half of us think it's downstairs and half say the orchard. The orchard is huge, even for the eight of us. We'd have to split up to check every place we just saw," said Toby.

"We can split up. And what I saw was very specific. I think we can do this," Mr. Stevens reasoned. His face very clearly reflected the surprise he felt in stating it.

"Do you really think Jonas is buried here? And Henry?" Jenna asked.

"Jenna, we saw Sylvia drag Jonas towards the door upstairs. What if she didn't get very far with him? Henry was already dead in the basement anyway," Will reminded her. His voice was even and fair but he was making a point to avoid eye contact and was keeping a tight rein on his emotions.

"That's a good possibility then," Sulis nodded. "That feels right."

"I don't think it would be Seth. I'm almost positive he moved out of state before he died," Jenna thought aloud.

"He did. I remember the research Mrs. Forrester did. He's not in New York," Mr. Jacobs confirmed.

"So that narrows it down and tomorrow is Halloween. Well, in a few hours actually." Mr. Levy sighed, looking at his watch.

"So, we dig tonight. We'll attempt the spell tomorrow. I have a lot of work ahead trying to transcribe the information Sylvia was giving me. I need to do some research too, and check on a few things I'm not familiar with. This is something I've never done before," Sulis admitted quietly.

"It has to be done, though, I know," Jenna finished. She didn't say out loud what everyone was thinking. There was no hiding the facts; all were fearful of not doing the spell correctly or finishing in enough time to see the spell through. They had less than twenty-four hours. No one asked what would happen if they didn't succeed.

They got up slowly, tired from what the day had brought and what the night would bring.

"I have some tools in my trunk," Mr. Stevens offered, reaching into his pocket for his car keys.

"I have a few things, too."

"Thanks, Toby, that will help."

"Let's split up and get moving. I think it's best to dig in the areas Sylvia showed each of us."

Mr. Levy paused. "We have a section for tools down in the basement by the power box. My arm hasn't healed enough for me to be able to dig, Sulis, but I'll do what I can. The vision I had was the same one Will saw by the storm cellar. I can help him, Toby, and my daughter on the opposite side of the room."

"I realize how difficult this is for you, Mark, and I appreciate it."

Jenna was going back outside to the orchard as that's what her vision showed her. She stood up with her dad and Mr. Jacobs. Both of them had seen the two trees that made a "V" formation. She was sure this arrangement made the parents more comfortable also. After what had happened at the beginning of the month, she knew it would be impossible for Tina to be separated from her father now. She also knew it probably was the same with her own dad. Privately, she was comforted knowing her dad would be with her if Will wasn't. Sulis was going to start working on the spell immediately. With several pieces of loose paper, she began to write down what she had seen from memory.

Two groups formed with Jenna's group getting on their coats and Will's group heading off to the basement. Will lingered behind, dawdling. He turned toward Jenna, who was at the front door. She was pulling the hood up over her head, tucking her hair in securely. She was the last of her troupe to leave and didn't notice Will's hesitancy in going downstairs with the others. He stayed behind for a moment, undecided. His jaw flexed and his face vacillated between determination and uncertainty. Jenna didn't look over and he turned, resigned, and slowly went downstairs.

Twenty-six

$\mathcal{J}$ENNA WRAPPED HER arm around her tightly while she waited. The fleece hoodie she was wearing did nothing against the sharp-edged wind that was blowing. The wind had picked back up and now the pitch black had turned icy. Mr. Jacobs and Mr. Stevens had located the two trees that resembled a 'V'. They had brought out a long orange extension cord and metal domed work light. Jenna held her flashlight on them as Mr. Jacobs climbed a nearby apple tree, yelling for her father to throw him a rope so he could tie down and anchor the light. It was difficult to hear them with the wind.

Jenna watched the beam from her father's flashlight bounce wildly as they tried to find a way to rig up the light. The sporadic brightness illuminated the shrubbery nearby, reminding her of her first dream of the orchard. Every time the wind blew and the bushes rustled, it triggered her peripheral vision, and she braced herself expecting something to come out at her. Their depths scared her. She paced anxiously in an area with less condensed apple trees, trying to concentrate on what the men were doing. She needed to stay moving to stay warm.

It was dark, and she didn't see the protruding root in front of her until she tripped. She landed hard on the ground and moaned as other roots jabbed into her side. It took a second for the pain to subside enough for her to want to get up. Suddenly, strong arms were around her. She drew in a deep reserve of air to scream but stopped immediately when she recognized the familiar scents of sandalwood, citrus, and lingering patchouli.

"Jenna, are you all right?" Will asked, his silky voice at once calming her fears. She bobbed her head, unable to speak until the adrenaline started to dissipate. He didn't wait for her to answer before embracing her in a suffocating hug, kissing the top of her head over and over.

"I hate feeling this way. I'm disgusted with myself for allowing you to feel so horrible. Making you keep the diamonds a secret wasn't fair to you, and I'm so sorry. I don't know what I was thinking. I can't bear to think of you out here walking on bones. I can't get that image out of my head, and it frightens me." The desperate look on his face was visible with the erratic light show.

"I'm sorry too, Will, I really am." Jenna sighed, clutching him tightly. They held each other for a moment before Jenna's dad yelled at her to come over. Neither he nor Mr. Jacobs had seen or heard her fall.

The bright work light was on now, shining brightly away from them on a small section of the ground about twenty feet from Jenna. It was anchored in the tree with bungee cords to keep it from being blown away. The apple trees in the orchard were scattered except for an area where they lined up and away from each other. The two trees that were side by side made up the bottom of a "V" shape. Mr. Jacobs was in the middle of the shape and Jenna's father was down from him, underneath the "V". They started digging.

Will helped Jenna up and hugged her again tightly. "I hate to leave you. I've realized how it pains me to be away from you. Please be careful," he breathed into her ear. Jenna nodded and he disappeared into the darkness only to reappear under the floodlights by the main entrance a moment later. He turned towards her and waved before going in. Jenna smiled and waved back. If everything else went wrong on Halloween night she hoped Will would still be by her side when it happened.

Exhaustion from digging came on fast from the manual labor, fighting against the wind, and having been awake all night. Discussions were kept to a minimum. It required too much energy to yell over the howling of the blustery gusts. Each took the briefest of breaks, mostly to go to the bathroom from all the coffee Mr. Levy was bringing them. No one who was using a shovel was complaining about the cold. Sweaty and dirty, the wind at times was refreshing.

At about three in the morning, the conversations of quitting started to become more frequent. Mr. Jacobs was frustrated, wrestling with tree roots in between damp, dank loam. That was when the ground Jenna and her dad had been working on changed in consistency. It had become softer. They hit upon an air pocket that provided a simple grave. The bones still had some fabric attached, but it was easy to tell it was the remains of Amelie. Jenna felt a shiver run up her spine through the sweat-laden layers she was wearing.

"I think this is it, Tom."

"I do too, Jack." Both men spoke quietly. Mr. Stevens leaned on his shovel, trying to catch his breath, shaking his head sadly at the small skeleton curled inside.

Jenna went back inside to tell the others and to find a towel or large clean cloth for Amelie's remains. She heard a lot of excited voices as she went into the great room and detoured downstairs to see what the commotion was about. The squeaking of the steep stairs alerted everyone to her approach. Will looked up, a tired but wild expression on his sweaty face. He climbed out of the large hole he and Toby were in. Mr. Levy reached down to Toby. He gently took the bone from Toby and laid it onto the tarp next to him. The tarp had been divided into two sections, each with its own occupants. Tina, who was facing the staircase, looked up and smiled. She was shining her flashlight on a raw jagged piece of granite the size of a small footrest. The reflection back was brilliant in its illumination.

"I think we have our guys," Toby panted. Will met Jenna at the bottom of the stairs.

"It's incredible, Jenna. Come and see! It's the largest Herkimer diamond we've ever seen. Mr. Levy says this thing is worth a bundle!" he said excitedly.

"It's worth enough, at least," Mr. Levy interrupted. Jenna was puzzled. She was unsure how to interpret Will's enthusiasm and tentatively walked over. From where she was standing it looked like a large, gray stone to her. When she got around to the side that was facing Tina, she understood. In the middle was a diamond the size of a saucepan, glinting in its crystal facets, hidden in its plain boulder layer. She stared, perplexed.

"Jenna, it's worth enough to at least make up a good portion of the missing funds from the cancelled Ball. The museum might not need to be shut down!" Toby called over.

It took a minute for Jenna to process the meaning. The relief that washed over her was twofold. Will hadn't changed his mind after all, and the museum would be safe to run for another year.

"It's a good thing the whole grounds are owned by the Historical Association and that I'm in charge of this kind of thing here," Mr. Levy commented. "We may need to make special arrangements for these skeletons, though. That is, when we're done doing whatever it is we're supposed to do with them."

Jenna looked back at the tarp, holding what was left of what she was sure were Henry and Jonas. She was hoping Sulis had some idea what to do now.

"We had just started uncovering the second body but were hitting nothing but dirt, so we thought we were at the wrong end. Before we were sure there were no more bones in that direction," Toby began, but was interrupted by Will.

"My shovel hit something hard. I told you I'd know the sound of that anywhere. Mr. Levy and Tina wanted to ignore it and turn back the other way. We had hit many large pieces of stone here, but it felt different. I don't think Sylvia realized she buried those thieves so close to their own stash."

"Sylvia buried them?" Jenna asked. She hadn't thought about that.

"Remember, she was pulling Jonas from the room after she got stabbed by her athame? She must have decided the best way to handle the whole thing was to get rid of the evidence. I don't think anyone would have come looking for those guys. The way Jonas talked, they were drifters."

"What about Amelie?" Toby asked, climbing out of the hole. He was now interested in the details he hadn't observed himself.

"I don't know. Maybe people got shot all the time back then," Will guessed.

"We found Amelie," Jenna said. "Sylvia didn't bury her with the enemy. That reminds me, is there another tarp?"

"We found something already, Jenna," her dad answered, walking downstairs followed by Mr. Jacobs. Sulis was behind them, a baffled look on her face, turning over and examining a turquoise-green candle. "We found this with Amelie."

"Another turquoise candle? Which one are we supposed to use?" Jenna asked.

"I don't know. This has made things exponentially more difficult," Sulis replied wearily.

Toby raked his forearm over his brow, frowning. "How so?"

"What information I gleaned from Sylvia spoke to using the turquoise candle. Now there are two. Do I do the spell twice with each one? Specifically use one but not the other? I don't know if more harm will come from using the wrong candle."

"Oh."

It took a few minutes for everyone to catch up on the finds. Sulis said she thought she was as ready as she would ever be for what Sylvia was giving her. All she had left was the research she couldn't do until she got home, consulted with her sisters, and looked through some books. It was fast approaching five in the morning.

"So much for shut-eye. I can't believe I have about an hour to get cleaned up and ready for work. Come on, Jenna, let's get home. I'm dead on my feet."

"If I sit down again, it'll be that much harder to get dressed for school," Tina said.

"Be realistic, kiddo. None of you are going to make it to school today."

"I think it would be a smart move to keep up with the pretense of normalcy," Will suggested, cupping his hand around his face to pull his hair back. "We'll get attention if all four of us stay home 'sick'."

"As much as I don't want to agree, I have to." Toby nodded, his eyes blinking slowly. "We can't afford to have people taking a closer look at what we're doing here. Especially since we'll be back out here Halloween night. I mean, tonight."

"Absolutely not!" Mr. Jacobs had folded his arms, much like his son did, shaking his head. "Sleep deprivation leads to poor judgement."

"And it impairs the ability to concentrate," added Mr. Levy.

"Isn't that the description of every teenager on a good day?"

"You've got a good point, Toby."

Jenna walked over to Will, yawning. He held his hand out at the same moment she reached for him. "It'll be dangerous enough for all of us considering it's Halloween, let alone nosy strangers poking their noses in on our business to see what's going on."

"True," Tina agreed, a small smile growing on her face as she took in Will's and Jenna's entwined hands. She took her glasses off and cleaned them with her underlayer shirt. "We need to stay under the radar. We can do it. I've pulled all-nighters doing English papers, Dad, and you didn't know about them."

"Until now I didn't know about them."

"So have I," Jenna, Will, and Toby said in unison.

"See? We'll be fine."

"I can't believe all of you are arguing about wanting to go to school," Mr. Levy admitted.

"That's just poor judgement talking."

"Go home, Toby."

The day passed in a blur. The kids that dressed up in costumes at school did nothing to entertain the four exhausted teenagers. They were tired and paranoid as this holiday consistently had surprises for them. Each of them had fallen asleep at one time or another throughout the day and had been yelled at and ridiculed by various teachers.

"I figure we can at least get in a good three or four hours of sleep after school before we get to the museum," Toby said during lunch. It was the one period they all shared a few minutes together due to overlapping lunch times.

"There's nothing good about three hours of sleep," Tina said, yawning for the fifth time. The first bell rang and Jenna got up with Will. Reluctantly, she let his hand go.

"Try not to stress. There's nothing we can do right now

anyway," Will encouraged her. The words were meant to calm her, but the look on his face said something completely different.

"Do you think your mom will find all the information she needs before tonight?" Jenna asked quietly.

"She will do her best. That's all we can ask for. Of anyone. We need to hold onto positive energy and let that guide us. Power of suggestion is very influential."

Jenna nodded, but wasn't convinced. It was too easy to forget about unimportant things such as school when her eyes tugged at her to close and her thoughts drifted to a mystery spell they were about to perform in a few short hours. With school life going on around her, it took energy she didn't have to concentrate on it. She nodded again and smiled weakly.

"I'll see you around seven," Will started to say. A classmate behind them tipped his chair over and the loud bang echoed in the cafeteria. Jenna's heart leapt into her throat and Will jumped. Their hands joined. Tina's arms crossed around her protectively as she gasped, and Toby's arm slammed down on the table so fast, droplets of chocolate milk flew out of the container. Will's eyes were hard and tense as he looked over at the table behind them. All of their nerves were frayed. He attempted to smile as he walked away. Jenna's stomach twisted itself into knots as they split up, thinking the next time she saw everyone they would all be in danger. Her head hung as she headed off to class.

The alarm went off loudly, music blaring, making Jenna jump. She had been sleeping, she was sure of that by her clock, but there were no dreams, and time did not seem to have passed. She had been out for three hours. How was it possible she felt more tired?

She dressed slowly for the evening, her balance failing her. Putting on her khaki pants, she matched it with a thick Irish sweater she usually reserved for the middle of January. Last night's cold hadn't crept out of her bones yet. She pulled a section of her hair back and braided it quickly. At least this way she had the length to keep her neck warm and it was out of her face. She could hear the wind shrieking outside already.

Heading into the hallway, she heard her mother and father in the next room. It sounded like a heated argument, but they spoke in low voices. She walked softly, trying to catch the gist of the conversation. It revolved around the fact that neither she nor her dad had come home last night. Her mom wasn't satisfied with his answers of where they were. Jenna heaved a heavy sigh and knocked on the unlatched door. She started talking before they could respond.

"Dad, we've got that last meeting at the museum, and it's already seven. Are you ready to go?" She couldn't discern what was said inside.

"I'll be right out," her dad answered. He came out a moment later, looking much older than he had two days ago.

Jenna made an effort to smile and look normal. "Mom, sorry about last night. The museum is so close to being shut down, we hammered out all our options. I think we've got a plan even though we can't announce it until later."

Her mother looked at her dubiously and turned to her husband and seemed to relax. "At least you're both going together. It's a museum for crying out loud. I can't believe this is taking so long to figure out."

"Trust me, neither can I," Jenna mumbled.

"You know I still don't understand your infatuation with that place. I wish it respected normal human hours. Well," she said, resigned, "I guess it could be worse. At least you're doing something constructive."

Jenna had to cough to cover the hysterics inside. No, it most definitely didn't respect humans at all. And it could be worse. The words constructive and destructive bounced around in her head, too, making her want to giggle. Her mother passed her and went into the kitchen ahead of them. Mr. Stevens looked at Jenna fiercely. He kissed his wife and grabbed his coat.

Jenna looked out into the darkness with the wind howling and suddenly wondered what she had found so funny just a moment ago. Grabbing her wool hat and a pair of gloves, she followed her father.

They turned into the drive a few minutes later, needing to drive onto the grass to avoid two huge signs that read 'Closed' blocking the entrance. They could take no chances tonight. Everyone was congregating in the great room, whispering amongst themselves. Will was sitting on the fourth step of the staircase, his elbows on his knees as he talked with Tina and Toby who sat two steps down. He had on a pair of black jeans, black boots, and an off-white, long-sleeved shirt with a Mandarin collar.

"Jenna's here. Hi Jenna!" Tina called, straightening the comb in her hair. She and Jenna still dressed a lot alike. Tonight, Tina had on cable-knit sweater over a turtleneck that matched her gray stretch pants. Her heavy coat was resting in the crook of her other arm. Her attention shifted back to Toby and Will, laughing at something Toby just said. He was wearing what he wore every day: jeans and a t-shirt. He had what seemed like a million tees. This one was in the school colors of brown and blue with 'Orchard Creek Rooks 'Restling' in varsity letters on the front.

Jenna could hear Mr. Jacobs and Mr. Levy in the corridor near the basement. They were deep in discussion. Even though it was obvious Jenna and her dad had come inside, the faces of all her friends turned again, anxiously this time, when the door shut loudly behind them. The nervousness that was emitted could almost be palpated. Tina made a squeaking noise, startled, and the other men rushed into view, craning their necks to see the doorway. The low hum of the voices in the room halted into silence.

Just then, Sulis walked out from the office with her hands full, books falling over her arm as she tried to catch the loose pencils that slid through her fingers. She was preoccupied with a distraught look on her face, muttering under her breath. Her face was scrunched with unease and the deep lines had drawn her glasses down on her nose. While she was securing all the items in her right hand, she dropped the small diamonds in the left onto the hardwood floor. Her cranberry cloak swished around her as she attempted to reach for them a moment too late. Jenna gasped, having a flashback to when she was in the Sewing Room with Jonas and Sylvia. She rushed over to pick up the diamonds and take the pencils.

Sulis smiled in her direction, but did not look at her. "Sorry. I'm trying to figure out what we need to do. I can cast the circle and do Sylvia's banishing ritual outside in the way I remember her telling me in my mind, but we'll need to light the turquoise candles and it's so windy outside…" her voice trailed off, in thought again, as she continued across the room and through the door without saying another word.

Will left the stairs and walked up to Jenna. Putting his arms on her shoulders he took inventory of her face. He noted how tired she looked, moving his hands to cup her head under her hat, his thumbs stroking her flushed cheeks. She looked so cute in that hat with braids off the end. He loved the fact that Jenna had natural beauty and didn't feel the need to wear a lot of make-up. The saying 'what you see is what you get' summed up Jenna perfectly. She hid behind no pretense; even her hair held her personality. Most times it was bouncy and light. Right now, her hair was held back and her dark eyes were pulled down with worry that had deep circles under them. Her face was drawn, and her usually full lips were pale and thin with tension.

"We're all together, and we can do this. My mom has backup plans to try the spell differently if it doesn't work right the first time. In fact, she has several. That second candle has thrown her." Will hesitated before catching himself. "We need to be centered and grounded. We need to believe," he finished firmly. His eyes were searching hers.

Jenna found herself staring back, relaxing into the deep chocolate depths that called to something inside her. She found she was breathing along with him, subconsciously, and had calmed down quite quickly.

The front door opened again bringing in a huge blustery gust with Sulis. She headed for the office not bothering with pleasantries or small talk. Stray leaves blew inside and dropped quickly once the force behind them was cut off. The night had been warmer than lately, but the wind that had picked up was frigid. Will grabbed both braids of Jenna's hat and pulled her in to him gently, kissing her lips. He directed her to the table to help carry things outside, rubbing her shoulders soothingly. She looked at the assortment of odds and ends.

"What are these for?" she asked, picking up very thin, long sticks. They were about six inches in length and looked like large tan splinters of wood, all even in size.

"They're just fancy matches for lighting our candles. They need to be brought out, too." Will shook his head as he noticed a set of notes his mother had left behind. He made a clicking sound as he reached to collect them. "We'll be fine, I'm sure of it." He said this last part mostly to himself.

Twenty-seven

THE FLASHLIGHTS AND floodlights still tied in the trees lit the area in the orchard just enough. Mr. Levy was yelling to Toby, and Tina was yelling back, motioning where to go. It was difficult to be heard outside with the windstorm. Sulis was lying out gems and the one Herkimer diamond they found the evening Will broke the window, to create one huge circle, almost eight feet wide. Her cranberry cloak billowed out around her. It reminded Jenna of Sylvia's skirt.

From where Jenna stood, she felt isolated with no landmarks or distractions. They were too far into the orchard to see any neighboring houses, and no headlights could be seen from the occasional passing car. Those that did pass didn't even slow down. Jenna wondered if Sylvia was responsible for that too. They had been sure they'd have to turn away at least a handful of people who hadn't heard the Halloween Ball was cancelled.

But they hadn't. It was almost as if they were in their own little bubble, hidden in plain sight.

Too many things seemed to have a mystical, unrealistic quality to it. Jenna thought at first it was the lack of sleep, but even the fresh night air did nothing to wake her up from this dreamy state. She willed herself to stay in the present and stay focused. She couldn't afford to be passing out now.

Mr. Jacobs and Mr. Stevens had brought out the thick blanket that contained Amelie's remains, following where Tina was directing them. They laid her down carefully inside the circle where Sulis had made a makeshift altar. Small holes had been dug in the ground to support the candles so they stayed upright.

The paper Tina held in her hand was being whipped mercilessly. She rolled it up as best as she could when she didn't need it, so it wouldn't tear. What was left of the bodies of Jonas and Henry were brought over. One of them was in a blue tarp, and the other was wrapped up in the thick, clear plastic the office's hard drive came in last April. They were put off to the side, out of the circle. Jenna stood there with the seven others. At last all the elements were there.

Suddenly there was luminosity to the area that hadn't been there before and everyone looked up. The moon had come out from a break in the clouds. It was a cherry moon with a creamy, pink hue. Just as abruptly, it waned as the wind blew more cloud cover in. Five seconds later it was back, throwing the moonlight on the clouds and all round them. The moonlight and the stark brightness from the work light illuminated the area to almost daytime quality. Outside the beam, however, where the bushes and trees were only partly lit, the shadows were thick and ominous. The wind whipped the bare boughs overhead and they rustled together making the sound of heavy rain. The branches, like limbs, reached and stretched as if trying to grab what was below.

Jenna wrapped her arms around her in a gesture to stay warm. The sharp wind blew at her face making her gasp to breathe, and it drove the loose braids of her wool chullo hat back behind her shoulders. She teetered on her feet from the strength and re-steadied herself.

As she looked at the anxious faces around her, worry colored her thoughts. She couldn't help but blame herself for the danger they all faced: the danger from five years ago, a few weeks ago, and now tonight as well. It had all started with her. Toby may not have believed it, but she did. He felt she did her best for the museum. Jenna knew it wasn't going to be enough.

Her reflections were interrupted by Will handing out copies of Sulis's notes. He stopped in front of her before giving her the paper. Mixed with the crisp air and rotting leaves was Will's cologne as he bent down and kissed her again, this time with determination. He continued on without a word.

At Sulis's urging, everyone was invited into the circle. They fanned out to form a circle within a circle, surrounding the altar and joined hands. Sulis held Will's hand who was next to Jenna who stood next to her father. On his other side was Mr. Levy, his daughter, Toby, and his dad. They began.

The wind had calmed a bit and Sulis no longer needed to shout. "First we open the circle. Doing this creates a safe space while we use our magic. It protects us because the energy is metaphysical and might attract entities that are negative or harmful."

"I'm already confused. We have the bones of murders right here," Mr. Stevens asked, using his head to indicate the two piles.

"Yes, but notice they are not in our circle, only the remains of Amelie are. We want to connect with her."

"Sorry, Sulis."

"It's quite all right. In fact, I'd rather you all know why we're doing what we're doing so you understand. Once the circle is open, we will not need to hold hands. Nothing can cross inside and harm us as long as we keep it intact. Breaking it will allow others in. If, for any reason, one of us needs to leave, that person must make a door for themselves. The doorway must be closed immediately after. They would have to re-enter the same way."

"Like Gina Davis did in Beetlejuice?" Toby asked, kidding. Sulis looked at him over her glasses.

"Exactly like that, but without the chalk. That's Hollywood hooey. As long as we make our intentions clear, the action will work."

"Oh, that's what you were doing for me when we shut the window for good a few weeks ago, right?" Mr. Stevens asked.

"Yes."

The wind picked up, shrieking as it streamlined around each person. Sulis spoke as loudly as needed. "Now then, to raise a circle we will recite only the words in the first paragraph on your paper in a round, like a song, as we walk around just inside the ground candles. I will start. Will will join after I've said the first phrase, then Jenna, and so on. We walk until we've all had a turn, lending and blending our energy with one another."

From memory, Sulis recited the words as she started to walk. Some of the candles around them had been extinguished by the wind. Noticing this, she waved it off with her hand, frustrated, and continued.

One by one, the group joined in, their voices weaving and overlapping until only Mr. Jacobs was left. The group all looked upward and around them at the same time. The winds had stopped as if listening to the rite. Jenna sighed. As foreign as this ceremony was, something settled in her mind; something that felt comfortable and right and gave her peace.

The ritual continued with Sulis and Will holding their athames and welcoming the elements. There almost seemed to be a buzzing in Jenna's veins. It was like a coming home of sorts. At one point, Will looked at her as if puzzling out a problem. Despite the reasons for the gathering, she smiled at him, a brilliant smile that left Will dazed for a moment.

"Focus, Will," his mother admonished. She finished the last few words in that section with "so mote it be."

Everyone expectantly turned towards Sulis as she attempted to light the turquoise candle she was holding. Again, it wasn't able to hold the flame. She shook her head and prompted the circle. They joined in where indicated, their voices both muffled and traveling on the wind. It didn't take long before things started to happen.

"Why do I feel warmer?" Toby hollered to Tina next to him. Sulis's eyes were still shut as she chanted the words Sylvia had given her.

"Because we're so close to each other?" Tina suggested.

"That can't be. We're still getting blown around, but I feel warmer too," agreed Mr. Levy. With that, the wind picked up, blowing everyone's jackets up from the bottom. The bones on the tarp started to make noise, knocking together.

"I smell apple again," Jenna stated. There were nods of agreement and concerned looks. Sulis opened her eyes and picked up the original turquoise candle. She tried to light the match, but the wind took the flame before it could ignite. Reaching down for Amelie's candle the wind blew her hood over her face. She debated for a moment and abandoned the idea. Discouraged, she tried a different paper after some difficulty trying to keep it from blowing out of her hands. Again, she started chanting. The bones on the tarp were now louder, the knocking becoming organized.

"We're not doing this right! We need to hurry! Who knows what's going on in the building!" Mr. Jacobs bellowed, looking across the circle at Sulis.

"Yes, I know! The Halloween veil has thinned."

Gusts were now coming at them from several angles blowing crisp, decomposing leaves at them. It threatened to blow over the slightest of the bunch as Tina and Jenna were buffeted to a point where they needed to re-find their footing. Sulis's cloak whipped against itself making a snapping sound like linen on a clothesline.

The energy buzzed around them, they could feel it. It was as if it was waiting for direction because nothing else was happening. Jenna looked over at the pile of bones that bounced around on the tarps. She wasn't sure if the wind was blowing them or if they were moving on their own volition. A sick twist tightened in the pit of her stomach and she cursed herself again for the mess she got everyone in. She started to think of everything she had seen in her dreams and experienced in the building. There was something they were missing, the key to make this work. Then it hit her. Toby had said it just a few days ago. She was the key; she always had been.

"I know! I know what to do! It's me. I'm the key! I need the candle!" Jenna yelled to the group. Everyone turned to look at her. Sulis's brow was creased, but then cleared with understanding. She leaned over to give her the original candle, but a big gust of wind came up, forcing her to wait until it had died down. At this point yelling was the only way to be heard. The focus of the group was being distracted by the contents of the tarps.

The blue and clear tarps outside the circle seemed secure on the ground with no hint that they would become airborne even though the small piles of bones were not heavy enough to hold them down. The individual bones jiggled and inched around looking for their neighbor to make a whole being. The rattling was distinctly bone on bone. Jenna's attention returned to the circle as Sulis called to her.

"Jenna, I can repeat the incantation again, but it's too windy to light! We'll try to do the spell as if the turquoise candles are lit!" Sulis hollered. She tried again with both her and Jenna speaking as loudly as they could but nothing happened with the circle. They watched as the bones on the tarp organized and moved together, forming.

"Hurry!" shouted Mr. Levy on Sulis's other side. Mr. Jacobs

looked over nervously at the building in the distance and at Mr. Stevens next to him.

Mr. Stevens glanced at his daughter then at Sulis. "We need something now! What can we do?"

Will was lost in thought, contemplating. He shook himself out of it. Jenna heard his voice above the howling. "Think Jenna! What do we need to do?"

She closed her eyes and tried to concentrate. She was the key. She was the key with Elizabeth and then with Amelie. What was she missing? Her brain seemed to have disengaged, her thoughts like sludge. Was it that they had worked in the building? No, Amelie didn't work there. They were about her age? No, she was only twelve when she helped Elizabeth. What were the similarities other than being mistaken for each of them? The pictures—she looked just like them. She looked just like them! She shared something more than just commonality. She was the exact image of Amelie as well! Jenna screamed for Sulis to trade with her the original candle for the one found in the grave only a few hours ago. They were almost out of time. Mr. Levy was rubbernecking. His hands held fast to Sulis's arm and Tina's hand as he tried to see around Jenna and Will across from him.

"We're in trouble here!" Tina yelled. Down the line heads turned from the tarps to the building. Mr. Stevens and Mr. Jacobs pulled the circle out a little further, still connected, to try to see anything in the museum. The building was barely visible from where they were. Nothing appeared out of the ordinary. They started throwing around suggestions. Mr. Levy and Toby began yelling to Sulis to break the circle as the tarp now held complete, cohesive skeletons.

As soon as Jenna had Amelie's candle in her hand, the energy stirred in her like an electric current from her head to her tingling toes.

"Whoa! What was that?" Toby asked, looking down at his hand.

"It came from Jenna," Will answered. "You could feel it from there? We're on the right track." He told his mother as Toby nodded.

"Now, now!" Tina screamed as the skeleton of Amelie started to move. The blanket stayed still although the fringe whipped back and forth as if alive. The wind doubled in force.

"I've done it the right way, I'm sure! We're still missing something, Jenna!" Sulis yelled to her. Jenna was just about to answer her when she froze. A white light tore through her mind, forcing her focus. As if fog clearing, her mind flashed visions of Amelie holding the candle, and Sylvia holding the candle. She knew they needed to do this together to complete the spell. The image changed from Amelie to herself. She saw herself holding the candle in front of her navy-blue jacket. It changed to Amelie holding the candle in front of a long linen dress.

"These guys are starting to move!" Mr. Levy roared.

"The candles are right this time! Why isn't this working?" Sulis shouted. The images replayed themselves in Jenna's mind, over and over, on top of each other, faster and faster. Soon the picture was the same, only one element was missing.

"We need to light these candles!" Jenna screamed into the roar of the storm around them. Sulis started to shake her head to indicate it wouldn't work. Then she shook her head as if trying to clear her mind. Her face abruptly went blank, her mouth open as if to speak. She didn't move from the position she was in, even when Jenna broke the circle and moved in front of her to grab the matches. The voice that spoke now was familiar to only two people there.

"These are special candles. They hold a rare magic that can be released only when lit on the windiest of days. This power has been safeguarded," Sylvia's voice reverberated through everyone's head. Each was still, preoccupied with the intrusion of Sylvia inside them once again.

"We never had the chance to complete the spells to use them. Quickly Mama, we're almost out of time," Jenna heard herself utter in a tone that wasn't her own. Her voice wasn't loud, yet everyone heard it.

Will snapped out of it first and broke away from his mother. Turning to the other side he took the candle from Jenna's shaking hands so she could light it properly. With their heads and shoulders together for shelter, Jenna lit the match into the candle itself. The flame caught quickly. It was a large brilliant green that stayed lit even when she backed away.

Sulis's eyes refocused on her son and she nodded. Will leaned into his mother to do the same with the original turquoise candle she was holding. Again, a strong green flame shone. Unexpectedly, the candles that surrounded them, that defined the circle, lit on their own, emitting a faint clover-colored hue. Faint twinkling shone from the diamonds that were placed next to them. The coats and cloaks that had been blowing in the strong zephyrs stopped dead. The wind did not affect them now.

Amelie's bones were still on the quilt, not just individual bone next to bone, but completely connected together. As the skeleton rose, it somehow stayed there as well. The bones that ascended blurred and faded as if transparent. When it came back into focus it grew and took on more of a solid dimension. It cleared even more and the silhouette of an outline became clothing. The body became brighter briefly, then subdued, resembling the others who watched. A jade-like gleam remained around the edges. Purposefully the figure moved, stepping in front of Jenna. It was almost as if seeing her twin. The image looked straight ahead and closed her eyes, shimmering silver and disappeared into a mist. It was very evident Jenna had been assimilated with Amelie as Jenna now took on a glowing aura as well.

Mr. Levy, Mr. Jacobs, and Mr. Stevens had stopped yelling about the skeletons on the tarps, turning their attention away from Jonas and Henry. They all stared, stunned, at the transformations of both Jenna to Amelie and Sulis to Sylvia. Sulis's crushed velvet cranberry cloak meshed into a thin, tan, linen robe. With that, her body shortened and slimmed. Her close-cropped hair altered from spiky auburn to smooth tawny brown, a tightly formed bun materializing in the back of her head at times. It looked like a light show projection the way it all flitted and faded.

The bones on the tarp outside the circle dropped to where they were before they were able to take on any physical mass. The apparitions of both women, like a blurry fog in front of Jenna and Sulis, moved together with the candles glowing brightly. They spoke together, but the timbre of voices was of four owners. Everyone's attention was on Jenna and Sylvia, and the circle re-formed and tightened with them in the middle. Tina had her arm linked around her father's for comfort. Mr. Stevens's eyes were wide and fearful, concerned with his daughter being out of his reach. He squeezed Will's hand intently.

The spell was finally cast. The pillars were raised towards each other and both flames united together. An explosion of green sparks flew skyward and sent chartreuse embers showering down on all of them. The force that detonated from the center of the altar had blown everyone backwards off their feet, a wave of bright light pulsing over them. The only ones who remained standing were Jenna and Sulis. As everyone's eyes became accustomed to the light, it became discernable that Sylvia and Amelie were together, separate entities now from Sulis and Jenna. Amelie's simple dress and apron accented her petite frame. In the glow of candles, she did look a lot like Jenna except Amelie's eyes were green. Her long, blond hair hung down past her waist in long ringlets. The two beings shimmered diffuse silver with green outlining them and the pillar candles they held. Sulis and Jenna had returned to a more normal image a foot away, glancing around awkwardly. Will walked into the middle of the circle and took Jenna and Sulis's hand. It took them a moment before they were reoriented.

Sylvia nodded at them, waved one hand over her candle as if capturing the smoke, then caressed the smoke from Amelie's candle to join hers. She rolled them together, dark green mixing with light green. She then threw it towards the carcasses of the others, muttering under her breath.

The tendrils floated with purpose to the bones on the tarp, settling over them completely. When the smoke dissipated, the bones started to move again. The long bones separated from each other and the skulls rocked back and forth disconnecting from the spine. The rib bones of the torso split in half and unfolded on the tarp. With bouncing and shaking, the pieces began to shrink and reduce. The vibrations sped up and the bones disintegrated until there was nothing there at all but fine, white ashes. The next gust of wind swirled them into the air and they were gone.

Sylvia did the same again, extending her arm towards the mill. The smoke floated in a thin wave, rising and floating slowly, cutting effortlessly through the wind beyond the circle. As it reached the building, which they could now see clearly, Sylvia's arms spread apart. The wisp split in two, half of it circled around the Sewing Room window and disappeared inside. The rest drifted around the side of the building, towards the cellar door.

Sylvia looked at Sulis, their gazes settling on the remains of Amelie. Her bones were still somehow on the blanket, motionless. Sulis nodded. Sylvia turned her attention to her daughter, who smiled up at her. The sense of their contentedness filled everyone. Mother and daughter embraced, their likenesses now just an afterglow. They walked out of the floodlight's path through the orchard toward the road and faded into the wind. The circle remained, Mr. Stevens and Mr. Jacobs were hesitant to move. Tina clung tightly to her father on one side of her and Toby's arm on the other. The wind returned inside the circle, but it had died down to a breeze. Will squinted into the darkness. He could just make out the candles still burning.

"So mote it be," Sulis finished.

Twenty-eight

"Is that it? Is everything okay?" Mr. Jacobs asked. Sulis nodded but frowned slightly. "We have just one obligation to complete,"

Mr. Levy groaned in frustration.

"Sylvia would like Amelie's remains to be buried next to her. Sylvia is in the graveyard across the road, next to the large willow."

Mr. Stevens took in a huge breath of air and released it. "I guess we can do that, too."

"Let's close the circle and get to it."

Everyone scattered to their position and scanned their papers. Sulis addressed each cardinal direction and element with thanks and blessings, asking each to depart in peace. "So mote it be," she finished.

Mr. Stevens walked up to his daughter, put his arm around

her shoulders and hugged her one handed, then started to walk towards Amelie's skeleton but stopped short. "Do you think we could check the building first? I'd like some concrete security that we're the only ones here."

"What about her remains? I mean, will it be okay if we leave them here for a few minutes?" Toby asked.

"I don't think they will be touched. We've asked for protection. It will be inside the circle, but let's do this quickly anyway," Sulis suggested.

The group broke up slowly, signaling with their heads in agreement. The stones, candles, and empty tarps lying on the ground were gathered. They headed back to the museum, craning to see the graveyard and two lit candles, which were just a dim light now.

Mr. Jacobs and Mr. Levy started downstairs to make sure everything was secure. The rest headed upstairs, pulling the ladder to the landing. With flashlights in hand, Will and Mr. Stevens climbed quickly into the loft. Everything was quiet. Nothing on the small altar had changed. Satisfied, they climbed back down the ladder and split up. Jenna, her father and Will went to the Sewing Room while Toby, Tina and Sulis went towards the Display Room.

The Sewing Room door was closed, the way it had been left. The tension was thick as they unlocked the door. Nothing was out of place. The only difference was the window. It no longer held the athame. The intake of Jenna's and Will's breath was audible. They hesitantly walked to the window.

"The window is definitely locked," Will said reaching out and gingerly touching the excess wax that bonded the double hung together. From end to end between the two windows was a dark teal scalloped design left by the liquid as it started to drip before it hardened. It connected both pieces of the wood together without a gap. The deep gash on the top of the bottom frame from the athame was the only evidence it had once been used there. "Sylvia is really something."

"Where did the athame go?" Jenna asked quietly. Will shrugged. They met the others on the landing. The Display Room remained untouched as well. They met up with Tina's and Toby's fathers who had collected shovels and flashlights.

"The basement looks good. What about up there?" Mr. Levy asked nervously.

"Well, the athame is gone. Not sure where that went. Whatever Sylvia did with her spell, it sealed the window with candle wax," Will answered.

"The Display Room is intact as well," Sulis added. They were all weary but trudged outside with the tools to complete the task at hand.

They walked quietly, split into groups of twos and threes. Toby and his father retrieved the heavy blanket with Amelie's remains, carrying it folded up so it could not spill. They had disconnected the work lights. Somehow, even though it was a quite a distance to the road and beyond, the green candlelight was visible. The muted light, like a beacon, directed them where to go. With flashlights in hand, the group walked back out of the orchard to the clearing by the entrance to the building. They saw no one as they crossed the road and walked the short way to the ancient cemetery. They made their way to the back of the graveyard where the oldest graves were. The wind picked up again.

"Wow. I hadn't thought about where Sylvia was buried," Jenna admitted.

They had come up to the corner perimeter, near an old stone fence. It held a very small marker that was almost invisible to the eye compared to the other, larger tombstones. It had both turquoise candles near it allowing it to be seen easier. Time had weathered it badly, and the etching in the stone was worn and impossible to make out. Behind the stone, directly in front of the fence was a huge willow. The tree's thickness was the width of three people with a canopy so expansive it covered a third of the deepest part of the burial area. It swayed and bowed in the wind menacingly. The light from the candles and their flashlights shone on it unnaturally against the black sky.

"This is it," Sulis announced.

"Hey, we can see our house from here," Will stated as an afterthought. Heads turned in the direction Will was facing. From the clearing behind the willow, tiny in the distance, stood a tall single house that sat on the corner of Miner and Fallow Road. The only sound now was the whooshing of the wind through the nearby trees and the tools being dropped to the ground.

The shallow grave did not take long with so many people digging. They laid Amelie's bones gently into its final resting place, still nestled in the soft quilt. They folded the corners over it.

"What do we do with the candles? Do we bury them with

her?" Will asked. He sat down with his elbows on his knees to catch his breath. Everyone was beyond tired.

"She didn't say," Sulis replied simply. "I don't think so. I'm sure I would know if they were meant to be with them. Let's finish this up and go home."

No more energy was put into conversation, though plenty of questions were still unanswered. Did the spell seal the loopholes for good? What if they were supposed to bury the candles with them? What would happen if they didn't? They would have to wait another day to think about all that concerned them.

Dirt was scooped and shoveled, narrowing the gap in the hole with the rest of the ground. The work was not difficult and was done quickly amid groaning and gasping mostly brought on by such a long, arduous day. Sulis blew out the turquoise pillar candles, and they extinguished with a pop, making Tina and Jenna jump. Slowly, the group walked back to the building following the angular beams of their flashlights. Will put his arm around Jenna's waist to support her. She was exhausted, weaving in and out of the path.

"Let's put the candles back on the altar upstairs for now," Sulis suggested when they finally stepped back into the great room. The lights, still on, were severe. Silently, everyone took inventory of each other. The men had taken off their jackets once they started digging and had them in their hands. Their sweaty faces were tired and apprehensive. Tina and Jenna remained in their coats, their gloves dirty from the soil. Tina had removed her hat and a halo of static drew her hair up on end. Most of her black hair had fallen out of the comb that contained it earlier. Jenna kept her hat on. Stray hairs stuck to her face from underneath it. Toby and Will had thick mud stains on the knees of their jeans. All looked worn out, physically and emotionally.

"This feels right to me." Sulis broke the stillness staring at the others, concern evident on her face with the silent unease. No one wanted to get their hopes up that they were truly done, but in the same regard, more problems were too much to even think about. Attention was turned to Jenna, who was fighting to keep her eyes open.

"Everything seems to be okay," Jenna stammered. She didn't know what to say. She didn't even really know what she was feeling. She felt drained, numb, empty. Toby and his father mumbled quietly to each other as they collected the tools and left to put them away. Mr. Levy and Mr. Stevens started towards the bathrooms to wash up when Mr. Levy put his hand out to stop his partner.

"Uh, Sulis?" Mr. Levy began quietly. Sulis, still holding the turquoise candles, looked over at him. "Thank you for everything you've done tonight. If you say we're okay here and there will be no more walking dead around, I'll take your word for it. I would be satisfied enough to say the museum is safe to be open to the public. What do you think?"

Sulis's face warmed into a smile. "My pleasure. I do believe we are all alone. That would be wonderful to know the museum can continue."

Tina smiled as she started towards the office with her hands full of stones, papers, and other supplies from the circle. Everyone in the room relaxed.

Sulis's nodded, her attention turning to Tina. "Hold on

Tina, and I'll help with those. I could use a hand taking these upstairs to the loft, Will."

Will took the candles as his mother walked away. He kept looking at Jenna, unsure if he should leave her. He was concerned that she might not be able to remain standing. He walked closer to her and slid his free hand to the small of her back. He let out a heavy sigh. Without saying another word, he leaned down and kissed her deeply. "Join me?" he asked in his gentle tone. Jenna nodded and smiled meekly. Will offered her the candles so he could guide them with the flashlight once they were up in the loft. He kept his arm around her waist.

Slowly up the stairs they went, distracted by their own thoughts. To Jenna, the weekend felt like a year. She corrected herself, the last month felt like an eternity. So much had happened. She wasn't sure what the future held, but she hoped it would go back to some normalcy. She was getting too old for this sort of thing to happen every five years or so. She laughed briefly. Will looked at her perplexed and she shook her head dismissively.

"I've got the ladder. Up you go," Will offered. Jenna made her way up, bending down to stabilize the top for him as he climbed. Will resumed his arm around her as they started walking. Their sneakers and boots on the floorboards were muffled but the only sound in the room. The flashlight roamed around them protectively as they crossed through the door into Sylvia's room. The altar was just ahead.

"Thank God, we're done," Jenna said tiredly, ready to put down the candles. Will's arm tightened around her, and the flashlight stopped moving, shining brightly on the center of the altar. She immediately looked up at him, his face surprised but intrigued. Her stomach did a flip in response to his expression. She closed her eyes briefly and bit her lip. She slowly opened her eyes. Confused, she saw two beams of light. One, a stark white, was from Will's flashlight and the other a diffused ivory that was its reflection. It was the light that bounced off the black metal blade of Sylvia's athame that sat quietly in the middle of the altar.

An excerpt from
Infinity Series Book Three
Spell Breakers

"**W**HAT...?" BEGAN JENNA, looking at the others. She was thinking there must be some part in the ritual where the candles are blown out as someone had just done with hers. It was only when she noticed that Mina was too far away that she started to feel uneasy. She was sure someone had just been at her shoulder; she had felt the invisible wave of coolness push against her as if someone had walked by quickly and very closely to her. The puff of air by her ear was tangible because it had moved her hair. Squeezing Will's hand with her right, Jenna looked at the candle in her left, the curls of smoke rising slowly, drawn to the center of the altar. The white wisps dissipated into thicker fibers and circled around with purpose. Jenna's attention went to Will as he squeezed her hand too tightly.

"Do you see that?" he asked no one in particular.

"Yes, we do," Mina answered. All eyes were on the shape of a face forming in the smoke from Jenna's extinguished candle.

"That's him! That's the man's face I see," Jenna whispered,

horrified. No one had moved, yet the threads spun and wound on, animating the expression on the face into a sneer that seemed to be looking directly at Jenna. It then dissipated into the air as a thin sheet before disappearing completely...

About the Author

REALM SPEAKER IS the second book in Laura Livingston Snyder's Infinity Series. Her first novel, *Dream Seer* was published in June, 2020, and satisfies her lifelong goal of being a published author. *Meditations Handbook: Four Revelations of the Solar Wheel of Meditations, Affirmations, and Guided Imagery for Pagan Sabbats* is a stand-alone book published in August, 2020, that delves into mindfulness techniques.

Laura is an RN and Certified Case Manager. She has several years' experience as a freelance writer for a local magazine, and occasionally blogs at FreshAppleSnyder.com. She lives in Upstate New York with her husband, children, pets, and lots of gardens.

Watch for *Spell Breakers*, the third installment in the Infinity Series, coming soon.